A DENIABLE MAN

By the same author

A DENIABLE MAN

a novel by

SOL STEIN

McGRAW-HILL PUBLISHING COMPANY

New York St. Louis San Francisco Bogotá Hamburg Madrid Mexico
Milan Montreal Paris São Paulo Tokyo Toronto

A Deniable Man is a work of fiction. All the characters in this book are creations of the author, and any resemblance to living individuals is coincidental and unintentional.

1 2 3 4 5 6 7 8 9 DOC DOC 8 9 2 1 0 9

ISBN 0-07-061010-X

Library of Congress Cataloging-in-Publication Data

Stein, Sol.
 A deniable man.
 I. Title.
PS3569.T375D4   1989   813'.54   88-32566
ISBN 0-07-061010-X

Book design by Eve L. Kirch

*To Estelle
for my life*

ACKNOWLEDGMENTS

I want to thank Daniel Chabris for improving my inadequate Italian, and Richard Graves for his demolition expertise.

I am especially grateful to the brave messengers who risked bringing me news about my earlier drafts: Pat, Elizabeth, Renni Browne, Jane Rafal, Virginia Brieant, Dan Weaver, and my law school, led by Judge Charles L. Brieant, his son, Charles L. Brieant III, and his daughter-in-law, Joy Beane Brieant, who, as I have watched the blindfolded lady with two empty trays, have lent me their own balance.

I sometimes think that if David Smith and I had been born earlier, who knows, we might have assassinated Hitler. If you think that wasn't possible, I'd like to show you my blue book. I've worked out four ways. That's what I do instead of chess these days, figure out how I would have rubbed out Caligula. I think of myself as the world's most underrated social worker.

—Sam Dracoff

BOOK ONE

CHAPTER 1

Farlan Amory Adams

The byword of my upbringing was *everything in moderation*. I had been preceded by six generations of wealth and accomplishment. My forebears were concerned with constraint and appearances, yet now I was trapped in the maw of an obsession that chewed away genes, schooling, ethics, and good sense because the demon in my heart had metastasized into my brain: Where is she now? What is she doing? What is she thinking?

She is Susan Sarah Whitcomb, once my student at the Columbia Law School, now an advocate practicing trial law as if the courtroom were invented for her. I have told myself that she is too young, yet how can one say that a woman in her late twenties is too young for a man just past fifty?

Was she a great beauty who turned the heads of passers-by? Not really. Her light brown hair, once blond I am certain, artfully tossed to make it seem windblown, cried out to be touched. Her thin-bridged nose was quite ordinary. Her blue-green eyes followed me about the classroom as if videotaping my words and gestures. If her head seemed exquisitely poised to me, it was because the head and face were hers. She sometimes moved her arms and hands as if she were conducting an orchestra in a subtle pianissimo, but that could have been because I was sometimes tempted to be that orchestra.

I am not a womanizer in the ordinary sense. While the externals that entice the eye give me pleasure, it is the output of a keen-edged brain that forces my priapic blood to stir. I told myself that her brilliance was not original, that she did well because I taught her to do well. The truth is I had never before had a student who extorted my best instruction as she willed. I wanted to tell myself that Susan Whitcomb is irremediably flawed, but I found no evidence to support my wish because by then the demon had corrupted my senses. I used to think words had power, and language was a sword, but the words that enabled me to seduce attention in the classroom and applause in the lecture hall now seemed as useless as an apple in Eden tunneled by worms.

You who have experienced requited love know that the mutuality of a happy mating will in time bring a certain peace. How I lust for that tranquillity. Yet I know the white water of my obsession will not be calmed until I rid the world of the man who stands in my way.

Who among you hasn't at a peak of anger wished for the death of another? The only obstacles I have are the moral law that all of us find gifted ways of circumventing when it suits our purpose, and the law of the courts, which as a lawyer I am doubly sworn to uphold.

It was early in the morning of the first Sunday of December that I went to execute my claim. Of course I had planned carefully. It was Susan herself who, in her innocence, told me what I needed to know. When Susan was with David, she said, the nurse took a break. On Sunday mornings, when the wicked overslept and the good, like David's loyal weekend nurse, took ninety minutes to pay her respects to the Trinity, David was alone for an hour and a half. Within a week he was being moved to some place in Washington, which left me very little time to do what I have to do.

The house, three stories built of an ochre-colored brick by an architect with taste, had a small brass plaque on its dark green front door that proclaimed S.F.A. NESBIT, M.D., F.A.C.S, and in smaller letters, OBSTETRICS, BY APPOINTMENT ONLY. It was all quite clever because the inscription on the plaque was too small to be read from the street even by someone with perfect vision. Your curiosity had to be sufficient to cause you to lift the latch of the wrought-iron gate and walk fifteen feet to the door. And if by chance you were interested in what Dr. Nesbit had to offer and wished to make an appointment, you could search the phone directory under Nesbits or Physicians till doomsday and not find any at that address.

The ground floor did indeed have a doctor's office, but the doctor was present only twice a week and usually went directly to the third floor to make his examination of the solitary patient there. That floor had had all the sills removed so that a wheelchair could be rolled readily from room to room. It was perfect, Susan had said, for someone who could not stay long in a public or private hospital or nursing home. She said it was so peacefully sequestered that she had even thought at one point of moving in there with him!

I came in precisely as I had planned, through the gate of what had once been a thriving garden, down the back basement steps to the door, which was locked, of course. People test doors to see that they are shut. But to the door's immediate left was a window from which, with foresight, I had removed the latch a week earlier when I came with Susan ostensibly to visit the sadly crippled man.

The bottom half slid up easily enough. I looked around. Not a soul. It was awkward clambering over the windowsill like a thief, but once inside I lowered the window and let a breath of satisfaction escape. What man as a youngster has not felt the fearsome pleasure of trespassing?

I heard the music, a Gregorian chant. It sounded like the Deller Consort, and I couldn't help wondering for a moment how a man with David Smith's proclivities had trained himself to listen to something like that. He would, of course, be in the room with the music. The door bottom, which looked strangely nude without a sill to meet it, let a fan of light into the darkened hallway. Wearing gloves, of course, I turned the knob.

He was sitting amid the clutter of medical apparatus in his electric wheelchair, staring straight ahead as a man will do who cannot hold a book in his hands. He may have thought it was his nurse come back early, for there was the definite perk of surprise in his eyes, immediately replaced by what could pass as a smile, as if he might have been expecting me to return. The thought occurred to me that a witness who knew of David Smith's heroism might want to defend him, and I would say: What good is his heroism now that neither he nor the world can benefit from it?

And so we support our sins with reason. I once heard a hunter say that it is easy to kill a running animal, particularly if it is running away. But if an animal stops and turns and fixes its eyes on you, how difficult it is to pull the trigger.

Smith was silhouetted against the bright light from the window. I moved a step or two to the side so that I might see him clearly.

His eyes followed me. Should I pull the blinds? No one could possibly see into that window.

I suddenly realized I was dallying and that it was perfectly possible for David Smith to charge me in his electric wheelchair, in which case my mission would be found out but its object not achieved. What a waste!

"You expected me," I said.

He nodded.

"You can perfectly well use your voice," I said.

He nodded.

"There is absolutely nothing you can do to make Susan happy," I said.

Again he nodded, his silence more frightening than any sound. Was this a trap?

I quickly looked about to see if the pistol Susan said they'd discovered under his mattress was anywhere within his reach.

"Don't be a fool," he snapped, "my hands don't work. Besides, they took it away."

"Look, I'm terribly sorry about your condition," I said, "but one must face the facts. Susan won't be able to live her own life while you're around. I can't have her following you to that place in Washington."

"Let Susan alone," he said, his face looking cadaverous compared to that one romantic photograph Susan imprudently carried of him.

"I have no intention of hurting her," I said.

I'd reached into my left pocket for the capsule. "I brought this for you," I said, extending my hand until it was inches from his mouth. Suddenly he twisted his head, the one part of his body that seemed to respond adequately to his commands, and butted the cyanide out of my hand.

I had to get down on all fours like an animal to retrieve it from under the white metal supply cabinet.

"Why incriminate yourself?" he said. "They'd know in a minute that I couldn't get my hands on something like that. They don't even trust me with aspirin."

The hubris of that man, thinking himself still in charge!

"You're a fumbling idiot, Adams," he said. "Use the Coke bottle."

I saw the empty bottle. I didn't understand his instruction.

"Just smash the bottle on my head, then heave me out the window. They'll think my fractured skull was from the fall. Just be damn sure you take the bottle away with you."

"I've never hurt anyone," I said.

"Bullshit."

"I mean I've never tried to kill anyone. You've killed many times."

"That's right, chum. Pick up the damned bottle. Hold it by the small neck like you hold your thing when you're whacking off."

I seized the bottle by its neck.

"That's it, baby," he said. "Don't leave any glass behind. Raise the bottle, or can't you get that up either? Aim right here," he said, bobbing his head. "Between my eyes."

"You bastard!" My trembling hands swung the bottle at his head with all my living strength.

CHAPTER 2

Susan Sarah Whitcomb

Maybe it wasn't a fluke. Maybe some higher power buzzed my buzzer and said Hey, why don't you register for Professor Adams's crowded course? If he doesn't live up to his rep, you can always switch. They say Adams doesn't bullshit you with high principles. He tells it like it is out there. Besides, he has the best rep in the Law School for keeping his students awake.

The clues I got came from Annie the night four of us decided to celebrate the beginning of a semester. It was our last night as law school grinds without an assignment that had to be completed by morning. Armed with six-packs, we chose a no-men evening so we didn't have to listen to the pitch of yet another male looking for a place to park his motorcycle for the semester.

I zeroed in on frizzy-haired extra-tall Annie because she'd already taken Adams's course in trial work. "What's he like?"

Annie squatted down Indian-style, facing me. "I got to warn you, Susie," she said, "Adams's taller than I am, dresses in Ralph Lauren, shoots his cuffs, and is the biggest snob south of Boston, but ..." Annie stood up to get her beer can, "... he is a Philadelphia mainline version of street smart. He'll tell you how to gut your best friend and make her think somebody else did it."

Annie clunked her beer up against mine in a toast. "Here's to you and not to him. Susie, this man professes the law but he's really a Svengali who'll make you wet just by talking. I had dreams about his tongue coming at me. I warn you, Susie, wear out a ballpoint in class, but don't go near his office alone or you'll get pregnant just listening to him."

We flapped away past midnight about professors past and professors to come, about the fate of the world, about men and how lucky we were not to have to carry all of that equipment around in our underwear. I faded first. At four a.m. I slunk off to my cubicle—a room I refused to call a room because it was smaller than the legal minimum for a jail cell.

I had three hours sleep, minus one bad dream about beer bottles that drank people. When I swung my feet out of bed and headed for the john, my slippers were encased in lead. In the mirror my face looked red and white like a big radish. What I wanted was: back to bed. I forced myself to take an ice-cold shower, which got me awake enough so I could pull on my light-blue V-neck with the front in front instead of in back.

I always thought of my father as just five ranks below president, which is an exaggerated way of describing a brigadier general. What I had in mind for myself was to be the first female Attorney General of the United States. It wasn't a question of ambition, it was a matter of natural selection. All I had to do was find the right loopholes to swim through, and one of those might be Professor Adams's course.

I got to the Fellows Lecture Hall just before showtime. It was a huge half-rotunda, with rows of seats going more than halfway up to the ceiling in the rear, and damn near full. What was everyone doing here? Who the hell wanted to be in a class this big? Luckily I spotted the one empty seat before someone else did. I was not about to spend an hour trying to stand up as well as keep awake.

No sooner had I gotten my ass squirmed into the seat than the man himself sauntered in. Like Annie said, Adams was tall, all right, and dressed with exquisite class. He had the walk of a man who owns the right of way. Arms outstretched to each side of the lectern, he eyeballed the rabble from left to right as if he were counting the house. Bunches of students were still chattering, their way of saying we pay so fucking much for tuition it's your job to get our attention.

He didn't shush us. He just froze as if he were posing for a photograph. When you noticed that, you stopped talking. I could see it happening, first in one group, then another. Finally, the last hold-outs noticed they were the only ones still talking and shut up.

"That," Professor Adams said, "is my first lesson in trial law. The jury is an audience. You can capture their attention, as I did yours, by standing stock still. If they are focused on you, everyone else's attention will be also."

My attention was on him all right. I noticed his cufflinks, which I hadn't seen on anybody in years.

"The first few sentences you speak," Adams continued, "are critical. That's when the jury starts forming its opinion of you. That opinion, for better or worse, will rub off on the client you are defending. If they think you're a jackass, they'll think your client is a jackass for hiring you. If you go in unprepared, take too long to make a point, muff your direct examination and then botch your cross, your client will have lost his money or his freedom, depending on what's at stake. Half the battle is that very first impression you make. Is that fair? Of course not. Is it fair if you go to a party dressed like a slob and strangers think you're a slob?"

Adams moved away from the lectern. "Let's try an opener." He held his hands up, palms facing us. "You are here," he said, lowering his hands, moving towards us, standing right up against the first row of faces that had to look up to see him, "to judge the truth or falsehood of certain facts. The future of a fellow human being who, under the law, is at this moment . . ."

Adams had lowered his right hand to rest on the bushy hair of one of the male law students in the first row.

". . . just as innocent as you are . . ."

He got his laugh, from me and everybody else.

"There you have it," Adams said. "If this young fellow were the defendant, I probably wouldn't put my hand on his head, I'd let it rest on his shoulder like this because I wouldn't want you to laugh. You know damn well you aren't innocent. I don't know you and I'd be willing to wager there isn't a student in this rotunda who qualifies for beatification. I'm saying that this defendant is probably as imperfect as you are. What have I done?"

For a scared second I thought Adams was going to point to me, but the target for Adams's finger was a lanky guy two rows in front of me.

"You're registering the idea that innocence isn't perfect innocence," said the student.

"And what else?"

"You've set us up to recognize anything negative in the defendant as a failing we might share."

"Which means you're identifying with the defendant, right?"

The mob of student heads moved to affirm.

Adams hardly paused before there was a rush of new energy in his voice.

"Now I'm the prosecutor," Adams said. He passed a hand in front of his face as if wiping a mask away.

"Ladies and gentlemen of the jury," he began, stopped, and strode over to near where I was sitting. He pointed a finger at the guy next to me, a cherub with a badly managed mustache that didn't fit his face. "Why am I addressing them as ladies and gentlemen?"

"It's a convention, sir," said the mustache.

"That expression," Adams said, striding across the front of the room in full performance, "compliments the jury because jurors by and large are *not* the ladies and gentlemen of our society but the soldiers of society who can be easily led. The ladies and gentlemen, if any, are removed by peremptory challenges. The function of jury selection is to remove anyone who shows signs of initiative, higher education, an ability to lead or to think for themselves because people like that try hard to keep prejudices in check. The aim of jury selection is to pick citizens susceptible to prejudice."

Of course we all laughed at the sting of truth. *Hey Annie, this guy isn't half bad.*

When the wave of laughter ebbed, Adams said, "As the prosecutor, I intend to play on your prejudices and lead you by the nose to a conviction. Why am I so intent on a verdict? I may tell the TV camera that I'm on a moral crusade, but the crusade I'm on is my career."

Adams got the silence he wanted. "None of you want to be somebody's assistant D.A. forever. We all want to fill our scorecard with convictions so some large firm with a need for litigators will snatch us out of our government job and put us where we can in due course share partners' gold. The person in the dock is a stepping stone in our career. And so we have to say, 'Ladies and gentlemen, a crime has been committed. A crime of violence. Not battery. Not mere assault. But the ultimate crime, the taking of a human life. The evidence we will put before you will demonstrate that there is not a scintilla of doubt among the experts, the police investigators, the forensic scientists, that John Doe, who had fifteen knife wounds in his body, did not die a natural death but was murdered by a hand not his own. We are here to examine the facts in order to conclude whose hand it was that committed the crime of Cain and took it upon himself to end the life of another human being.' "

Adams had walked over to the left side of the first row and stopped in front of a female student. He held his hand, palm down, inches above her head. "Of course," he said, "I would get as close as I could to the defendant without touching him or her, and say, 'What have we here?' What we have, of course, is a play with the following plot: A was murdered by B. The police identified B as this woman," he pointed down to the student immediately beneath his hand, "and the District Attorney thought the evidence against this particular person sufficient to pass the responsibility of determining the facts to you."

I was wide awake now, and yes I thought he was funny and dramatic and clever, and the combination of the way he looked and performed was a real turn-on. I was surprised to find myself holding my hand up.

The elegant man seemed to look me over carefully before he acknowledged my raised hand.

"Professor Adams," I said, "I thought the prosecutor and the defense counsel were both officers of the court."

"They are."

"Aren't officers of the court supposed to help discover the truth?"

Adams coughed gently into his cupped hand. "That," he said, "is a truly noble thought. I suggest you stow your noble thoughts in your locker. This is a course in the mechanics of the real world."

I started to protest but he cut me off. "Your definition is factually correct. But in terms of how our system works at trial, it is naïveté incarnate. The only way a lawyer can get away with the practice of that belief is to avoid having clients."

I couldn't be sure if they were laughing at his comment or at me.

"The fact is," he continued, "that each officer of the court has a client. One is the defendant's advocate. The other is the plaintiff's. And both have a much greater interest in winning for their clients no matter where the truth lies. Young lady," he was suddenly addressing me in particular, "the department secretary will telephone you to schedule a conference in my office. You cannot go on to a law career while seriously ill with innocence."

The son-of-a-bitch was a fox. In one stroke he'd pinned my ears in public and forced me to register for his damn course so I'd have a forum for fighting back.

Even his office proved to be a turn-on. Most of the faculty offices I'd been in looked out at the wall of the building next door. Nothing like that for this guy Adams. The double windows behind his desk could have been a framed portrait of the campus. To the right of the windows was a large plant, I mean a giant man-eating eight-feet-high plant tickling the ceiling with its topmost huge green leaves, dark green as if the plant had been cared for. In my dorm cell the leaves of the one plant still alive from last semester were turning a lighter green every week and showing their veins.

One side of the room was wall-to-wall books. Only one shelf was devoted to the sets you saw in law offices. The rest were real books that looked as if they'd actually been read.

He looked at me looking.

Okay, I'm a sucker for a room like this, nice view, big plant in good shape, lots of tempting books to browse through.

On the other wall was a gallery of photo-portraits, most of them signed. I recognized some of the judges and public figures. Who were those people to Farlan Adams? And he to them?

I felt I had to say something. "I like your room," I said.

"So I see." He said it as if I'd come out with something much more personal. A room could be very personal. This one felt as if it had a bed in it. Was it me reacting to him reacting to me? Or was I being influenced by Annie's cracks?

"Please have a seat," he said, with a quick glance up. I got a half-second forced smile. Then his gaze went back down to the card I'd had to fill out with my name, dorm, place of prior degree, parents' home, whatnot.

One thing I'd learned about the adversarial system is that you can say almost anything provided you say it in a soft voice. And so in my softest I said, "Why'd you pick on me, Professor Adams?"

"Please sit down, Miss Whitcomb."

The chair alongside his desk was one of those ancient bentwood creations designed to make sitting still an achievement. His own high-backed leather throne looked damn comfortable.

"You haven't answered my question," I said.

He looked up from my card. "Witnesses have to answer questions, Miss Whitcomb."

Of course people are supposed to look at you when they speak. But when they examine you with their eyes the way Adams was examining me, it's not exactly polite.

A significant percentage of any female student's energy is devoted to saying *no, not now, later, never* to predatory males. I'm not a prude, just particular. Did Adams think he was dealing with a high school girl?

He leaned forward in his high-backed chair, reached for a pipe, and started filling it from a black leather pouch.

"Your Honor," I said, "was finding fault with my statement that lawyers on both sides are officers of the court."

He seemed amused by my calling him his honor. He said, "Mind if I smoke?"

"As a matter of fact I do." Maybe it was rude. Well, it was rude of him to stuff his pipe first, then ask.

He put the pipe aside.

"Let us suppose," he said, "this was the medical school. Instead of your trying to live up to being an impartial officer of the court, the gospel held up to you is the Hippocratic oath. Now you know, Miss Whitcomb, that doctors honor that oath when it's convenient and profitable for them to do so and otherwise ignore it to the extent they can this side of malpractice. The percentage of enrollees in medical school whose primary goal is to serve the medical needs of East Africa or the Louisiana bayous, say, is too small to put on a graph. And even most of them come back from a first tour of duty feeling that the world had better help itself from now on."

I was going to respond but he did his hand-holding-up-traffic-cop trick that stopped me cold.

"I know," he said. "You've thought of being a public defender."

"As a matter of fact I have."

"That's an inaccurate statement. You've thought of being a public defender *for a while*."

"Of course."

"And then leaving the indigent to other inexperienced newcomers while you go off to become a high-priced litigator, having sharpened your talents on the poor."

"That's not fair!"

"Fair to you, or fair to them? Before you brand my views, please remember that I am here to share my experience as well as my knowledge, and both have made it absolutely clear to me that lawyers can't possibly serve as officers of the court if they want to do a good job for whoever hired them, even if it is the state. We don't give degrees in altruism here, we prepare brighter-than-average lawyers-to-be to make more money than the President of the United States."

I finally got my chance. "Professor Adams," I said, "if money is the goal you preach, why don't you set an example?"

"You're invading my privacy."

"Law professors don't make as much as practitioners, do they?"

"Are you always this outspoken?"

"Only when pushed. Or preached at."

"Young lady, I don't preach, I describe reality to young people whose heads are filled with idealistic junk."

"Do you give a short course in ambulance chasing?"

Adams actually laughed. "Not at Columbia. Not yet, anyway. Most of the lawyers we train go to work in the law factories, their time clocks ticking away."

"And what you do is waste your life training them?"

His eyes wouldn't let go. I looked away first. "I'm sorry," I said. "I didn't mean to be impudent."

"No, no, no," said Adams, "the ability to ask a question like that is the mark of someone who might do well in the courtroom. Most successful trial lawyers can contrive questions that go well beyond impudence if they help win a case."

For a moment he looked longingly at his pipe, then said, "Have your questions at school always had a cutting edge?"

"Yes."

"I like that," he said.

"Most teachers haven't. The best have."

"Thank you for what I presume is a compliment."

"It was intended."

"Well then, you have charmed an answer from me. The fact is that I am here because my family has been well-to-do for several generations, which gives me the freedom to accept Columbia's pittance instead of five hundred K a year from Skadden Arps. I elected to teach because I enjoy the pleasure of seeing my best students out there occasionally setting precedents. I like guessing how each will turn out. I hope when you find your niche, whatever it is, that you savor it as much as I do mine."

"Professor Adams, I appreciate your attention, but if I don't have the makings of a trial lawyer, I'd be wasting time in your course. Isn't time what lawyers sell the most of these days?"

He smiled his smile. "I think you might possibly turn into quite a tigress as a litigator. An occasional surge of naïveté may hobble you at first, but unlike chronic idealism, naïveté is curable."

I wanted to write down exactly what he said. I was sure I'd forget it the minute I left his office. Worse, the man was talking to my head and I was feeling it in my body. *Annie, what do I do?*

Annie would say *What does a mouse do when it sees a cat?* I stole a glance at his wall of books, and then at his wall of pictures. Why should I escape? I am not a mouse. He's a handsome tomcat. Why should I jump back into a hole in the wall? This could be fun.

He was still looking at me. Was it my turn to say something?

CHAPTER 3

Farlan Adams

During the first of our private meetings, I committed the details of her face to memory. And the contours of her body.

She caught me staring.

"Miss Whitcomb," I said, "what made you choose the law?"

As she began a detailed answer, her words could not compete with the questions churning in my head. Why have I never been able to bring myself to say to a young woman *I am a hunter not a fornicator, I enjoy the chase more than the catch.* Why do women think of the chase as a male ritual, and that the woman's role is to twirl away like a dancer, to deny, thwart, block, delay, and then finally give in to the pre-ordained? The exquisite agony of pursuit if managed cleverly can be stretched indefinitely. How superior a pleasure is exploration compared to the mere minute or two of friction and ten seconds of spasm that passes for lovemaking! What is the difference between one lover or another if not his ability to make foreplay a long-lasting delight? Anticipatory relish can be an art with a woman who understands its endless potential.

I suddenly realized Miss Whitcomb had stopped speaking.

"What made you choose the law?" I quickly said.

She smiled. That was the question she had just answered at length.

"In a word?" she asked. "Lawlessness."

"That can be a clever answer or a wrong answer, depending on what you mean by it."

She said, "We have come around to admitting reluctantly that children long for discipline. Don't you agree that most adults also long to know where the boundaries are?"

It was clever of her to put a question to me.

"I do."

"And," she immediately continued, "don't you agree that since the Enlightenment each generation has removed some of the disciplines?"

"True."

"Isn't it also true that the main discipline left in society is the body of law that says if you get caught you will be punished? Professor Adams, I firmly believe that the only web that keeps society from disintegrating into anarchy is the law, which is why it fascinates me."

"Excuse me," I said, "but is that something you memorized?"

"Of course not. I just thought of it."

"Then I congratulate you," I said, wondering what it might be like if instead of sitting across a desk listening to her, I would come home each evening to sit side by side with her on my blue velvet couch, so that as she spoke I could feel her thigh against mine. If circumstance, at the end of an evening, put me in the same bed, it would thwart my plan for the prolongation of desire. What fools are the married men for whom a mere flicker of the satyr's flame in the middle of the night makes them reach out to their bedpartner for instant gratification. If they only knew as I know that ecstasy is the stretching out of two lovers' desires in parallel lines that meet only in infinity. There was danger in letting this conversation continue!

I stood to tell her that the meeting was over.

Once upon a time my bachelorhood might have been suspect. I might have felt it necessary to impose a union on my pleasure to keep my colleagues from gossip. Now marriage and parenthood have both become options, releasing me from the need for public deception. I am surrounded by a plenitude of unmarried females as targets of opportunity that I can dally with, and yet postpone—exquisitely postpone—the inevitable. Fools wonder why I exclude attractive married women from my endeavors. Because, my dear fools, married women cheating on their husbands seek to shorten the chase and to get to it. Oh no, the single, unattached female is my ideal.

Why was she smiling? As I moved around the desk, she moved

her chair back as if to safety, then stood up, allowing more space between us. *I must not frighten her.*

I walked her to the door and put out my hand. I felt her palm against my palm, my thumb interlocking with hers for a mere second.

"I believe you'll make a fine lawyer," I said, then realized I was still holding her hand and let it go.

She said, "I hope I can be half as good a lawyer as you are a teacher, Professor Adams."

I opened the door for her, stepped aside, and said "Good-bye" in a way that sounded more like hello.

She turned and walked down the hallway rapidly as if she couldn't wait to tell her friends about our meeting.

The beginning of a semester is always ripe with opportunity.

The department secretary had made an appointment for me to see in my office a certain D. Halpern, an undergraduate who was torn between the law and another discipline and wanted some advice.

D. Halpern proved to be a young woman, very petite with blond hair that was gathered in back and fell halfway to her tiny waist. She wore high gray leather boots, but above them her legs and thighs were bare up to the bottom of a very short skirt not then in fashion. As my eyes took her in, I tried to listen intently as she described the forces that pulled her in opposite directions.

I had to say something, if only to relieve my pulse. "Why do you call yourself D. Halpern?" I asked.

"You assumed I was male."

I nodded.

"Therefore you were surprised when you saw me."

"Yes."

"And in that moment of surprise I had the advantage, right? An advantage that usually belongs to the interviewer, not the interviewee, correct?"

"Young woman," I said, "we need go no farther. Anyone who thinks as you do would make an excellent courtroom lawyer."

I was flying on automatic pilot, imagining long hours with my new find, when suddenly I caught myself. Was I betraying my hoped-for relationship with Susan Whitcomb? A lure was safe, I told myself, a tie frightening.

Nevertheless, I decided not to pursue D. Halpern any further.

In my silence, it was she who stood up. "I want to thank you," she said, holding out her hand.

I shook it, of course, and felt the firmness of grasp that always pleasures me in man or woman. She turned to go. I watched the slow roll of her derriere as she walked to the door, smiled, and closed it behind her. *Pity.*

Later that same afternoon near Low Library I saw Susan at a distance, walking with a young man. I wanted to run across the campus, swing the young man around by his shoulder, and shout *What are you doing with her?*

Was I, who previously cared not one whit about whom my Beatrices actually went to bed with, jealous of Susan Whitcomb walking on the campus with a male who wasn't me? This first twitch of exclusivity was both foreign to me and incredibly exciting.

I did something I had never done before. On some idiotic pretext, I got her telephone number from the bursar's office and recorded it in my book of private phone numbers at home.

I began to look forward with keen anticipation to each hour in which she would be part of my audience. I searched for some reason to entice her into the privacy of my office again. Then, after the passage of weeks in which longing wormed its way through my body and into my brain, one day Susan failed to show up for my lecture class. I broke my rule and didn't start precisely on time, hoping she would come in late and breathless. I looked insanely across each row to make sure I hadn't made a mistake. Was she ill? Had she abandoned me? The students were restless. I had to start. My tremulous voice hardly carried me through the hour. When it ended at last and students clustered around me with questions, I waved them away. I all but ran through the crowded corridors to my office, afraid of being knocked over, of falling, of tearing a rent in the knee of my trousers like a boy. Safely inside, I phoned Susan's room. It rang for an eternity, three, four, five times. Had she left school without telling me? On the ninth ring she answered in a voice thinned by sleep.

"Who is it?" she said.

Who indeed? Why was I calling?

"I didn't see you in class," I said as calmly as I could.

She was silent for a moment, thinking what?

"Sorry," she said. "Woke up with the flu."

I wanted to say that I would come take care of her, sponge-bathe her feverish body, prepare broth, juices, whatever she needed to get well fast.

"Anything I can do to help?" I asked helplessly.

"Sorry I missed today's lecture."

"I'll let you see my notes. If anything's unclear I'd be happy to elucidate."

"That's very kind, Professor Adams," she said. "I'd better get back to bed now." And she hung up.

What must she think of my strange call? What must *I* think?

Susan next visited me in my office without an appointment. She just opened the door a bit, stuck her head in, and said, "Busy?"

I still had half a dozen or more papers to review. "Please take a seat," I said. "I see you're well."

"Much better."

I was tempted to tell her *I* wasn't much better.

"I'm sorry to burst in like this," she said, "but I was reading the Weinstein horn book and getting the drift that opinion evidence is generally inadmissible except for experts. Yet in reading excerpts from trial transcripts, I see a lot more opinion than fact. Is Weinstein right?"

I wanted to crawl up to her. To touch her ankle, her leg, perhaps even her thigh.

"Well, Miss Whitcomb," I said, "an ambitious, energetic young lawyer can move to strike every opinion, but a motion to strike, if sustained by the judge, calls attention to what has just been said. If not sustained, it calls just as much attention. Therefore a smart or experienced lawyer will minimize his motions to strike."

Susan suddenly stood up as if to go. Quickly I said, "I would like you to remember that every trial is really two trials taking place simultaneously."

She sat back down.

"One of these trials, you might say, is a simplification of the issues designed to persuade the jurors that your cause is just and that the other side is wrong. At the same time, a quite different second trial is taking place, designed to convince the judge that the law and precedent are on your side. My advice is to conduct the second trial at the bench so that only opposing counsel and the judge hear you because you don't want to confuse the jury."

Had she glanced at her watch? "You know what every judge wants?" I asked.

"A raise in salary," said Susan. "If he's not rich."

"Twice wrong," I said. "Even independently wealthy judges want a raise in salary. What all judges want even more is not to be reversed by a higher court. Where are you dining this evening?"

The words just came out, surprising me.

"I wouldn't call what I do dining. I usually grab a bite at a fast food place."

"One of the great pleasures in life is to relax over a long meal with pleasant company," I said.

"Well, you can guess what my life is like."

"Meaning?"

"Cramming, reading, preparing papers, stuff like that."

"No social life?"

"Oh, I sometimes let loose with friends. You have to or you go nuts. But whenever I stay up late, I regret it the next day."

"You find law school a grind?"

"Not in your lectures."

Why was I suddenly so cheered? I've been buttered up by scores of students and taken the flattery for what it was. "Do you have a best friend?" I found myself asking.

She hesitated. Had I intruded upon some clandestine relationship? "I'm sorry if—"

"It's okay," she said. "It's just that I have two. Close friends, that is."

"Male or female?"

"One of each."

"Is the man the one I saw you walking on the campus with?"

"When?"

"It doesn't matter," I lied. I put my hands below the level of the desk so that she wouldn't see them tremble.

"I know you've got work to do," she said. "Thanks so much for clarifying."

Nothing is clarified.

"I must go," she said.

The hell with the papers, please don't go.

"Thanks again," she said.

And she was gone.

CHAPTER 4

Susan

A few months before we were due to get our law degrees, Annie said to me, "I'll ask you once more. The big bang happen yet?"

I told her, "You keep confusing me with the solar system."

"I'm not confusing anybody with anything. You've been dating Adams for nearly two years."

"I have not dated him once. I see him."

"I've seen you seeing him." Annie grabbed a strand of my hair, which is her trick for keeping me from fleeing. "You listen to grandma. I feel responsible."

"For what? Let go of my hair."

"For inducing you to sign up for his class." She let go. "I'm not the only one who's noticed you two."

"There's nothing to notice, Annie. Farlan Adams has never touched me."

"You're a liar, Susie. You two take twice as long shaking hands as anybody else does. Honey, he's double your age. What gives with you two?"

"We like each other."

"Oh sure. You two stroll on campus as if no one else existed on earth. You'll end up fucking away your law degree."

"You don't understand, Annie. We are not lovers. We are friends."

Annie put her face twelve inches from mine and said, "Susie, you and I are friends. You and Adams are something else."

*   *   *

Early in my last year Farlan had invited me to a dinner he gave at the faculty club for ten people. I was the only student present. I found myself sitting next to the Manhattan District Attorney. In introducing me Farlan simply said, "Susan will make an extremely able litigator. She wants to start out as a defense counsel, without being a prosecutor first. Maybe you can talk her out of it."

And so the D.A. spent his time trying to get me to think about being a prosecutor, which is what I wanted in the first place. I worked like hell to make an impression. By ten o'clock I'd even agreed to visit the Manhattan D.A.'s offices and let a young Assistant D.A. show me around so I could rethink the error of my choice!

I got the tour at the hands of a red-headed Assistant D.A. named Manny Brustein, who believed that women shouldn't be prosecutors because their voices are too thin. He didn't hide his resentment at being assigned to show me around. I decided to show him. By the time we were finished he knew my voice wasn't thin and that if I ever defended anyone he was prosecuting, he'd better do his homework. He was now saying maybe the boss was right, and I should consider getting some experience by joining the D.A.'s office. I think what young Mr. Brustein wanted me to join was him in bed.

Even if Brustein had attracted me, my bed was filled to capacity. Unlike some of the people I hung around with, for me capacity was two people, me and someone else, and the someone else at the time was Al Papamongian, an actor. I know—Actors Equity says 96 percent of actors are unemployed at any one time. Papamongian, during the five months that we were kind of a thing, was unemployed 100 percent of the time as an actor and employed 100 percent as a waiter in a Sixth Avenue delicatessen. His great gift was being funny, a full-time off-duty role player. We'd be walking down Broadway looking for a movie we might want to see and Al would spot a New York cop, drop my arm, walk right up to the cop and say, "Excuse me, I'm Al Papamongian, Miami District Attorney's office, up here on a lead, and I want to say the detectives here have been very cooperative and super-smart. I hope you make detective one day soon, officer, it's a pleasure meeting you."

Al would walk off at a brisk pace. Breathless, I'd catch up to him around the next corner so we could laugh our heads off like kids.

The night I met Al he came straight up to me at a party and said, "I'm Al Papamongian, I'm an actor and I need to come up with a stage name by next Friday, can you help me?" How can you resist a come-on like that?

I had about four months of this with Al. I liked him but the funny stuff went lame. Al was a comic, not a wit. In my time with him I got convinced that part of growing up was to chuck the ha-ha stuff. I didn't want to be a captive audience for somebody else's never-ending, top-of-the-head script.

It took me nearly a month to shake Al off. "You can't stop seeing me," he'd say, "I haven't got a stage name yet." He eventually landed a bit part in an off-Broadway play and sent me a postcard saying, "I carry a switchblade in this play and if I don't see you in the audience on opening night I will step up to the footlights and put the switchblade between my ribs in full view of everybody while yelling your name."

I went to the opening with my new escort, who paid for up-front seats. When Al was onstage I tried to catch his eye, but throughout that lousy play his gaze meandered everywhere except toward me. During the first intermission I was wandering up the aisle and, would you believe it, I saw a girl showing her date a postcard exactly like mine!

What do you do about a crazy nerd like Al? Forget about him, right?

I have twice kicked the habit of reading obits. They're in the same class as horoscopes. All they tell you is that you're nervous about tomorrow. Leave it to *The New York Times* to change the location of its obits and catch me by surprise. And there it was:

AL PAPAMONGIAN, ACTOR

Albert Papamongian, 27, an actor in a short-lived off-Broadway play earlier this year, was found dead in his room by his landlady Tuesday after she failed to see him entering or leaving the building for a week. According to police, the body was on the floor halfway between the bed and the bathroom. Mr. Papamongian, who had told his landlady that he was currently in a play, actually worked the 4 p.m. to midnight shift in a brokerage firm as a word processor, according to police. No suicide note was found. An envelope addressed ''To All My Friends'' contained a piece of blank paper. On the floor next to the body were snapshots of eleven young women, some with messages on the back. An autopsy has been ordered by the medical examiner's office. Mr. Papamongian has no known survivors.

People should have funerals. With Al there wasn't even someone to phone and say I'm sorry.

Was I the last of his lovers? Or one of the eleven? Was there anything I could or should have done? When I passed a policeman on the street, I wanted to go up to him and say, "Excuse me, I'm a friend of Al Papamongian from the Miami District Attorney's office . . ." How else keep alive the memory of Al F-for-Funny Papamongian, who made everyone notice him except the people who could take him off the streets and put him in a show?

I didn't know whether I was grieving or just plain scared. If it could happen to jokey Al Papamongian, it could happen to anyone. I sat in front of open books I wasn't studying.

Farlan, ever the gentleman, happened to spot me on the campus sitting on a stone staring into space. He had to pass a hand in front of my face to get my attention.

"You look like you lost your best friend," he said.

I bit my lip. *He didn't know.*

"Not my best friend, but a friend."

I told him about that night in the theater and then seeing the obit.

"I'm so sorry," he said. He seemed to mean it. I could feel a crying jag coming on.

"Why don't we walk a bit," he suggested. "Blue sky, sun, not to be wasted."

We walked in the direction of Morningside Park. It's the kind of time you say dumb things. "I've known you for going on three years? I knew him for just four months!" My seams gave. I bawled like a kid. Farlan put my head against his shoulder. "He acted alive," I said, my nose running.

Farlan gave me a neatly folded handkerchief that looked cleaner than anything I've ever laundered. I didn't want to spoil it, so he took it from me and wiped first my eyes and then my nose.

"Better?" he asked.

I nodded.

"Have you ever lost anyone before? Dead, I mean."

I shook my head.

"Like everything," he said, "it takes practice." I was thinking about that when he said, "Is there anything I can do?"

Sure, you can walk up to a policeman and say I'm Farlan Adams of the Miami District Attorney's office.

I didn't say that, I just tried to keep my eyes dry.

"Were you lovers?" Farlan asked.

Not yet knowing all of Farlan's flash points, I opted for convenience. "Not really," I said. "He was entertaining." I could see Farlan the Wise was tense, so I added, "in a sophomoric sort of way."

Forgive me, Al.

Annie knocked on the door one evening. I said, "Come in," without looking around to see who it was.

"That's some 'come in,'" Annie said. "It sounded more like stay out."

"I'm sorry," I said, waving her toward the other chair. Instead, she sat on the edge of the bed and let her legs swing loose.

I said, "How can someone you had sex with over and over for months just go off and die?"

Annie cut me off. "I know all about that. There's absolutely nothing you could have done about it."

She'd gotten right to the point of death, the damn guilt you feel about how, in your most elaborate fantasies, you might have thwarted it. Then Annie said, "I've lost my mother, my father, my only brother, and both sets of grandparents. I didn't need all that experience, but now that I've got it, let me tell you something, Susie dear."

I hated being called "Susie dear." I waited for the word.

"Life goes on," Annie said.

"Is that all?"

"Don't be crazy, girl. The one thing a death teaches you is that life is all there is. Grab it. Use it. Fuck it. Do anything with it, but don't let it lie there like a used tampon. Aren't you supposed to be studying for the beloved bar like the rest of us?"

The short of it was that Annie was so alive you couldn't remain a drag in her presence. I made coffee for us on my illegal hot plate.

When she left, at the door she said, "Next time somebody dies, call me."

I sweated out two months of no dates, no sex, no anything except cramming, sleeping, cramming. Sweet Farlan once again asked if he could help. "Sure," I said. "Want to put on make-up and take the bar exam for me?"

"I wouldn't worry about the exam," he said. "You'll pass. If not the first time, the second time."

Was he nuts? Who wants to cram like this twice?

By exam time I was convinced all my internal support systems including my brain had failed. The normal people applied for jobs before the exam. The cocky ones took jobs, figuring they didn't need to study all that much. Me, I was so sure disaster awaited, I didn't do a damn thing except cram.

I waited forever for the results, wishing my mom and dad weren't in Europe. I needed parenting.

Okay, I passed. The first thing I did was to buy Annie a box of sinful chocolates. The morning after a party sixteen of my friends threw I took my second Alka-Seltzer and phoned Assistant D.A. Brustein to tell him I was ready to join up. I got as far as a voice with a Spanish lilt to it saying, "Mr. Brustein is no more with this office."

"Is he in another office?" I asked, and the Spanish lilt said, "Sorry, Mr. Brustein is in private practice now."

Shit! I felt like I'd run the law school marathon only to find there was no tape at the end. My first instinct was to run to Farlan for help. My better instinct said to me, *Girl, life is a hands-on experience. It isn't a classroom.* What the hell, I sat down at my typewriter, and made myself write a semi-forceful letter to the D.A. himself and tell him that he and Brustein between them had persuaded me to start out on their side of the adversarial fence. I wasn't applying for a job, I was just giving in to his persuasiveness. I didn't think he would even remember me.

He not only remembered me, he remembered I wore a locket above my decolletage that evening!

After an all-too-short briefing period, I was allowed to handle some misdemeanors and boring arraignments, but I sure as hell didn't want to spend a couple of years paying my dues. I pitched the D.A. to get a felony case.

"Don't be greedy," he said. "You can assist on a felony case."

"I'm not greedy," I said. "I'm good."

"If you screw it up, it's your ass."

All I did was smile my smile, and wouldn't you know three weeks later I get handed a felony case, and it scared the hell out of me. *This isn't law school, this isn't a mock trial, this is for real.* It wasn't a bottom-of-the-barrel car theft case. Car thieves, when caught, go right through the sieve. Mine was a hit-and-run-driver, and it got to the Grand Jury fast because the victim was the wife of a Council Member and she died of her injuries.

The doorman of a building at the scene of the accident had noted only three of the six numbers and letters on the license plate of the white Buick. The defense counsel, an experienced courthouse hack, could argue that several hundred plates have those numbers and letters. I could argue back that a much smaller number of plates were on white Buicks. That's not the kind of evidence you get a conviction out of.

The accident had happened about five-thirty on a Friday afternoon on Park Avenue in the 80s, where uptown traffic begins to thin out. A very smart detective named Spitzer had figured there was a chance the driver was returning from work, so he positioned himself on the east side of Park facing uptown and just behind a hydrant space so he'd be able to move out into traffic fast.

Detective Spitzer sat facing downtown in his uptown-facing car on three successive late afternoons looking for a white Buick or a car that might look like a white Buick to someone who didn't know cars. On the third day he spotted a white Olds with a badly broken grill and a dent in the hood driven by, in his words, "a young white male who drove in traffic as if there weren't other cars around." The detective had a difficult time moving in and out of traffic trying to get up alongside the car he didn't want to lose sight of. When he did, he sounded his siren and motioned the guy over, but the guy kept going because, he later contended, the detective wasn't in uniform and was driving an ordinary car.

Detective Spitzer finally cornered the white Olds at a red light, got out and shoved his badge in the driver's face. According to the detective, when both cars were around the corner on a side street, he took the young driver to the front of his car and asked him how come the damage. Spitzer was experienced in what a detective encounters every day of the week, liars. So he read the Miranda to the young man, who was shaking a bit, and said, "Son, why did you drive away from the accident?" And son told him some cock-and-bull excuse but never denied that he was the driver and that was the car. The problem now was that the kid, after due consultation with his hack, was saying he never heard any Miranda, and you know what happens to that kind of case.

So I phoned Farlan Adams and with a touch of honey in my voice asked if he'd be free for a cup of coffee at Billy's Java. He answered as if I'd invited him to massage the small of my back.

I told him the alleged facts. I didn't have to tell him I wanted desperately to win my first case. He took his time thinking. I watched him. He wasn't getting rid of me with top-of-the-head stuff. Finally, he said something like "Ahem," which meant he was ready. So were my notebook and pencil.

He gave me point after point in rapid fire. I scribbled like mad, determined to get it all down.

Suddenly I felt his hand on my hand. It felt like a man's hand, not like a teacher's hand. I looked up.

"Susan," he said, "the small points aren't as important as understanding your strategy. If the jury starts out wanting to let the man go, they'll look for the holes in the evidence as it's presented and vote for acquittal. If they start out wanting to convict, they'll see past the holes to the equity. That's why the opening statement is crucial."

He looked at his hand on my hand as if he was seeing it for the first time and pulled it away. I didn't give a damn about his hand, he could have laid it anywhere on me he wanted to so long as he kept talking.

He said, "Try this. Ladies and gentlemen, an accident is an accident. The people are not saying that the defendant intentionally took the life of a woman trying to cross the street. They are saying that after he hit her instead of stopping and trying to get medical help he took off, hoping no one would ever link him to this death. The taking off, leaving the scene of an accident, compounds the crime he is charged with, vehicular manslaughter, in plain words, killing with a car. The defendant's counsel will try to make you believe he didn't know he had hit anything. You will see photographs introduced

into evidence of the extensive damage to the defendant's car. He'd
have to be dead not to notice the kind of impact that would cause
such damage. What did he think he hit on Park Avenue, a deer?"

He paused for effect, as he'd want me to. Then he continued.

"What he hit was a human being. He hit her so hard she died
within an hour. And he took off. Did he later decide to report in and
say he was sorry? He went to work the next day, and the next day,
and the next day, until coming home the third day an astute detective
spotted his car, and when faced by the detective he admitted his
guilt. You will hear his lawyer speak. What his lawyer says is not
evidence, any more than what I am saying is evidence. Your job is
to listen to the evidence and to determine the facts and see that
justice is done. Otherwise, you will be sending a message to every
driver in this city that pedestrians are fair game, that if you hit someone and drive right on, leaving the person to die in the street, all
you need is a good lawyer and you'll get away with vehicular homicide, which is another name for murder with a four-thousand-pound
weapon that no pedestrian can defend himself against."

I kissed Farlan Adams on the cheek. Oh I realized my mistake
the minute I'd done it. I could actually feel his cheek quiver. He
turned red. He looked twenty years old.

"Thank you, thank you," I said, and tried to finish my second cup
of coffee fast while Farlan sipped his forever because he was inter-
preting my kiss as a thousand decibels louder than what I'd intended.

We parted company on 116th Street. I put out my hand. He took
mine in both of his. There were Columbia people all over the place,
but he didn't seem to care who saw. The color in his cheeks made
him glow. He was handsome. With a slight bow, he said, "Please give
my love to General and Mrs. Whitcomb's daughter." Then he turned
and strode away like a man who had achieved something remarkable.

That is the best teacher I've ever had. And the best advisor a young
lawyer could ever have. I would lose him the moment his head
cleared.

Four days later I got the letter.

My dear Susan,
      Ever since our last meeting, my mind's been in a mael-
strom. All this past year I struggled to calm my feelings,

as you had cautioned me to do. Apparently all I'd accomplished was to isolate them in some hidden compartment of memory and pretend they didn't exist any more. Thursday, the simple act of seeing you and responding to your need for advice ruptured the walls of that compartment and flooded me with feelings I haven't had since I was a very young man. How I wish I was that young man now so that I wouldn't feel like a trespasser on your youth. The truth is I have not been able to sleep a night through since seeing you. I have imagined the indescribable, and am suffering the exquisite pain of the unrequited. Would that I had been struck by temporary blindness when you first raised your hand in class.

Who was it that said that love letters should be written and thrown away? If I do that I will never know if there is the smallest possibility that you might ever return my affection. I could not bear that. Please do not laugh at this letter. I beg you not to show it to your friends. It is difficult enough for me to parade my naked spirit before you alone.

I wish I had met you in a different context years ago. What a life we might have led! Have you ever wondered how cruel time is that it does not allow us to redo the past or let history be history? I am bereft.

As ever,
F.

CHAPTER 5

Brigadier General Harold H. Whitcomb

I enjoy the beautiful mornings we get in Rome. This very morning I was tempted to have my driver drop me off at the park entrance instead of taking me to the stone building that housed my office. Playing hooky isn't easy for someone in my uniform.

As I passed Lieutenant Daniels's desk I spotted on the top of my in basket a letter from Susan marked PERSONAL. I picked it up immediately, said "Good morning," and headed straight into my office, leaving Lieutenant Daniels looking as if he were trying to retrieve an objection from the slow disk in his brain.

I suppose I hurried past Daniels a bit faster than usual so that I could open Susan's letter. An only child should write more often. Or phone. Did PERSONAL mean there was something she didn't want my aide to see? Was she pregnant? Getting married? I was about to slice the letter open with a souvenir stiletto when I heard a commotion in the outer office, and Lieutenant Daniels yelling, "You can't go in there, sir!" The door swung open and a captain I'd never laid eyes on before shouted "General! Don't open that letter! It'll blow your arms off up to your shoulders!"

The captain's hands reached for the letter.

"It's from my daughter," I said.

"Please, sir," the captain said. There was something in his voice that made me think perhaps he knew something I didn't know. I held the letter out to him.

With two careful fingers he plucked the letter from my hands, held it up to the window light, felt around its perimeter, said *Jesus* under his breath, and ran from my office with the letter and without saying another word.

I went after the captain, yelling "Where are you going with that?"

The captain paid me no more mind than if I were a buck private. He headed straight for the men's room. I followed him in. In a sink filling with water he was holding the letter down as if he was trying to drown it.

"Sorry, sir," he said, looking down at the mess.

He finally took the remains out of the basin and laid them out on a paper towel. I saw tattered paper, soaking wet cardboard, some gray, putty-like stuff rolled thin as a playing card, a button battery, and one thing I recognized: a very thin brass detonator the length of half a cigarette.

I folded my arms so the captain wouldn't see the stupid tremble of my hands. Like everyone else, I'd attended the lecture on letter bombs. I'd been suckered into damn near opening this one because of Susan's return address on the envelope.

The captain dried his hands on a paper towel, picked up the one with the pieces on it as if it was a hammock and said, "I didn't mean to be rude, sir, but that was pretty close."

"I appreciate your rudeness, captain."

"Can we go back to your office?"

I led the way.

The captain put the paper towel with the remains of the letter bomb on my desk, reached for his wallet, and showed me his I.D.: CALVIN MOORE, CID. I shook Calvin Moore's still-damp hand.

"The person who really deserves the thanks, general, is a smart young female security-checker assigned to the immigration section at Leonardo da Vinci. Night before last a dark-complected fellow caught her eye because his forehead was wet with sweat and it was cold in that reception area. She spoke to him in Italian and he answered in bargain-basement English, flashing a Lebanese passport. These days the last person you expect to use a Lebanese passport is a Lebanese. She made him open his carry-on. No weapons, no explosives. She asked if he had enough money to cover his stay in Italy. He took out his wallet, and showed lots of lira, drachmas, and Syrian money. The Syrian bills increased her suspicions. She checked everything in his wallet twice. Nothing. Except his international driver's license had four typewritten names fastened to its back. The second name was yours."

"Jesus!" I sucked in a deep breath. "Who were the other three?"

"I'm sorry, sir," the captain said. "You don't have a need to know."

"Just curious about who else around here is worth killing. How the hell am I going to piece together what's left of my daughter's letter?"

"Don't worry, sir," he said. "We'll do that for you and give you a photocopy of the reconstruction. We have to preserve the original for the trial."

"What trial?"

"The Italians are going to try this man as a way of getting to Monteleone."

He could see I was as uncomfortable as a bat in daylight.

"After two hours of interrogation, the man with the Lebanese passport got hysterical. He thought his mission was safe because he only carried names. What worried me was that Monteleone always gets his list of targets twice, just in case one gets waylaid or doctored. We believe the four people were supposed to be executed by resident terrorists."

I sat down hard enough to feel the jolt in my tailbone. When I first got here, I used to worry about being targeted. Nobody bothered me, and I finally decided I wasn't doing anything important enough to be in anybody's gunsights.

"Who thought of checking the mail, captain?"

"That was me, sir."

"I have to thank you once more."

"It's my job, sir. Monteleone's a smart cookie. He'd figure his targets wouldn't open their own mail unless it was marked *personal* from someone they knew. I phoned the ADC's of all four people and asked if any incoming material didn't look official. Lieutenant Daniels said you had a letter from the States. I told him not to touch it, I'd be right over. You apparently overruled me, sir."

Dammit, I hate being suspicious, but you have to choose between being suspicious or dead. Whoever named this field "intelligence" couldn't have imagined the ironies contained in that one word.

"I suppose someone in the central post office waylaid my daughter's letter."

The captain stood. "That's as good as any scenario we've been able to put together up till now. I'll be off now, sir. Please be careful till we put this particular thing to rest."

"What about my daughter's letter?"

"I'll have a copy of that in your hands in under two hours."

You better believe I tried to dig into my morning's work just to get my mind off what might have happened. *Do I tell Heather about this? Do I phone Susan and tell her not to put her name or address on envelopes?* She'd ask why. She's been a why girl since day one. If I tell her I want a grandchild she says why. There're some things there's no answer for. I didn't worry when Susan was twenty-two or -four, but she's twenty-seven now and time's running out. The one time I mentioned the subject out loud, she said, "Don't worry, Dad, if I don't get married in time, I can always pick up a deposit at the semen bank."

She inherited that smartass tongue from Heather, who was running off at the mouth just like that when she was Susan's age. The truth is I wish Susan weren't still seeing that professor. She was never one to go ga-ga over a teacher, though she did talk a lot about him. These days every army post has got young women running all over the place saying, "Yes, colonel, yes, major" to men who take advantage of their rank. I wouldn't be at all surprised if that professor does. No use asking Heather if she suspects any hanky-panky in that relationship. She'd only laugh, like she did about my needing to have my rabbit's foot in my left pocket. Last week I couldn't find the damn thing anywhere and now look, nearly got my arms blown off.

Heather says I don't like the professor's attention to Susan because I'm prejudiced. Well, prejudice is one subject I know cold. I go lots of places out of uniform. The army wants it that way. No World War II haircuts, no dogtags showing in an open-necked sport shirt. For certain kinds of official functions, of course I have to put the gear on. Anyone wants to sniff prejudice in five seconds flat should accompany me into a room full of educated civilians. They see my uniform, the three rows of ribbons, and they've got me typed. The worst snobs are the raised-consciousness embassy think-tank types who could be knocked flat by a wet glove. One thing I've learned is that it's easier to judge the character of a woman wearing a dress full of sequins than to get an accurate fix on what's inside a uniform somebody else picked.

Heather gets hit with a prejudged view all the time. People can't understand what a woman with two graduate degrees in the humanities and a profound love of painting and music and ballet sees in a career officer. As a class we've had some lousy PR. When Ike got to be President, I fidgeted every time I saw him on TV trying to end a sentence in grammatical tune. And that pre-Rambo maniac Patton with his pearl-handled balls didn't help the image any. Of course you find you need both types when there's a war on.

Heather says she couldn't have married a man like Ike, she'd go crazy waiting for him to finish a sentence. As for George Patton, she said she encountered one of those hyperventilating testosterone problems in high school and never wanted to meet another. She says she needed someone like me. But does she know me? She sure doesn't know much about what I do.

I used to tell her about my work. When I stopped she had to guess that I was now doing something I couldn't talk about. She notices the way Audley checks out underneath my car in the mornings. And that non-regulation automatic in the night table.

"You're not afraid of burglars, are you?" she said.

"No," I said. By rights I shouldn't even have said that. Nothing would be gained by Heather's knowing, except gray hairs.

I've seen the reports. If the Iranians don't love me, I'm in good company. If the Syrians get nervous about my Bekaa Valley photos, let them. But the people who really hate me are the ones Heather used to dote on, the French. Their penchant for appeasement is masochistic. Every time they kowtow to some terrorists, the next half dozen bombs turn up in France.

With several hundred thousand Americans in Europe, being one of four shortlisted for removal is a goddamn compliment to my work. Sure I could be rotated back to the States, but the man who replaced me would have my files and not my memory. Besides, Heather just loves living in Rome or Paris. Sometimes I'm convinced the bastards think she's part of my cover. I go to the museums with her. I sit next to her at concerts. She listens to the music, and I'm tuned into my peripheral vision, waiting for some sudden movement, afraid they'll miss me and get Heather. Or they'll get both of us, and where'll that leave Susan? She hasn't a clue that the army moved me sideways out of the chain of command and gave me a role in intelligence that scares the hell out of me because the other side knows we're at war and we don't.

I decided not to tell Heather what happened this morning. She'd just worry.

It was damn near three hours before the copy of Susan's letter arrived. By then I expected it to say she was pregnant by a black man from China. Maybe that's what she did say for all I know. Did you ever try to puzzle out a letter that's been drowned in rain? All that handwriting with whole patches missing?

"Dear Dad," it said. "I didn't . . ." and the rest of the paragraph couldn't be made out for love or money.

Then it went, "Which was enough government work to last me a lifetime. Dibble Lowe now has me working my ass off, but I slavishly love it because it's got two of the best litigating partners in the business. One of them is a handsome, thirty-six, divorced, presently unattached Protestant New Englander, all of which should warm the cockles of your impatient heart. No, I didn't land the job through *The New York Times*, it was a tip from Professor Adams. We keep in touch."

What the hell exactly does "in touch" mean?

The next two pages she was either describing a case or a disease, it could have been either. I was looking for more mentions of that Professor Adams. Adams's damn near my age. Liberal-minded Heather thinks age doesn't matter, wants me to relax about it. I'll relax when I know what the hell's going on with that girl.

CHAPTER 6

Susan Whitcomb

A CID man came around at work and asked did I keep any of my personal stationery in the office.

"Sure," I said. "Why?"

"Your father's General Whitcomb, right?"

"Right."

"All I want is one sheet and one envelope. You can write *not to be used* across the sheet if you don't trust people."

I repeated my question.

"They're investigating some kind of letter bomb incident over in Italy."

"What's that got to do with my father?"

"I sure don't know, Miss. Maybe your father does." When I gave him the blank sheet and an envelope, he asked, "Want a receipt?"

The second he was gone I reached for the phone. When Dad was on this side of the Atlantic, it was easy enough to pick up a phone and chat, but overseas phoning still puts me on edge. You can't just chitchat for half an hour, you feel you've got to keep it short and important. The last time I phoned, I ran out of things to say in maybe twenty seconds. *Hey, Dad, what's this about a letter bomb?* He'd say, "I don't know what you're talking about." End of loving conversation. Dad has always been too damn closed-mouthed for his inquisitive women. He was too young for the good war, still underage for Korea, and in Vietnam, thank heaven, he never got further inland than Saigon, where the joint chiefs sent him on some excuse or other. Mom and I both knew it smelled of an intelligence thing.

Mom must have guessed. I remember something happened to him that touched off the only loud squabble I ever heard between them, with her saying did he want to get himself killed, and him saying this was peacetime, and her going on about she didn't want a widow's pension, she wanted both of them to retire right then. They sure shut up when I came out of the bathroom. I said I vote for retirement, and they both turned on me as if a teenager wasn't supposed to have a vote.

My mouth used to get the better of me then. Will I ever forget the day I was playing the terrific stereo Dad got for me and he opened the door of my room without knocking and told me to turn the damn thing down, he had a headache, and I went and turned the volume control until nothing came out, and he said, "You don't have to turn it off for spite, just turn it down." Like a jerk I started to say, "If it gives you a headache—" and he cut me off. "I came home with the headache," he said, "that noise just makes it worse." That's when I said, "If your work gives you a headache, Dad, why don't you retire like Mom says and stop playing soldier?"

He slapped my face hard.

His eyes looked frightened afterwards. The truth is I felt scared for him from then on, because by slapping me he had broken his own code of discipline and he must have feared, as we did, what might now be let loose.

CHAPTER 7

Heather Paley Whitcomb

This morning I woke with the lilt of Mozart in my head. Some mornings it's Vivaldi, sometimes Gershwin, sometimes the third Brandenburg that I imagine being conducted by Bach himself, who, I must say, is much more handsome in my mind's eye than in the drawings by his contemporaries. How can I trust an artist who makes Bach look, well, uninteresting?

I trust myself. Over the years I've found my instincts to be far more reliable than the army or newspapers or other transient authorities. Hal says quite lovingly that I don't even trust God, which is just not true. I trust God to guide my instincts every single day.

Hal claims to hear nothing except the alarm clock when he wakes up and bounds out of bed for his wash-up, shave, coffee, and out of the house into his waiting car. It's just as well he doesn't hear music. The only possible accompaniment to Hal's morning rush would be John Philip Sousa played at triple-speed.

I truly do not understand people who say they are zombies until they've had a cigarette or coffee. Why shouldn't the first minutes awake be the day's appetizer? Morning ought to be viewed as if God were holding a fork with one bite of a delicious dish inches from one's mouth and saying *take a taste of today's special.*

This morning, on the way to showering, I caught a look at my body in the full-length mirror on the bathroom door. It's an expe-

rienced body, I said to myself. It sure as hell doesn't look the way it
looked when I was eighteen, but it'll damned well do.

Mozart played all through my shower, then invited me to sample
deep breaths of good outdoor air before it got polluted by the day's
traffic. My morning ritual included buying a *Herald Tribune* from
the vendor outside the hotel, who gives my name a lovely cadence.
I glanced at the one photo on the front page, some men in an iron
cage in a courtroom. Terrorists on trial? For what? Oh Lord, they're
the ones that shot Robbie Baker on his doorstep in front of his kids.
I tossed the paper into the nearest basket. The world would just have
to get along without my knowing the news today.

I found myself on the small side street off the via de Tizio, where
the bakery produces what I would have to call very-non-Italian bread,
a wonderful mixture of all the grains on earth. The baker knows I
don't like to carry unwrapped bread in my hands the way most of
his customers do, so he kindly puts some newspaper around it.

The baker was just handing me my wrapped loaf when a man's
voice next to me said, "Are you not General Whitcomb's wife?"

The women doing their morning shopping turned to look at both
of us. What in heaven's name is wrong with being an American? Or
a general's wife, for that matter?

The man, fortyish, sported a dark blue velvet jacket, a silk paisley
ascot, and flashed perfect teeth in the kind of smile that in Italy makes
me think *gigolo*.

"Excuse me," he said, "I thought perhaps for a moment you were
General Whitcomb's wife."

Hal sometimes gets me almost as suspicious as he can be, especially since General Beach's wife had acid thrown in her face by
someone she'd never seen before. This dandy seemed harmless
enough. Despite his smile, he seemed strangely sad, as if he'd once
been a proud man. I decided to take the risk and said, "I am the
general's wife."

He put out his hand and of course my quick reflex was to extend
mine also. In a second he was holding the back of my hand up to
his lips. I was certain that what I felt was the tip of his tongue.

He mumbled his name and said, "We met . . ." and launched into
something completely indecipherable, then released my hand from
its warm captivity.

My move was in the direction of the door. Of course he followed, and so, outside, I turned and said, "Forgive me if I hurry off, but the general is waiting for me." I nodded toward the bakery. "I'm afraid you've lost your place in line."

His attempt at smiling made him look much older, as if he were used to being rejected and was trying to keep the pain to a minimum.

"Good-bye," I said.

"Good-bye," said the sad man, and in defeat turned back into the bakery full of onlookers.

Maybe I had met him at some reception. Had I been rude to a diplomat? Did he kiss all hands that way? I could hear my heart all the way home.

In the bathroom I peered into the mirror. *Heather dear friend, don't let a European's hand kiss go to your head. Hal will tell you the man is some male Mata Hari working for the enemy!*

There was no reason to tell Hal anything.

Something made me glance in the mirror at what was behind me.

It was just the door of the bathroom slightly ajar. What was I expecting? Punishment for liking the way the man kissed my hand? Well, I was not going to let the remnants of a puritan conscience interfere with my breakfast.

I cut myself a slice of the bread, spread some lovely soft cheese on it, and had it with rich black coffee.

I wasn't alone. As I ate, I listened to the street sounds, the babble of people with tireless energy in their voices, and somewhere in the background, Mozart playing loyally. Europe is still Europe. The piazzas and boulevards are as lovely as ever. Hal has his work to do here. My advice to all of those who want us to leave is *tant pis*. We are the descendants of pioneers, we have gumption, and your retreat into violence may frighten a coward or two here or there but you had damned well better keep clear of me.

When Hal called me just after five to say he was headed home, did I want to eat at Luigi's, I asked, "Could we eat early enough to make the Mozart concert?" He said could we save Mozart for another night? I told him Mozart would keep, he's kept well for a couple of centuries. Then Hal asked did I mind if Milford Burns joined us?

General Burns—Hal calls him Millie, which drives Burns up the wall—is Hal's closest friend. What could I say—no? That a gigolo had stepped on my accelerator this morning and I wanted some private time with my husband? General Burns is a widower. Whenever the three of us have a meal together I catch Millie looking at me with the eyes of a satyr. Right in front of Hal.

"Is Millie coming home with you?" I asked.

"He'll meet us at the restaurant later."

Well, I thought, we may just get to the restaurant a wee bit late.

Extraordinary the way memories drift to mind. When Susan was three or four, she'd stand facing Hal, then step up onto his highly polished shoes. Then he would sort of walk her, left, right, left, right. We would all laugh, and Hal would say something like "She'll learn to stand on her own feet soon enough."

In Frankfurt we'd had a lovely private house with a slate roof. Hal's car was kept in the locked garage. As soon as his driver, Corporal Audley, arrived every morning he'd check underneath Hal's car even though it had been locked up for the night. He'd make sure there were no wires linked to the wheels to explode a bomb when the car was moved. Audley always started the engine and backed out so the car would be at the curb when Hal was ready to go. "I'm like the general's taster," he once said to me. "If the ignition was wired to a bomb, it'd blow before the general got into the car."

I'm certain Audley's intention was to ease my mind.

For Christmas Millie Burns gave Hal something he'd ordered from a catalogue, an anti-theft alarm device that plugged into a car's cigarette lighter receptacle. If anyone lifted the hood, or fooled around underneath the car, or tried to open the door, the sensor would wait fifteen seconds and then flash a strobe light on the dash and emit a banshee siren that would wake the neighborhood quicker than an earthquake. You couldn't turn it off by yanking it out of the lighter receptacle. Only a key could turn it off. Hal had one, Audley the other.

Hal certainly appreciated that gift. He said to Audley, "You're not at risk anymore. General Burns gave us an early warning system that's a dilly."

Audley continued to check out the car every morning. He didn't trust gadgets.

When we were relocated to Rome, we were put up at the Hotel Tantillo until a house became available. It wasn't as if we were living in a Hilton. The two-story hotel lobby had marble columns. On each of three walls, lit by an overhead light, was a painting. I don't mean a hotel painting, I mean a work of art worthy of a sensitive private collection. Our two-room suite had a painting in its large living room and a Chinese cabinet in which we kept liquor for guests. Atop it was an antique clock I would have liked to own.

The doorman always got a taxi for us while we waited in the lobby. Hal said it wasn't safe just standing around in front of the hotel. Audley, who had been transferred to Rome with Hal, would come by each weekday morning in a car that had been checked out at the motor pool. Driving the general, Audley never took the same route two days in a row.

Hal is almost never late. This time he was half an hour late. An hour late. No point in calling his office. I called anyway. No answer. Two hours. I was getting frantic. The knock on the door jarred me. *Hal never knocks, he uses the key.*

It was Millie Burns, still in uniform. He and Hal always change to civvies when dining out.

"I thought you were going to meet us at the restaurant," I said. Then I saw his face.

"Let's sit down," he said, closing the door behind him.

CHAPTER 8

Brigadier General Milford Burns

Despite my recent command of nearly fifteen thousand men, I've been as lonely as Robinson Crusoe since Abby passed away three years ago.

My estranged son tells his friends I'm an executive in some international cartel. He says I don't understand his music because all the guns I've heard go off have made me deaf. I'm not deaf, I'm just not trained to hear the kind of music he composes.

A general-grade officer can't mingle for more than a minute or two with lower-ranking officers without spoiling their good time. When I go into the john at the officers' club, whoever's telling an off-color story stops dead. They leave quickly as if it would be unseemly for them to see a general piss.

If it weren't for my friendship with Hal Whitcomb, I'd have asked to be transferred back to the States just to preserve my sanity. I realize it wasn't just that Hal and I got along as if we were brothers. It was Heather.

It took a long time for me to acknowledge that I had a stirring whenever I saw her. Heather and I once spent two hours talking when Hal was called away one evening, and I think we both realized that if Hal hadn't been such a good friend we'd have gotten ourselves in trouble.

When Abby was alive, I didn't feel so bad about my Heather fantasies. After all, it was Abby in my bed, not Heather.

This afternoon Sergeant Hart knocked and came on in before I said "Come in!" From the look of him, if Abby wasn't already dead I'd have thought something had happened to her. The corner of Hart's eye was ticking away.

Abby was safe. That's the only good thing about death, nothing that bad can still happen to you.

"What's up?" I said.

"It's General Whitcomb, sir."

"Where?" I stood up. I was expecting to meet Hal at the restaurant, not here.

"They got his car on his way home."

"Somebody stole his car?"

"No, sir." The sergeant seemed afraid to speak out.

"Then say it."

"General Whitcomb is dead."

"Are you crazy? I just talked to him an hour ago. We're going to have dinner."

I must have been shouting because Sergeant Hart stepped back. "There's an M.P. lieutenant outside who knows the whole story, sir."

I shoved Sergeant Hart aside. I'd never so much as touched an enlisted man in my life.

The M.P. officer standing in the anteroom came to attention.

"What am I hearing?"

"It's true, sir."

"What's true?!"

"General Whitcomb's been killed."

I wanted him to take back his words. I motioned him into my office. My chest hurt with the pounding.

"What the hell happened?"

Then he told me, step by step.

My double-crossing brain had two thoughts at once, a pang of shock and a sense of opportunity. "Has Mrs. Whitcomb been told?"

"Not yet, sir. Major Crouse thought you might be the right person to tell the widow."

"I see. What about the assailant?"

"I was told that's under control."

"What does that mean?"

"I don't really know, sir."

"Thank you, lieutenant. I'll take care of things."

I ran scenarios in my head. When someone died overseas, the army tried to speed things up. They'd want the widow to travel with the casket. On what earthly pretext could I persuade Heather to stay in Rome? Or, failing that, to come back quickly?

As a young officer I several times had had to write a letter to the parents of a young serviceman. I never had to make a house call.

The moment I was in Heather's suite, I pecked her offered cheek as I always do and said, "Please sit down."

"What is it?" she said, still standing. Heather isn't the kind of woman you argue with, so I stood there, telling her.

Hal's car had stopped for a light on the via Cardinale.

A goggled man in black leather on a motorbike had pulled up alongside the car, plunked something on the roof and sped off with the light still red. As Corporal Audley got out of the car to see what the thing on the roof was, it went off in his face. The main force of the blast was set to go downward into the rear seat area. Where Hal was.

That's how the lieutenant told it to me. Just the facts.

"Is he dead?" Her face pleaded with me for an answer she could live with.

"Yes, thank God."

"What the hell do you mean by that?"

"I meant given the extent of his injuries."

"I want to see him," she said.

"The morticians will need a few hours. They weren't too optimistic."

"I won't believe he's dead unless I *see* him, Millie!"

Then Heather shattered like a pitcher breaking. She was sobbing, her chest heaving, her hands clasping and unclasping. I didn't know what to do with my hands.

I tell you it was a shock. I'd never seen a great proud woman suddenly crack like that.

Just as suddenly, she dried up, took a tissue to her tears, blew her nose, took control, and said, "I'm sorry, Millie."

I did what I thought was the natural thing, I put my arms around her, held her head, wondering if I'd said everything the best possible way. Heather's a smart woman. She probably knew before I started talking.

I was holding pressed against me the wife of my closest friend, having delivered the most awful message in the world. I hardly realized what was happening, but she must have felt it because she looked up at me with pure hatred and told me to get the hell out.

CHAPTER 9

Heather Whitcomb

Once, when Susan was just four, I took her with me to the central library's large reading room.

"What are all these people doing?" she asked me in full voice.

Several of them turned around to shush the little girl.

"They're reading," I whispered.

She wiggled her finger for me to bend over toward her. "Are all of them reading everything?" she whispered.

I shook my head.

Loud enough for everyone to hear, Susan said, "I am going to read everything!"

Outside, I squeezed her hand in approval. Susan squeezed my hand right back to show she approved of my approval.

If I call Susan in her office, she'll still have to go home to pack. I'll wait till she's home.

Was I being considerate or cowardly? I wanted her here. I gave the hotel operator Susan's office number. Yes, person-to-person. The operator said she'd call right back.

Waiting, my memory was of Hal and me in the evenings, listening to Chopin over a glass of wine, letting the waves of the day settle. Over dinner we gossiped with each other like cronies. From time to time at the end of an evening Hal would put his strong hand against the hair at the back of my head, patting it gently. He'd touch my ear as if it was something forbidden. That's the way he started lovemaking, something that might seem irrelevant to an onlooker, but not to me.

The phone's insistent *blah*-blah, *blah*-blah jarred the memory away. I picked up the receiver. The operator said my party was not available at the present time.

"Please tell them it's her mother calling," I said. "It's an emergency."

I could hear some conversation at the other end, not clearly, then the New York operator was back on, saying, "Susan Whitcomb is not on the premises. I'll leave my operator's number to call back when she returns."

"Thank you." I put the phone down, got undressed, put a robe on, and scrunched myself deep into the armchair Hal had sat in last evening. If I were a cat, I thought, I would still be able to smell his smell.

I awoke with a start when the light came in through the window. It would be past midnight New York time, only a few hours until Susan would find out from a newspaper!

I told the hotel operator I needed to place a station call to the United States and gave her Susan's home number. She said she'd get back to me as if I was being a pest.

I wanted to brush my teeth, such an ordinary everyday thing to do in a crumbled world. No sooner had I a mouthful of toothpaste than I heard *blah*-blah, *blah*-blah, *blah*-blah. I quickly rinsed and hurried to the bedroom phone. Would you believe it, the operator wanted to check the number I'd given her. She'd transposed the last two numbers!

Milford Burns, breaking the news, must have felt what I feel now. I really should phone him later on. The poor man'll want to see me through whatever it is that army widows have to do. I'd better apologize for shooing him out of here. He wasn't making a conscious pass. Old Millie is just strapped to his physiology. It must have embarrassed him as much as me.

The next time the shrill phone rang, I picked it up and could hear what must have been the sound of ringing in Susan's bedroom four thousand miles away.

CHAPTER 10

Susan Whitcomb

I groped for the clamoring black instrument and snatched it from its cradle to stop the sound. Whoever says they have never experienced a second's terror from the ringing of a telephone in the middle of the night is a liar. My voice still thick with sleep, I said, "Yes?" and I heard an Italian accent that seemed like singing, "*Un momento*," and then immediately Mom's voice saying, "Susan, it's me."

"Where are you?"

Why do we first assume that a call from overseas is a call from nearby? Is it because we still cannot credit the clarity of sound bouncing off a satellite and coming down to earth in the exact spot next to your ear that the caller was aiming for?

"What is it?" I said, wide awake.

Her next words were like dry biscuits breaking.

I said, "I can't hear you."

"I have to . . . to talk to you, Susan."

"You *are* talking to me, Mom."

"I don't know how to tell you."

"Tell me what?"

"Love, Dad's been killed."

I must have misheard. "Mom, would you say that again."

"Oh Susan, I don't want to."

"Did you say he's been killed?"

"Yes."

"Did you say yes?"

"Yes."

It was as if a deep, round, endless hole had opened in the world and I was plunging down it like a doll dropped down a well. People didn't die in their fifties anymore, he could live another twenty, thirty years.

I heard Mom crying. When I'd thought of the possibility of death, it had been hers. That formidable woman's lungs from childhood on were a place of danger. She caught pneumonia from simple colds, she sometimes had a cigarette cough without ever having smoked. I thought she would one day die gasping for breath with Dad and me standing over her helpless to help her. She was now telling me that the general, with the physique of a much younger man, "fit as a cello" he would say patting the slight arch of his midsection, had, in the euphemism he himself used, "disappeared off the radar screen."

Still struggling against a wave of disbelief, I stupidly asked, "How did it happen?"

Mother said, "Excuse me." I heard her blow her nose. "He was killed by a terrorist."

"Where?"

"In his car, coming from work."

My bedside clock said just past midnight. Early morning in Rome. *Why do we care what time things happen?*

"His driver, too. Please come."

"Oh Mom," I said, and called on God to twist the rules and bring him back. "I'll get the first plane I can. Where are you?"

"At the same hotel. Tantillo. They still haven't found a house for us."

"Is anyone there with you?"

"No."

"What is the army doing?"

"Nothing. I suppose they are doing things. I don't know."

"I'll be there."

"Hurry," she said, as if my getting there sooner might somehow still save his life.

* * *

I lay back, my head on the pillow, seeing my father eating his breakfast cereal. It was how I had seen him most often in the morning when Mom and I traveled with him, always a cloth napkin tucked under his chin to spare his tie. I wanted to reach out and hug him hard.

The sound of an automobile in the street pulled me back. That car was going too fast. I had to move fast, too. If I was desolate, how must she be?

I had to get to her.

The good thing about calling airlines in the middle of the night is that they don't leave you hanging on the line listening to Muzak. Why did all the damn airlines fly direct to Rome only in the evening? The British had a flight to London that connected to a flight to Rome. Yes, they had room in business class for the overseas leg. Yes, I had a credit card. I was told to check in two hours before flight time because of new security measures. *They didn't help keep my father alive.*

Daddy used to say that when trouble struck it was useless to churn over what had already happened unless you were an historian. Soldiers had to focus on the battles to come. Only when the war was finally over could a soldier relive the past. When I asked him if he, the closed-mouthed one, would ever jot down his memoirs for his grandchildren, he came back at me with, "What grandchildren?" Now, when I had a child its grandfather would be somebody in a photograph, not warm arms and a lap. If he could talk from wherever he was now, he would say, *Susan, stop chewing cud like a civilian. Get on with it.*

I hated waking my secretary. Her husband almost always answers the phone. Betty said he refers to me as "your female boss."

Before calling her I showered, dressed, packed with a checklist taped to the inside top of my suitcase, delaying my call to Betty to the very last.

"I'm sorry to call so early," I said to her husband.

"I'll get her."

When she came on the line, I said, "Sorry about the hour." I told her I was off to the airport, would she please call Judge Ballin's clerk and get a continuance, yes I knew there'd be hell to pay because you couldn't just abandon the jury, yes he'd always wanted to hold me in contempt, here was his chance.

"Hold the fort," I said. "Reinforcements are coming."

"Who?"

"Me. I'll be back in a few days at most."

I'd forgotten to mention that the reason for the emergency was that my father had died.

In the taxi on the way to Kennedy, my thoughts tumbled like clothes in a dryer: Dad and me when I was young. Mom in Rome counting the hours. My answering machine. I'd forgotten to turn it on! If Farlan called he'd get no response. If he kept trying, he might go on one of his jealousy binges. Poor Farlan, I could feel his hurt. He might call the office. Betty would tell him I'd gone to Rome, but she didn't know why. He'd think she was holding back on purpose. . . .

At Kennedy, the moron going through my carry-on bag was like a raccoon grubbing for morsels. Because I was late in arriving, did I fit some hijacker's profile? What did he expect to find, some lingerie to feel, a gun? *Listen, the gun is in my head.*

After clearing security, my first thought was to phone Farlan. All seven public phones were in use, my flight was being called on the public address system, the flashing light said "Boarding . . . boarding . . . boarding." I'd have to remember to phone him from Rome. Or to send a cable.

On the plane the stewardess gave me the morning paper. There it was: U.S. GENERAL KILLED IN ROME. It had really happened.

I turned to the obits. Not yet. He wasn't old enough or important enough for an obit to have been prepared in advance.

I leaned my left temple against the cushioned vibration of the plane's curved wall, and hoped for sleep. Memories of Dad kept crashing in like November waves on the Montauk shore. It was in Montauk that he'd made his last try at converting me to a military career, anything, even the navy. "Look what Rickover accomplished."

I'd told him I wanted to do battle in courtrooms, where nobody died except in small places in their heart.

Annie, my old chum, where are you now? Why did we lose touch? The deaths aren't over yet.

* * *

From home I'd cabled my flight number and arrival time to Mom at the hotel. *Stupid*, David Smith would tell me later. *You could have been met by the wrong people*. A cable is as public as shouting from a rooftop, anybody can get access to it, David would say. I had not yet entered the world where phones are bugged without bench warrants and letters steamed open, a world in which "against the law" simply means "clever" or "professional."

Have you noticed how normally polite people will stand up in a plane when it hasn't stopped yet, jostling for a place in line to get off as quickly as possible in order to be surrounded again by walls that don't fly, as if merely being on the ground wasn't enough? I let the pushers push. I needed to prepare my face for Mom.

In the crowd outside the gate, I spotted her immediately, hurried to throw my arms around her, hugged her hard, all of my Protestant restraint dissolving in the babble of Italian reunions surrounding us.

Mom introduced me to the young sergeant escorting her, explaining he'd been Audley's immediate superior at the motor pool.

"I'm sorry," I said to the sergeant. "Is Audley's family coming to Rome?"

The sergeant did a kind of shuffle with his feet and said, "He grew up in a Texas orphanage, ma'am." He volunteered to carry my bag for me, which I let him do because I wanted my arm around Mom as we walked the endless mile to the baggage collection area. And there, at the Rome airport, an exposed location where people had died at the hands of terrorists, I waited in a crowd for my bag to come around the carousel. As I reached for the bag, the sergeant plucked it up, his face triumphant like a sportsman's. He then led us away from the long customs lines to a station off to the side.

Outside, I expected the sergeant's vehicle to be an olive-drab sedan of the kind I'd remembered my father being driven around in, but it was a stark black car without military markings.

In the car Mom showed me the Italian paper. The front-page picture displayed the shattered vehicle and the bodies under tarpaulins. I wondered what they had showed on *Today* and *Good Morning America* while I was at the airport in New York.

"Will I be able to see him?" I asked.

Mother carefully explained why we couldn't.

I cursed whoever had destroyed my father's face so that even the skilled cosmeticians of death could not restore it for me to see it one last time. I'd have to rely on memory, jogged by the contents of the shoebox Mom had stuffed with a lifetime's photos.

We were driven not to the hotel but to the headquarters of the military liaison team. Inside the major's spartan office, the quick condolences over, the major said in a voice that was doing us favors, "General Whitcomb's body will be returned by air at government expense. You may accompany the body on the same plane, or take another. The government will pay for Mrs. Whitcomb's fare but not Miss Whitcomb's since she is technically not a resident dependent."

Get it over with, fucker. I said, "I understand."

"The general will be buried in Arlington with military honors."

For getting himself killed?

Mom said, "I don't know that I want him in Arlington. I'd rather have him closer to me."

The major looked as if she'd spurned something no one had ever spurned before.

"I'll let you know in due course," she said.

I squeezed her hand under the level of the desk.

"Mrs. Whitcomb," the major continued, "would you please fill these forms out to get the pension in motion?"

Mom started to write when the major abruptly stopped her. "No, no," he said, "please print."

"My handwriting is perfectly legible," Mom said.

"It doesn't matter. Please print or the forms will have to be re-done."

"What is this thing about hazard pay?" asked Mother.

"Don't check that box," the major said, "the general's duty in Rome was not considered hazardous, therefore there's no hazard pay."

Mom managed to say, "Wasn't the killing a proof of the hazard?"

When Mom was through the major stood up smartly and held out his hand. I turned my back on it, trying to control an adolescent fury at the insensitivity government people sometimes brandish as their sole sign of office.

Outside, still livid at the major, we found an NBC-TV crew waiting to ambush us. Mom tried to sidestep them, drawing me away, but I'd had it with the incursions of unfeeling strangers plying their trade.

The TV reporter next to the camera said, "Do you have any comment on the general's death?" and I turned to him and to the camera and said, "I'm going to get the sons-of-bitches who did this and kill them with my bare hands." I could see the headlines: SPUNKY GENERAL'S DAUGHTER SEEKS REVENGE. Mom pulled at my sleeve, but I was in no mood for retreat.

"I'm not kidding," I said. "I swear to God I'm going to get the bastards."

He had nerve, the newsman in charge. He said, "Isn't that just as bad as what the terrorists do?"

"Go to hell!"

"Don't you want to see your father's killers brought to justice, tried, convicted, and jailed? What about the law?"

"Fuck the law!" I shouted as Mom pulled on my arm to drag me away.

I bet they didn't use that on the air, the cowards.

That long night of our first grief, not sleeping, we sipped at the cognac Mom had in the flat. Unaccustomed to drink, she talked on and on about things she and Dad had done together before I was born, and then about how he'd throw me up in the air, frightening her and delighting me, always catching me in the safety net of his arms.

I held her, as if I was the mother.

"You owe your life to him," she said.

"I owe my life to both of you," I said, refilling her glass, which was a mistake.

"No, no, no, I meant literally. When I was in the hospital in Paris, having you, it was the American Hospital and I thought I was safe, but I couldn't get them to show me my baby. Your father barged right past the nurse who tried to block his way to the nursery. He saw a gaggle of them around a newborn on an examining table. Hal pounded the palm of his hand on the glass so hard the nurses thought it would break. One of them came out and he said, 'What's wrong?' and the nurse said, 'She seems to hold her breath from time to time.' At the top of his lungs he bellowed, 'You mean she's having trouble breathing? Where's the damn doctor!'

"They told me later that Hal literally yanked the doctor off his bed where he was reading a paperback and virtually frog-marched him to the nursery. We were told he got there just in time. You could have had permanent brain damage. I can't imagine you without the brain you have. Oh, Susan, I still need him!"

Helpless to help her, I cracked and cried.

I had never let her see my tears as an adult. At first, she didn't know what to do with her hands. Then in a rush her arms were around me, nestling my head against hers, the tears from her face mixing with my tears. Though our faces were joined like Siamese sisters', neither sorrow nor cognac could join the separate webs in which we each in silence spun memories of the man who had been the force of my childhood and of her life.

Our bodies, unlike our minds, are quick to reject the intolerable. Mother got sick from the cognac she wasn't used to drinking. When she went to heave in the safety of the john, I offered to hold her head, but she wouldn't have the humiliation of it and shut the door hard.

Afterwards she stretched out on the bed, her forehead damp. I got a washcloth and patted the sweat from above her eyes, which opened to look at me. A droplet had run down to the bridge of her nose. I folded the washcloth carefully to get an edge, touched the droplet. It disappeared.

Her barely audible "Thank you" seemed no louder than her heart, or was it mine? I found myself quietly singing *Flow gently sweet Afton*, the words with a feather of melody. I held her hands tight, whispering my song until I felt the tension in her hands wane and I was sure she was asleep.

When the phone rang I jumped at it, hoping to catch it before it rang again. I don't know what people say in Italy when they answer the phone, but it didn't matter because I spoke before thinking, saying my name, Susan Whitcomb, as if I were in the office taking a call.

A remarkably sonorous man's voice said, "This is David Smith. I've been assigned to you and your mother. Could I come to see you now?"

"It's very late," I said into the phone.

"Tomorrow morning, then?"

"Who are you?"

"I'll show you my I.D. when we meet. Say the lobby of your hotel at nine?"

"I don't know what you look like, Mr. Smith."

"I'll recognize you."

"Have we met?"

"I was at the airport when you arrived."

"You didn't introduce yourself."

"I just wanted to make sure everything went all right."

"Are you with the army?" I asked.

"I'm a civilian, but I've got nothing against the army, don't hang up!" He'd read my mind. "I am," he said, "your official baby sitter."

"Now what's that supposed to mean?"

"I'm your bodyguard. Your mother's too."

"What do we need a bodyguard for? I don't—"

"We'll talk in the morning." His voice had the tone of an order. "Be in the lobby at nine sharp, please."

"I'll be there when I'll be there," I said.

"I don't want you hanging around the lobby unnecessarily. Keep to your room in the meantime. Make sure the door is locked. Don't call room service. And come down at nine sharp."

He hung up, leaving me holding the dead receiver. I looked over at Mom, who'd slept through the conversation.

In bed I closed my eyes and saw page after page in an album of memories, Daddy holding me up in the air with both his arms, saying, "Fly, fly," or sitting in his lap, asking about each of the ribbons on his uniform, "What's this one for?" Would he now get a Purple Heart for being wounded beyond redemption? The devil take his enemies, I wanted *him* back, not a photo album! I opened my eyes to dispel the memories, but the sound of my heart thumping in anger still kept me from sleep. I lay awake for the longest time, hoping that the shadows on the ceiling would drift away.

CHAPTER 11

Susan

In the morning I dressed as quietly as I could. I was adjusting my collar in the mirror, when I heard Mother's voice.

"Good morning," she said. "I hope the inside of your head isn't trying to fight its way out the way mine is."

I quickly went to her bed and hugged her. "I shouldn't have let you have all that cognac. Want me to fix you an ice pack? I could ring—"

"No, no. I'll be all right. I have something Hal used to keep for other people's hangovers."

"You sure?"

"Where are you off to? Are you meeting someone?"

"Just to the lobby, Mom," I said.

"Who are you meeting? Will you be long?"

"A man who phoned last night. He says he's supposed to be looking after us. I'll be back in a jiff. Then we'll have breakfast."

"I'd better get busy. Tell the man we women can look after ourselves."

"I promise I won't leave the hotel," I said.

David Smith must have spotted me the moment the elevator door opened, spewing seven or eight of us out into the brightly lit lobby. A six-footer in a tan suit came straight toward me, blinked through oversized glasses that didn't fit his face at all, and, in a sonorous voice I recognized, said, "You're late." The large clock on the pillar showed two or three minutes after nine.

"Not very," I shrugged, but he had already taken me by the elbow in a way that made it awkward to resist without attracting attention.

He ushered me to a sofa between two oversize tropical plants, and sat down beside me. "I'm really sorry about your father," he said as if he meant it, but his gaze seemed fixed on the other end of the lobby.

"Are you expecting someone else?" I asked.

He looked at me only for a split second, then turned away. "You might say I'm watching for the unexpected. Right now the only one I'm concerned about is the man fiddling inside his briefcase. He's taking too long."

I said, "Would you like me to ask him to hurry up because he's keeping you from telling me why I'm down here?"

That was when David Smith first let me see for an instant what I now think of as his characteristic smile. It appears in three places at once, at the sides of his eyes, in his dimpled cheek, and in the slight movement of his lips. Then his gaze swung back to the man puttering in his briefcase, and from there to the hotel's front doors.

"Aren't you being a bit paranoid?" I said.

Without turning toward me, he said, "I give the devil his due. Your father had too little paranoia." Then immediately he turned to me and said, "I'm sorry. He was a good man."

"Oh, did you know him?"

"Benefited from his work twice," he said, standing up. "Never met him."

The man with the briefcase found what he'd been looking for, closed the case, anchored the straps, and strode toward the reception desk holding a large passport wallet in his other hand. David Smith, with obvious relief, sat back down.

"Mr. Smith, you said you would identify yourself."

Like a blind man, his eyes focused on the lobby entrance, he lifted a flat wallet from inside his jacket and flipped it open with his left hand. Much later I learned why, as a right-handed person, he always did things with his left hand.

The I.D. card that showed through the transparent plastic had his photo on it. With his left thumb he flipped the plastic over to show an international driver's license, name also David Smith.

"My father told us where those are made," I said.

Smith laughed like a human. He actually took his eyes off the hotel entranceway and looked directly at me. *There was something wrong about his face.*

"How can I check you out?" I asked.

"Maybe you can't."

I stood up. "In that case there's no point my staying here." But I didn't move to get away. *What was it about his face?*

He said, "You can pinch my cheek to see if it's real."

"Would Milford Burns know who you are?"

"General Burns?"

"He's a good friend of my father's. Don't all you generals know each other?"

"That's how a lawyer digs out information, isn't it? I have no rank."

"Not even private?"

"Very private."

The officers my father associated with were not given to word play. "Well, what do I ask General Burns?"

David Smith removed a tiny leather case from a side pocket of his tweed jacket, tore off a blank piece of paper, and carefully wrote a local phone number on it. When he handed it to me, he was standing much closer to me than strangers stand to each other.

"I'll bet you're CIA," I said.

"Like hell," he said. "I have never bungled a job."

"How do I know your I.D. isn't fake?"

"Most people don't question it. Go ahead, call that number, they probably won't give you the time of day. They might speak to General Burns, let him try it. I'd like to know what they say about me. There's a phone booth right over there."

I said, "I could telephone from my room."

"Don't be careless, use a public phone every time you can. And don't give the number I gave you to anyone except the general, understood?"

I must have shown that I didn't take well to his saying *understood*. "Please," he said. "Now."

"I'm going to find out who you are," I said and shut myself into the phone booth. I'm not in anybody's army, who the hell did Smith think he was giving orders to? Why should I ask General Burns to make a phone call I can perfectly well make myself?

I dialed the number Smith had written down.

"*Pronto*," said a woman's voice.

"*Parla Inglese?*" I asked.

"*Certo*." If she can speak English, why doesn't she?

"*Mi può dire chi è David Smith?*"

"Who is speaking?" English at last.

"This is Susan Whitcomb."

You'd think I'd said Typhoid Mary from the silence my name drew. Should I have identified myself as General Whitcomb's daughter?

"This is Susan—"

Whoever it was hung up on me.

I wasn't even sure I had reached the right number. I dialed it again, carefully put in the correct coins, counted the rings, once, twice, three times. By the twelfth ring my nerves had spiderwebbed. I hung up.

David Smith was standing just outside the phone booth, a demonic smile on his face, shaking his head.

CHAPTER 12

General Milford Burns

When Susan Whitcomb called me about David Smith, my mind had an image of her, of course. In Hal's photos she looked like a young version of Heather. I'd wondered why a girl that nifty-looking hadn't married, or was that old-fashioned of me? Hal said she was a hard-assed lawyer. In my day if you heard a woman was hard-assed, you ran like Jesse Owens. She certainly didn't look like a tough broad. But Hal said he'd seen her in a courtroom when she was a D.A. slicing some witness's ego like it was a roll of baloney.

When Heather told me her daughter was on her way to Rome, my first instinct was hey, be helpful to them both in their time of sorrow, a kind of substitute Hal. I know Hal's thing here was a cover for whatever he did for the intelligence people. Whenever I alluded to it, he changed the subject. I wasn't a congressman. I didn't need to poke around where I wasn't wanted.

When Susan asked me to check on this David Smith fellow, I was glad to help her out. I phoned the number Susan'd given me. It was answered by an Italian woman who put me on to a woman who spoke English and sounded American. I identified myself, told her I was checking on the *bona fides* of one David Smith.

She said, "Hold on"—abruptly, I thought—and the next voice I heard was that of a man who apparently knew who I was. What a relief! "How can I help you, general?" he said. I asked him to identify David Smith, was that his real name, was he in any of the services, what was his rank if any, what command was he in, and who would have assigned him to his alleged bodyguard role, all legitimate questions, and what I got was a smartass comment. "If he exists, he's on our side, general."

"You aren't telling me anything," I said, my voice raised.

"Believe me, sir, I'm saying as much as I can say."

"Is he or isn't he one of us?"

"One of who, sir?"

"He's an American, isn't he?"

"Does he sound like an American, sir?"

"I haven't spoken to him directly."

"I see, sir. Then perhaps you should."

"Is he a soldier?"

"Oh you'd know that in a moment, sir. One way or the other."

"This is most frustrating."

"I'm sorry, sir."

And he hung up, just like that.

CHAPTER 13

David Smith

Sam Dracoff makes me wear these phony eyeglasses and the damn wig. He says nobody can tell. *I can tell.* When I meet a woman like Susan Whitcomb, I want to wear the face I see shaving, not this rig. Once I said to Sam, "How come you don't disguise your face?" and he said, "I don't go on missions anymore, kiddo."

That's a lie, too. When he doesn't trust a team to do a job right without his personal supervision, Sam is squat in the middle of things. I think the real reason he doesn't camouflage his puss is that his woman here likes the way he looks. I love to shout him down, given half the chance. Once I said to him at the top of my voice, "How come a steady is off limits to me and not to you? How come you don't follow your own rules, Sam? How come I have to?"

Sam looked down his nose at me in that special way he has of pulling rank. "My woman here is not permanent," he bellowed.

"Can I tell her that?" I shouted back.

"You're looking to get your face lifted by the back of my fist, boychick. I said no permanent attachments, I mean no permanent attachments. Any link puts both you and the woman at risk. Discussion over."

I know women in every country I've had to work in for any length of time, but they're nobody you'd want to spend more than an occasional evening with getting soused, and then to bed.

Susan Whitcomb mistrusted me. I found that tempting. She was off limits. I found that tempting, too.

We were waiting for General Burns to call her back.

"My stomach's growling for breakfast," she said.

"Hang in," I said.

"My mother's up there alone. Why doesn't the damn phone ring?"

"Any second," I said.

Wouldn't you know an Italian in a businessman's uniform barged into the booth. He talked so loud you'd have thought he was giving a speech to a crowd. I knocked on the glass door of the booth. He waved me away. I was on the boil. Finally he hung up and had just stepped out of the phone box when it rang. The son-of-a-bitch turned back to the phone box to answer it but I stepped in front of him and said, "I think that's for me."

He looked like he didn't understand a word, but he read the expression on my face just fine and skedaddled on his way.

I grabbed the phone before it decided to stop ringing.

"Hello," I said.

An authoritative male voice said, "May I speak to Susan Whitcomb, please."

"General Burns? This is David Smith. She's just outside."

"Smith, I didn't get anywhere with those people at the number you gave Susan. Who the hell are you?"

There are some people who've been in the army all their lives without learning what really goes on in the world. I had to tell him something so I said, "I'm involved in the Whitcomb case."

"Involved? How? Are you C.I.D.?"

Dumb is dumb. "No, sir."

"On whose authority are you acting?"

Times like this I realize how little patience I have. "Sir," I said, "one point concerns us both now. The man who planned the attack on General Whitcomb is well known to my people. We've all studied his m.o. Given his way of working, we expect him to go after Mrs. Whitcomb and her daughter. If you can expedite getting them out of the country quickly, it'd be a help."

"You sound like all you want to do is dump the problem into someone else's jurisdiction."

"Sir, they are not safe here."

"What's the name of this man you say had General Whitcomb killed?"

"I didn't say."

"Well, what the hell's his name?"

"Monteleone."

"Where do I know that from?"

"Giovanni Monteleone. The Aldo Moro kidnapping. The knee-capping of the police chief in Sicily."

"Why'd he go after Hal? Was Hal onto something?"

"That's clever of you, sir."

"I'd better speak to Susan and her mother. You say Susan's right there?"

I turned to look outside the phone box.

Susan was gone.

"Hello," he said. "Hello, hello."

What could I tell him? I placed the receiver on the hook as quietly as I could so he'd think we'd been disconnected.

CHAPTER 14

Susan

Leaving David Smith in the phone booth was like escaping from custody.

In the packed elevator, I scrunched my shoulders to help make room for the last three people to get aboard. They looked perfectly normal. But what about the people behind me I couldn't see? Once you start imagining danger ...

Listen, counselor, I told myself, back home isn't safe anymore either. Don't the judges in the Foley Square courthouse rise to their chambers in special elevators whose doors open only when security code numbers are punched in? Does that make the judges paranoid or prudent?

What about the judge who got a box of poisoned chocolates for Valentine's Day and whose wife ate four of them before she collapsed?

If back home isn't safe either, where the hell do you go?

I stepped off the elevator. Before turning right or left, I waited to be sure no one got off after me. One man did. He went in the other direction, thank God.

I didn't want to knock in case Mom had drifted off to sleep. I fumbled in my purse for the room key.

She was sitting in a chair pulled close to the window. *The most dangerous time in a person's life is when a spouse dies.* "Mom," I said, "aren't you sitting too close to the window?"

"It's the only way to get fresh air in this room."

"Your head . . . how are you feeling?"

She looked at me as if I'd laid the words out in front of her to study. "Oh," she said, "the headache's mostly gone. It might do me some good to eat something."

Was that a slight tic vibrating her left eyelid? "I'll order up," I said.

"Just some toast and tea for me. I can't imagine why none of the people who know us here haven't called. It must have been in all the papers."

"Perhaps they've ordered that no phone calls be put through."

"They can't cut us off from people just like that. Hal would never permit . . . oh Susan, I can't believe he's gone."

I hugged her.

"I'm so glad you're here," she said.

I gave it time, then slowly disengaged myself to phone room service. I figured if they put up Americans, they must be used to the American idea of breakfast. I ordered orange juice, scrambled eggs, crisp bacon. Coffee. "Sure you won't have something else?" I called out to Mom before hanging up.

"I'll pilfer some of yours if I'm up to it. The bacon won't be crisp. Hal always asked for it crisp. They don't know how."

Suddenly I remembered. *Don't call room service,* David had said. But that was only for last night, wasn't it?

"What is the matter, Susan?"

"Nothing," I lied. "Absolutely nothing."

I didn't know if she had heard me. She seemed awash in thoughts of her own.

After a moment, she said, "Did I ever tell you I first met your father at a roller-skating rink?"

I shook my head.

"And that he picked me up?"

Her smile flickered one bright second and then was gone. "Susan?"

"I'm listening, Mom."

"I loved your father, not the army. At the beginning I was sure I could talk him into quitting. 'To do what?' he would say. To me, wearing rank on your shoulders was like boasting. My fear was your father wasted his brains. And mine, too."

I was moving toward her when a sharp rap on the door stopped me.

"That was quick for room service," Mom said.

I opened the door to find David Smith striding in past me as if he thought I might stand in his way. He closed the door behind him and double-locked it.

"You didn't even ask who it was," he said.

"I thought it was room service."

"You didn't think."

"May I introduce my mother?"

Mom rose from her chair to shake his outstretched hand.

"This is David Smith, Mom."

"Please sit, Mrs. Whitcomb. I don't mean to be rude. I need to speak to you both."

Mom sank down into her chair. Smith sat down on the ottoman close to her, shutting me out. "Mrs. Whitcomb," he said, "I want to explain why the danger isn't over. The man who organized the killing of the general—"

"And who is that?" I interrupted.

Smith turned to me as if I were a child asking for needless information. "His name is Monteleone."

"Doesn't mean a thing to me," Mom said.

"He heads a group that split off from the Italian Red Brigades because he thought them too soft."

"Too *soft?*"

"Monteleone goes after NATO officials, the military, intelligence officers in particular. With one specialty. He follows up by getting at the families of victims."

I saw Mom's hand move up to her lips as if she were trying to keep a sound from escaping.

Smith went right on. "If after having the general killed he took you out also, the dependents here would skitter for home. The morale of husbands left behind would plummet. Experienced professionals would ask to be rotated. Wives—"

Mom said, "We're not all cowards."

"Mrs. Whitcomb, if you had met your husband at his office as you sometimes do, and you had been with him in his car, you would both be dead. Monteleone probably planned it that way. Now he has to go after you one at a time."

Mom said, "Mr. Smith, what is your role in this?"

"I've been assigned to keep you from harm."

"Assigned by whom?"

David moved his shoulders, not a shrug, not a denial, just a physical means of avoiding an answer.

"If you don't tell us," Mom said, "how can we trust you?"

David looked at me. I wasn't about to help him.

"I'm not very good at baby-sitting."

"We're not children," Mom said.

"That's what they call what I'm doing. I'll tell Dracoff to get someone else."

"Who is Dracoff?" I asked.

"Nobody. Forget I said it. Look, I'm no good at this, I belong in the field."

"Before you do anything rash," I said, "perhaps you can tell us why my father was killed."

It was a lawyer's trick. I could guess at the answer, but I wanted the jury, my mother, to hear it.

"He was good at his job. He was . . ."

"He was what?"

"He was up to his neck in evaluating information for a raid on terrorist training camps by special forces. They killed him to stop his work."

David pressed his palms together the way they do in India, not in a gesture of obeisance but as if his left hand and his right hand were restraining each other.

"I'd rather have prevented the assassination in the first place. The damn army gets around to using us when it's too late."

"Is it too late for us?" I asked and immediately heard Farlan berating me. *Never ask a question of a witness if you don't know the likely answer.*

"It's not too late," he said. "That's why I'm here."

Whatever I was about to say was stopped short by a sudden double knock on the door.

David had the most astonishing reaction to the knock. He moved to the hinge side of the door like a dancer on silent feet, reached to the bottom of his left trouser leg, and removed a gun from a holster strapped to his ankle. Mom was about to say something, but David held the gun vertically across his lips for silence as he would have held a finger. He nodded to me, then toward the door.

"Who is it?" I asked.

"Room service." Not an Italian accent.

David, not more than four feet away, nodded.

I opened the door, concealing David, and let in a very short, curly-haired waiter who couldn't have been more than twenty years old. He pushed his trolley into the room, lifted the sides up, pulled over two chairs, and was about to start removing the metal dish covers when I said, "That will be all." I signed his check, including a tip in lire that was probably too much. The waiter smiled and said, "Thank you, miss, thank you very much yes," and left.

Mom's eyes were on David holstering the gun.

"I'm sorry," he said, "it pays to be careful."

"The waiter's an Arab, isn't he, Mr. Smith?"

"Waiters here are as likely to be Arabs or Turks or Spaniards as Italians. Not all Arabs are terrorists, Mrs. Whitcomb. Fewer than a thousand, in fact, but they manage to hamstring NATO. Your husband was quoted as saying they were the most cost-efficient army in the history of the world."

Had that remark cost him his life?

David the mind reader said, "They don't pay much attention to what we say. Just what we do." He took a small spoon that came with the marmalade and dipped it into the teapot, held the spoon up to his nose to smell the tea. With the tip of his tongue he tasted it. He broke off a small piece of toast and sniffed it, poured a little coffee into the spoon and tasted. He then took a knife to move a small amount of scrambled egg onto his spoon for smelling and tasting.

"It's okay," he said finally.

"I don't see how anyone can live this way," Mom said.

"As a matter of fact," David said, "this is the way to stay alive. The food's getting cold. You'd better eat."

I sat down, hoping if I started Mom would too. I'd had two forkfuls of scrambled egg when there was another knock on the door.

"Stay put," said David. "I'll go."

By the time he reached the door and said, *"Chi è?,"* he had his pistol in his right hand behind his back.

Was there no answer? Or did we just not hear it?

David opened the door a bit. We could see it was one of those midget white-gloved bellboys.

David held out his left hand for the large flat envelope the bellboy was holding. The bellboy was reluctant to give it to him. David's left hand went into his pocket for some coins, and the boy released the envelope.

David closed the door, put his pistol away, and felt the envelope all along its perimeter. "Courier from the States," he said. "Expecting anything?"

"No," I said.

He felt around the edge and held it up to the light from the window. "If it comes from the States, you don't expect a letter bomb. This one's okay." He handed it to me.

Inside the large envelope was a smaller one with my name on it. In the upper left corner was handwritten, Farlan Amory Adams. *I hadn't cabled him!*

"We'd better eat," I said. "I'll read it later."

It was hard to concentrate on eating with David moving about the room like a jungle cat, checking behind the sideboard, under the armchairs, out the window, then in the politest of voices asking, "May I go into the bedroom, please?"

Mom said, "Of course," but the moment he was out of the room, she said, "Whatever for?"

We ate in silence. David came back in. "I assume," he said, "that the other door in the bedroom leads to an adjacent room?"

"I suppose so," Mom said.

"You've been living here for some time, haven't you?"

"Oh yes," Mom said. "I've seen people go in and out next door a few times. Never the same people, no one either my husband or I knew. They weren't American military personnel. Scandinavians, Germans, British. Tourists and businessmen, I suppose."

"There's a deadbolt on that door. Please be sure it's always locked."

"I haven't opened it since we've been here."

"Please check it out every time you go in. A maid or a waiter or the valet could open the lock from this side so that an accomplice could later get in from the adjacent room. ... I'll only be a few minutes." And he was off.

"It's like prison," Mom said. "I think we need to shuck that man and get ourselves home as soon as arrangements can be made. I'll leave that to you, darling. That breakfast I said I wasn't going to eat wants me to lie down a bit. I'm going into the bedroom to rest."

Not to rest, I thought, to remember.

I stopped my thoughts from drifting like a boat through fog. I'd have to read Farlan Adams's letter sooner or later, why not now?

Via DHL Overnight

Dear Susan,

I'm sending this by courier so that my thoughts can catch up to your grief as soon as possible. Though I never met your father, knowing him through you made me feel as if my own father had died a second time.

From the photo in the paper, your father looks younger than I do. My father at least died in bed *en famille*, with my aunts and uncles as well as my mother and me at his bedside. The only comfort I can think of in your father's case is that in one second it was over. I feel so clumsy trying to comfort you with words when what I would so prefer is to embrace you and provide whatever comfort you might find within my arms.

On reading the news my immediate thought was to get Albertson to take over my lectures for a few days and fly over to be in the same room with you.

Does your mother know how close you and I have become? If she doesn't, the fact of my presence might disturb her. That restrains me more than anything. A teacher doesn't fly across oceans to be with a former student whose parent has died. It would mean confronting your mother with the truth about us at a time when what she requires least is the turbulence of a new and unexplained presence. Perhaps what you both need to hear is a few lines of uncharacteristic Hopkins:

> *... I have asked to be*
> *Where no storms come,*
> *Where the green swell is in the havens dumb*
> *And out of the swing of the sea.*

Think of me as staring at the second hands of a clock till you come home. Do you know yet when that might be? If you would cable your flight number and time, I will meet you at the airport, glad of heart and full of welcome.

Meanwhile I live in a desert. Oh I know that even though we both reside in the same city and sometimes months go by when we do not see each other, because you now are so far out of reach, not seeing you fills me with loss. Perhaps some higher power knows that I am destined to share your anguish as well as your joy.

My nerves have been too overwrought for me to give anyone competent advice right now, so I have been avoiding private meetings with students. Except for my lectures, I am almost always alone, it seems by choice because I have left a vacuum next to me that I now know can only be filled by you.

Do you realize how many thousands of days it has been since we first met? I have to confess something. When you were in the District Attorney's office, I arranged through a good friend, someone whose picture is on the wall in my office, to get an illicit photocopy of every brief you wrote. I wanted to reveal this to you earlier. What a wonderful excuse that would have been to sit next to you hour on end, discussing your briefs line by line, but the fact is that your work is so good that I would have added little. My great dread is that the time will come when you may no longer need my advice on the law. Or has that happened already? When you left the prosecutor's office, I felt betrayed. I no longer saw your work. But you know, my dear, for an academician I am not such a bad investigator. I looked up the names of each partner in your firm. I couldn't find any who'd taken a degree here, but I did find two who had gone to Columbia College and then went on elsewhere for their law. I got in touch with one of them, a younger man. He said that he had surreptitiously monitored my lectures for a full year when he was still an undergraduate. I told him you were my niece, that I was most anxious to know how you were doing, and that you, out of modesty, were unwilling to let me see your work, could he oblige? I stupidly offered to pay for these, and the young man quite correctly said I'd lost my good sense, did I want to leave evidence of his transgression? I assume the photocopies—there were many of them in time—were charged off against one or another client's account.

So you see I am once again examining your every work word, as it were, and wishing it were the other words I could hear, the spoken ones that have nothing to do with the law but with the care and affection that we have felt for each other since.

I know that a time of grief is also a time of change. Therefore I am certain you won't misinterpret my intrusion of a question into your life at this time. Will you marry me?

With affection, as ever,
Farlan

CHAPTER 15

Susan

I sat rigid as rock until a quiet knock on the door caused a reflex in the hand in which I was holding Farlan's letter. At the door I asked, "Who's there?" and heard back "David." I quickly folded the letter, returned it to its envelope as if it were an obscene photograph, and let David in.

"Sorry to skip out so suddenly," David said, "but that other door into the bedroom worried me."

"Did you arrange to have it nailed shut?"

"I arranged that whenever someone is checked into that room, the desk will notify my office. Name of party, origin of passport. If anyone asks for that room in particular, the reception manager will cause a delay and we'll have someone here within minutes."

"Why not just ask them to leave it empty? Mom said the hotel is never quite full up."

"An empty room can be a greater danger."

"Aren't we overdoing this precaution stuff?" I asked.

"Your father underdid it."

"You are a son-of-a-bitch." *Dad wasn't careless. Nothing he did would have saved him.*

David's eyes were blue anger in a suddenly blanched face.

"I'm sorry," I said. "I didn't mean—"

"It's okay. It's okay."

It wasn't okay. I said, "Is your father alive?"

"I don't know."

"What do you mean you don't know? You know who your father is, don't you?"

"Yes, of course."

"And you don't know if he's alive or dead?"

"He's alive. I try not to remember him."

"Was he awful?"

"No."

"Was he . . ."

I stopped. David wasn't hearing me. He was somewhere else.

"David," I was saying, "while my mother is out of the room, would you answer a couple of questions?"

"I don't know what I'm allowed to tell you without consulting my lawyer." He flashed his three-point smile for a millisecond.

"You don't much like lawyers, do you?"

"I haven't had all that much experience with lawyers, male or female. I get the impression most people don't like them. They manufacture trouble."

"But people like soldiers, right?"

"Sure. Soldiers fight their battles for them."

"That's what lawyers are supposed to do."

"I agree," David said. "Supposed to do."

I couldn't keep from smiling. Farlan had said *Be prepared for buckshot. The profession gets it all the time.* I noticed that David's chiseled face had changed. "Softened" was the way I put it to myself.

"Would you rather they'd given this assignment to someone else?"

"Not anymore," I said. "Do you know why they picked you?"

"Because I know Monteleone's tricks."

"Better than others?"

"For your sake I hope to hell I do."

"At least you're not self-effacing."

When I said that he came over closer than people normally stand to each other, the way Farlan does. Very quietly, looking straight into me, he said, "If my neck gets chopped, and anyone asks after me, they'll say, 'David, who?' as if I never existed. My job isn't self-effacing. It's self-extinguishing."

I turned to get away from the closeness of his physical presence. "There's one thing I'd consider a favor," I said.

"And that is?"

"I want to learn whatever you know about my father, good or bad."

David's mouth clenched as if he were physically trying to prevent himself from speaking. "You're pushing me to break the rules."

"You don't strike me as someone who obeys rules any more than I do."

"Your father . . ." he started to say. I felt that tiny zing of elation when a witness first breaks down.

"Your father, not too very long ago, had a decision to make. The intelligence we were getting from sources inside the terrorist groups was useful. We were able to abort half a dozen outrages you never read about in the papers because they didn't happen. They were pre-empted."

"What's that got to do with my father?"

"The plastic explosive several of the groups have been using comes from Czechoslovakia. Your father had three agents in position, two Slovaks and a Czech from Prague. Their mission was to sabotage the factory making plastic explosives that got into the hands of terrorists all over Europe. One of your father's sources inside a terrorist group was able to pass a signal that the three were under surveillance by the Czech military. Your father had the choice of warning the agents so that they could save their skins or not warning them."

"Why wouldn't he?" I'd raised my voice loud enough to disturb Mother in the next room.

"Because if he did, the Czechs would know there was a leak, that somehow their communications were being monitored and their code broken. Your father let the agents go."

"What the hell does that mean in plain English?"

"He let them be taken and disposed of."

"Killed?"

"It was the right choice."

"How could it possibly be? How—"

"Dozens of lives were spared because of the advance warnings we were receiving. We couldn't kill that source for the lives of three men who knew they were as expendable as I am."

Mom was standing in the doorway of the bedroom.

"What's going on?" she asked.

I looked at David.

"I'm afraid we woke you," I said.

"Oh I hadn't gone completely off yet. But I will now. Why don't you two go get some fresh air while I nap?"

"I don't want her outside," David said.

I was not going to let him give me orders. "Please, Mom," I said, "you rest. Leave this to me."

As soon as she was out of the room, I turned on David. "I am not going to stay cooped up here. I'm going for a walk. You can stay here and play bodyguard to mother, or you can come with me. Take your choice."

"I can't let you out."

"Try and stop me."

I have always walked faster than anyone I know. Outside, David kept pace with me. I could feel his energy.

"If you're going to risk the out-of-doors," he said, "I don't want you strolling just anywhere."

"I don't care where we go as long as it's out of that hotel room."

Whenever we turned a corner David had the habit of slowing down and glancing back just long enough to see if anyone turned after us.

"Do you always walk as if you're being followed?"

"I'm not always being followed."

"Are you now?"

"Not that I can spot."

"Good. Maybe you'll relax a bit."

We ended up in a part of Rome I'm sure few tourists get to see. It smelled and looked working-class, foreign. We were surrounded by a polyglot buzz. I noticed a huddle of Arabs.

"Don't worry about them," David said. "These have been here for generations. Even the Libyans here don't bother anyone."

"Are you sure?"

"No," he said, laughing. "But I'll tell you one thing. If anyone is out looking for an American woman, they won't start in this part of town."

"Slow down," I said, winded from the pace.

In a moment David had led me by the arm into a café, past the small round white tables to one against the wall in the back. The huge, mustachioed bartender nodded to him. David held up two fingers.

"What have you ordered?"

"You'll see."

"You like this place?"

"What I like," said David, "is that I can see anyone enter from here, and the hallway right there leads to the kitchen, which has a door leading out to another street."

"How do you know that?"

"I checked the parallel street before I ever came in here the first time. Don't look at the bartender, but I think we've given him a bit of a shock. The few times I've been in here I've been alone or with another man. He's surprised to see me with a woman."

We found ourselves conspirators, laughing.

"A very attractive woman."

"Thank you."

"And smart."

"I'd have thought you'd always be around smart women."

"When you move around the way I have to, you're lucky to meet someone whose IQ even registers on the meter."

"Perhaps you should wear your uniform. You know how women are supposed to be about men in uniform."

"Very clever. Next time I have to debrief a terrorist, I'll bring you along." He sighed. "I don't own a uniform."

"You have to be a member of the armed forces. I saw the armament."

"You draw conclusions from superficial evidence. Did your father carry a weapon?"

"No."

"And he was in the so-called armed forces, wasn't he?"

The waitress put two camparis in front of us.

We clinked glasses. David sipped at his. I put mine down.

"What's the matter?" he said.

"Nothing. Just thinking. About my father, I mean."

"Want to talk about it?"

I didn't say anything.

"Better out loud than inside your head."

"I can't."

"I'm not a complete stranger."

"Are you going to tell me about yourself?"

"Sometime. Maybe. Depends."

"On what?"

"I envy you."

"Because I can talk freely about anything I damn please?"

"No. Because you liked your father."

"I love him. It's easier for a daughter, I suppose. In recent years, I didn't get to see him much. He slapped me once."

"Why did you say that?"

"It just came to mind."

"Did he hurt you?"

"The slap? Not much. It was the fact that he slapped me that really stung."

"I know."

"Know what?"

"My father slapped my face once, too."

"Once?"

"Once is enough if you never get around to sorting things out."

Were we talking about fathers, or ourselves?

"Tell me," I said.

He put his palms together hard.

"All right." He turned to look at me from just a few inches away.

"A man like my father," David said, "spends most of his time being an authority over cows and pigs. When his wife has a child, he's got to learn it's not just another animal to have authority over. When I was four years old I saw him cut a pig's throat, and whenever he'd sharpen up that butcher knife of his I stayed clean out of his way. Sure he said he loved me, but didn't he love those pigs?"

CHAPTER 16

David Smith's Father

I can damn well guess how David talks about me off wherever the hell he is. He doesn't even use my name. My name isn't Smith. Folks hereabouts know who we are.

They don't ask after David anymore. If they do, Josie'll say, "Still in the army," and I'll add, "They tamed him, they might as well keep him."

People in these parts grow wheat, keep a few pigs and cows, or work in town, selling hardware or groceries, or sitting by the phone in the funeral parlor waiting for the good news of someone dead.

Even some folks in North Dakota never heard of Scaville. The town was small when David was born. Half that size now. The smart kids migrate like geese, come back for Thanksgiving or Christmas or funerals. Best investment I ever made was saving up to send David's two sisters to college back East, pretty girls they were, settled down with fellows make more cash money in a month than I do in a year.

I always wanted a son and what I got was David. Other boys around here all had automobile oil in their veins, take anything that moved apart and put it back together so it'd run better. But David, he'd take his lacquered-up Chevy out to the straightaway beyond Scaville and push the pedal to the floor till the bearings popped. All that drag-racing and playing chicken was just show-off to the girls. Josie knew whenever David was going to try some new piece of hell-raising. She'd pray the Lord bring him back alive and I'd say, "Josie, the Lord don't pay no mind to David anymore, he's the devil's champion kid in this county, and if that Chevy don't take him straight to hell, he'll build something that will."

Josie said, "Talk to him." You ever have a teenage son who wasn't deaf? Sure I tried and he cut me right off. "Dad, what you wanted was three girls." I told him playing Russian roulette with automobiles didn't make him a man. . . . He wasn't listening. He was out the door.

In eighth grade David rang the fire alarm in school. After the commotion, Mr. Phillipo, the principal, said to him, "David, you've got decent grades, you've got a good mind, you come from a right decent family, why'd you pull the alarm?" And David he said, "Give the firemen some practice getting here fast. They ought to have fire drills same as we do."

Mr. Phillipo was a kindly man, could keep his temper a year for every minute I could keep mine. He said, "David, I'll have to punish you," and he swears David said, "Then, sir, I'll have to punish you right back."

You can see why when David decided to enlist, Mr. Phillipo and the whole town, including me, heaved a breath of relief, figuring the army'd make him grow up like it did me in my war. It was Josie who worried about the danger. The first month he sent one postcard a week saying, "Dear Mom and Dad, love, David" with nothing in between and only the postmark to have us guess where he was at. First postcard with anything to say said, "Army tamed. Moving to Special Forces."

He came home on furlough looking better than Gary Cooper did in uniform. He shook my hand, put his arms around Josie and kissed her as if she was some woman not his mother, asked one question about each sister, and rushed out to bedazzle the local girls. I was trying to figure out what to say to him now that we could talk man to man, but he slept through till midafternoon the next day, and sudden-like said good-bye, he was finishing his furlough someplace the clock moved faster. "Don't worry about me," he told Josie, "they'll send you a telegram if I get hurt bad. No news is good news, Mom," and he was gone.

Josie and I had a fright when a federal man showed up at the door one day. He knew our real name, which is how he found us, but he kept referring to David as Mr. Smith. Said he was just taking

some notes for a security check. He said no he didn't know what
kind of work David was doing, he just gets these checks to do and
he does them.

Josie, which is where David gets his spunk from more'n from me,
said to the man, "If I tell you David's a Russian spy, does that get
him back home?" The man—he wasn't a man but a kid himself,
really—looked at Josie as if she'd be a lunatic, then realized she was
joshing and said, "No, ma'am, we'd just have to shoot him, that's all."

David stopped by only once more, four years later, wearing civilian clothes. He brought me a pipe that said *Brière d'Afrique du
Nord, Fabriqué en France*, which he taught me to pronounce. He got
Josie a little round thing with a cover that he said was genuine
Wedgewood, but it wasn't wood at all, it was like porcelain, and Josie
said it was the most beautiful blue color she'd ever seen on anything.
He sure knew how to pick gifts. He even brought along two silk
scarves made in Paris for us to send to the girls. "You out of the
army?" I asked him. "You getting rich?" He took his wallet out and
asked did we need any extra money, was that the question, and I
said we were doing fine, but I saw the I.D. card and held his arm
before he could put the wallet back. That was the first time I felt his
strength since he left home. He could have forced me to let go, but
he didn't. Maybe he wanted us to know, because the I.D. card with
his picture said DAVID SMITH, and I said "Why in hell don't you have
your own name on the card? Isn't my name good enough for you?"
He apologized real polite and explained that David Smith was a work
name, but after that he didn't come by any more. It hurts me to see
the way Josie misses him. It would have been better if she'd never
borne him. Josie says, "Whatever he's doing now, I sure hope it's the
Lord's work, not the devil's." I keep my opinion to myself.

CHAPTER 17

Susan

I said, "I know most boys wage war with their fathers. But doesn't there come a time when you shake hands like two men and forget the past?"

"I suppose so. I think if my father hadn't been in the so-called good war, it might have been different. You know the people from that war are actually nostalgic about it? Whenever some old wartime tune played on the radio, he'd start to tell stories. The girls would scatter, but Mom and I stuck out the nostalgia. By the time I was a teenager, I used to encourage his reminiscing."

"So you could bait him?"

"Sure. His pet peeve was the 82nd Airborne. 'Them rednecks,' he said, 'didn't take prisoners.'

" 'Dad,' I'd say, 'If the drop zone has got enemy on all four sides, what the hell are you supposed to do when one of them surrenders, take one of your own men out of action to guard him?' "

"You'd have killed him?"

"They'd have killed me under the same circumstances. My dad had the same law-and-order mind set you have. He blew my gasket once by throwing the Geneva Convention at us. 'Hey, Dad,' I said, 'you told us about all those civilians stuffed in ovens. Did you make that up? Did you make up that stuff about the Nazis killing prisoners at that Malmédy place? Did you make up that shit about the Bataan death march? Where the hell did you spend the war, Dad, in a canteen?' That was when he slapped my face."

"If I'd been your father I would have done the same thing."

"Sure, I deserved it," David said. "He'd been a soldier with a civilian mentality. What did he do when a kraut surrendered, read him his rights and tell him to phone his lawyer? You can't argue with his so-called principles. That's one reason I don't visit home."

"I can't believe you talked to your father like that."

"Believe what you like."

"I believe you're wearing a wig."

I thought I saw a flash of anger vanish as quickly as it had appeared.

"Look," David said, "maybe I'm completely bald."

"I wasn't being unfriendly. If anyone observant gets this close to you, they could tell just as easily as I did. When I have someone on the witness stand I look for things like that."

"Things you can trip somebody up with?"

"Sometimes."

"To make someone tense?"

"Sure. If a witness is concealing something, it's my job to rattle him. A jury's lie detectors are its own eyes and ears."

"You must be a real sweetie to have around. Let's get the hell out of here."

David got up, and went to the bar to pay. I went outside. The sun had come out and I had my face up to it.

"You should have waited for me," David said, glancing right and left. He took me by the arm and led me between slow-moving cars across the street. "I'd hoped you'd be friendlier," he said.

"It's hard to be real friendly toward someone who pretends to be secretive."

"Your father had his secrets, didn't he?"

"My father wasn't paranoid. Do you really think if almighty David Smith went everywhere with him he might still be alive?"

"Maybe."

"You *are* arrogant," I said.

"That's me. Truthful and arrogant."

"Well where the hell were you when he needed you?"

"That wasn't my job. I don't usually bodyguard."

"Then why are you being so damn protective of my mother and me?"

"Because I don't want to risk my neck having to deal with whoever gets you."

"That's it?"

"That's it."

"David, who the fucking hell are you?"

"I didn't know lady lawyers use four-letter soldiers' words."

"It's seven letters and it's coming from an army brat. I've got a closet full of words and I'm prepared to use all of them unless you tell me who you are, where you come from, what you do, and why I or anyone else should pay attention to your instructions."

"Are you finished?" David asked.

"Maybe just beginning."

We went the rest of the way in silence till we were almost back at the hotel.

"You still haven't answered me," I said.

"One of the things I'm paid for is not to talk."

"You are exasperating."

David gave me a one-second shot of his three-point smile. "Why thank you," he said, then took my arm and led me through the crowd at the front of the hotel, checking right, checking left, making sure, I suppose, that I was safe from everyone but him.

At the door to Mom's suite, I turned my key in the lock. When it wouldn't open easily, I started to twist it with force. Immediately David's hand was on my hand, pulling it away from the key.

"Before you break it," he said. "She's got the door double-locked."

A match of anger flared in my head. *Men aren't the only practical people on earth.* If he'd given me another second, I'd have realized it was double-locked.

"Guess I should have let you break the key," said David the mind reader, tapping lightly on the door.

We heard footsteps, then Mom's voice saying, "Who is it?"

"Susan," I said. "And David Smith."

"Welcome to the fortress, Mr. Smith," she said, opening the door. "Come on in, Susan, I've been preparing lists like mad, your father's winter things, his summer things, my things, memorabilia, souvenirs, all the things that need to be shipped home."

Home, of course, was Scarborough. Dad had said, "There's not one retired military officer living in this hamlet, thank God. I'll be the first and last." The real reason Dad loved the place is that he grew up there. "I knew every pothole in the road till they started repaving." Mom was right to want him buried in the Sleepy Hollow Cemetery, just minutes down the road.

"While you were out," she was saying, "I was trying to make plans about where I could stay. The house is rented till the end of next month."

"You could stay with me."

"Your apartment's small and you're gone all day."

"Who's renting the house, Mom?"

"Dull sweet people called Webster. Their kids had trouble in the city schools, and they wanted to move back to Scarborough while looking for a house. It was a perfect arrangement for them and for us."

"Did they keep our phone number?"

"Yes, why?"

"I'll give them a ring and see if they could put you up in the guest room for whatever time's left on their lease, maybe for some concession in the rent."

"I really couldn't impose—"

"If they're dull, they could use your bounce around the house. And you could have the company of neighborhood people you know."

"Maybe I should stay here. I mean until the Websters' time is up."

"No," David's voice cut in. "I'm afraid Rome isn't safe for either of you."

I spotted the split-second distention of Mom's nostrils. *Watch out, mister. The general would have told you neither of the women here take orders.*

"I'm sorry," David said. "I didn't mean to sound peremptory."

I felt as if he was using one of my words without permission. "How soon were your overlords planning to fly us out?" I asked.

"Not sure. I'll have to make a few phone calls. The custom is for you to be on the same plane."

"Same as what?"

"The general. The casket travels in the hold. In the old days, they'd fly you all back on military aircraft. At least you don't have to worry about choosing a funeral director. The army takes care of that, all the way to Arlington."

I saw Mom's face, with one breath, age.

"I'm sorry," David said. "I'm being clumsy."

"No, you're not," Mom said, "you're being practical for us. Thank you. But my husband's not going to be buried in anonymous Arlington. I've made my plans to keep him close to home."

"It's supposed to be an honor to be buried in Arlington."

Mom said, "I don't know if it's an honor to be buried anywhere."

"My mother deciding where and when she want my father buried isn't a subject for debate. It's her decision. Period."

David did that half-shrug of his. "I'm not going to argue with you. I have to find out if they want me flying back with you."

"Whatever for?" I said.

"In case . . ."

"In case what?"

"If they decide I shouldn't go, I'll have to pass you on to someone else for the trip."

Mom said, "I don't understand why."

"We have lives to lead," I said.

"So did your father. I don't mean to sound callous. We have to be cautious until we nail Monteleone."

"How do you mean nail him?"

"You both please listen to me right now," David said.

I was about to answer him in kind, but I heard the beep. So did Mom.

David looked embarrassed. I was glad. "May I use your phone?" he asked.

"Take the one in the bedroom," Mom said. "You'll have some privacy."

The second he was gone, Mom said, "What was that all about?"

"His beeper went off. He's been summoned."

"Another odious invention."

"We have them in our office, Mom. They can be—"

"I think the United States needs a ten-year moratorium on inventions, Susan."

David was back. "I've got to go," he said. "Please, both of you stay here, keep the door locked, wait for me. I'll return as soon as I can."

And he was gone.

CHAPTER 18

Sam Dracoff

David had better get his ass here fast.

You have to understand that a man who's on the other side of fifty like me doesn't shove himself off on every lunatic operation that comes up. David's forty, and personally I think that's already too old. Your reflexes start to go at twenty-seven. And if there's killing involved, you're better off with teenagers, like every army in the world.

On the other hand, in this success-or-else business, you need experience which teenagers don't have. They love a pinch of violence now and then. A little blood, terrific. They don't believe in death. They make toughness into a magnetic field. It attracts girls and trouble. What could be better? I'll tell you. Religion. You got a crusade, you've got yourself an army. You got the Ayatollah, you've got martyrs reaching for pie in the sky and ending up in body bags on prime time back home.

The reason our little bunch here has a track record is that among the terrific boys we have a few men with long experience, by which I mean they know not only how to keep from being killed, but recognize it as an advantage.

Think of the *pishers* the terrorists use. They have trouble opening the buttons on the front of their pants. How much of each of their brains do you think is like a chess player's, figuring out a few steps ahead how not to die? The Ayatollah can have his pimple-faced masturbators ready to take on houris in heaven before they ever get properly laid down below.

Sure, we have some younger men, you've got to. For hostage-relief operations we give them more practice than a kid learning to play chopsticks. But with grownups leading them. For solo operations, I use old hands who've decided to live a little while longer. Like David. I sometimes think that if he and I had been born earlier and gotten together, who knows, we might have assassinated Hitler. If you think that wasn't possible, I'd like to show you my blue book. I've worked out four ways. That's what I do instead of chess these days, figure out how I would have rubbed out Caligula. I think of myself as the world's most underrated social worker.

Where do you think I get my people from? We can't interview the graduating class at Yale and entice them into a job where the odds on surviving are worse than being an infantry shavetail in wartime. I pick up my recruits from on-the-job training. I've got a few people here and there looking out for my interests. Whenever they spot a young David Smith, they give a whistle and I take a look. Oppenheimer wanted young physicists willing to do anything; he found them. I find mine.

I'm not a pessimist. I think we can show young terrorists that there's a better way to get to heaven. When one of them sees his friend with his gut open, he doesn't think of Allah, he thinks of his own gut. That was God's genius, making people selfish. Otherwise there'd be nobody left on earth after all these centuries.

My theory is that beneath every burnoose burns a practical brain thinking how can I save my ass. So my thing is to make terrorism impractical. Right now what those fuckers do is knock off seven or eight people and scare the shit out of hundreds of millions. The government people—French, German, British, American—they've all wished their hostages dead at one time or other. Hostages invite policy fuck-ups. You rescue one hostage, they take another. Think of all the people who've been killed rescuing hostages. How many lives is a life worth? Find me a politician who volunteers to trade himself for a hostage, and you've found a man who isn't really a politician.

Mind you, democracy has its martyrs. Isn't everybody in this end of the business a prospective martyr? If I had a son I'd feel no different about him than I do about David. *If I had a son.* People in this business don't have children if we can help it.

You see, I call it a business and even that is wrong. A business is supposed to make money, right? You can't call a counterterrorist a mercenary. Very few Davids are in this for the money compared to some of the civilian buck-chasing professions. You say counterterrorists are heroes? Who are you kidding? In death, we are nobodies. What can we be in life?

Maybe George Washington did more for his country than David Smith has, but I can name a lot of Presidents who've done less. How many of them since Washington have put their lives on the line every other week? The first year I was in this, when I was a punk of nineteen, some son-of-a-bitch said to me, "Hey Isaac'l, why aren't you in the Quartermaster Corps?" I told him because I didn't want to be led into an oven, by him or anybody else.

When David finally showed up, he was puffing, probably because he'd been running part of the way. I said, "What's the matter, boychick, you getting old? Sit down."

"Don't talk to me about old, Sam. When's the last time you got it up without outside help?"

"Pour yourself some coffee. Tell me about the younger one."

"The daughter?"

"I wasn't talking about Shirley Temple. What's she look like in person?"

"She looks all right."

"I caught her on TV. I think you're in trouble."

"Sam, what the fuck are you talking about?"

I put a finger near his face. "You see to it she and her mother get back home in one piece, period. Keep your prick in your pants."

"You're a vulgar hebe, Sam."

"They gave you a pedigree in South Dakota?"

"North Dakota."

"What's the difference? When you settle these two in, maybe you ought to take a couple of days off and get some R and R back home."

I shoved my cup toward David.

"Warm this up, will you?"

As he topped my coffee up from the hot pot, he said, "I haven't been home for fifteen years."

"That's what I figured. Your father alive?"

"Probably."

"You could use some fatherly advice from someone besides me."

"My father never got any advice to me in time for me to use."

"No teenage punk ever listens to his old man. Now that you're a grown-up punk, maybe you ought to pay your family a visit. You might surprise yourself."

"It would sure as hell surprise *them*. Sam, you didn't pull me in for a back-home travelogue, what's going down?"

"My morale." I shoved the thick envelope in his direction. "The three of you are booked on a commercial flight out of Leonardo da Vinci. I should have said the four of you. The general travels in the hold."

"Sam, why don't you put somebody else on the baby-sitting detail?"

I reached way over so I could pinch his cheek. "Because I trust you to keep Monteleone's score down. You want me to send a twenty-year-old?"

"You know anything I don't know?"

I had to laugh. "Lots. As for this little adventure, I'm sharing. I've ordered that plane to get the most complete going-over for bombs and guns that any plane ever gets this side of Tel Aviv. I tell you, kiddo, if it wouldn't give people the wrong impression, I'd send all three of you to New York on El Al. I've put out the word that every piece of checked luggage goes into a pressurized container. If anything blows, I want it blowing on the ground, not under you."

"How come you're so considerate, Sam? Getting soft?"

"I'm considering the general's family, not you. You're expendable."

"Thanks," David said. "Thanks a lot."

I stood up and put my hand against his cheek. "Be careful. I don't have the patience to train another idiot."

CHAPTER 19

David Smith

Somebody stupid suggested a brief ceremony over the casket on the tarmac for propaganda purposes, weeping widow, daughter, flag-draped coffin, the living victims of terrorism, ta da da. I told them if they wanted to keep the American community in Rome calm, they'd better put that idea in the toilet and pull the chain.

At the airport, after all the other passengers had been loaded, a full-dress two-man escort took Mrs. Whitcomb, Susan, and General Burns over to the plane, which was about a hundred yards away from the terminal. I tagged along. They ushered us around to the far side where the hold had just finished being loaded except for the flag-draped coffin.

In Nam we put a raincoat over somebody till they could find a body bag. It couldn't mean a damn to whoever was inside. I guess the brass-handled casket the general got is a final camouflage to make us think he'd died in his sleep.

Looking up and around, I spotted a TV camera crew two hundred feet away with a long lens. Those bastards would crawl up someone's ass to get a picture. I didn't want them taking my picture in my get-up as I approached them. The best I could do would be to hurry this leave-taking along.

Mrs. Whitcomb and Susan, separate from the rest, had their arms around each other, their hair whipping in the airport wind. I didn't realize how much Susan looked like her mother. Both stunning

women. They . . . I noticed the coffin lid seemed just slightly askew.
Shit! I quickly stepped over to it and felt around the rim of the lid,
first one side, then the others. *My God, they must have used a timing
device. The plane's more than two hours late taking off. The thing
could go off any second.* I grabbed the arms of both women and
yelled, "Run like hell!" At General Burns and the escort I bellowed,
"Get the hell away from the plane! Run!" *What a jerk I'll be if I'm
wrong.*

As we all scattered fast in the open, I knew the damn TV camera
would get us. The women were in front of the terminal when, by
what instinct I'll never know, I stopped and turned at the exact
moment the casket blew up in a shower of wood and God knows
what else.

Mrs. Whitcomb screamed. Loud. For a second I thought she'd
been hit by fragments from all that distance. Then I saw Susan, in
shock, like the grunts in Nam when someone stepped on a mine and
you saw body parts flying in a cloud of blood and dirt.

"Keep them here!" I yelled at General Burns, and streaked for
the plane. Susan, disobedient, followed in my tracks. A baggage loader
who'd been standing too close had a piece of wood or metal in his
thigh.

Glancing up, I could see the frightened faces of passengers at the
windows of the plane. I ran around to the other side and up the
stairs. No fire. Lucky. If the fuel tanks had been hit, the plane might
have blown.

I scooted back down the stairs and around. There wasn't enough
left of the coffin or the flag or the general to gather up. *My God, I've
left the Whitcombs alone.* I double-timed across the tarmac. When I
got to them, winded, I put my arm around Susan.

"Jesus I'm sorry," I said.

Her color was coming back. Her eyes were wet. "You saved our
lives," she said.

"I just wish I could have saved his."

Back in the terminal we were told there'd be room for most of
the passengers on a light-loaded 747 coming in from Bahrain. I could
name at least seven people in Bahrain who would pay a lot to see
me dead.

As usual, the seating of a lot of unexpected passengers was handled by three frazzled passenger agents who had something less than a single functioning brain between them. I got nowhere trying to explain that the three of us wanted to sit together. Susan and her mother ended up with seats on the starboard side of the plane, next to a young man at the window seat whose fingers were dancing on the keyboard of a laptop computer. I was able to get the aisle seat just behind Susan. I could look at her hair when I wasn't looking around to see if I could spot trouble. The man on my right seemed hypnotized by a copy of *Business Week*.

After the plane took off, I loosened my tie. Mrs. Whitcomb turned around just once. She said, "I can't believe that to get at us more than three hundred people might have died."

The businessman sitting on my right looked at her and at me, then all around the back of the cabin, searching for an empty seat somewhere behind us.

The stewardess distributed peanut packs and paper napkins.

I popped a couple of peanuts in my mouth. They had some kind of sweet coating. I pushed the rest aside and doodled on the napkin with a ball point pen, then closed my eyes. I didn't want to think about passengers, or the plane, or the cretin I hated most in the world.

"Who's M?" asked Susan.

I opened my eyes. Susan had turned and was looking over the back of her seat. On the paper napkin, without thinking, I'd scribbled the initial of Monteleone's name.

"Nobody," I lied. "Nobody."

BOOK TWO

CHAPTER 20

Monteleone

Everything changed when Gino met this girl Maria, the most gorgeous chick he ever saw.

I'm busy cleaning my nails with my knife. "If she's so terrific," I tell Gino, "she's too good for you. She needs to meet me." I swipe at Gino's balls with my blade. Gino knows it's just a joke, I didn't get to be who I am by forgetting who's a friend.

Gino arranges a meet in some coffee joint near her place. "No way," I says to Gino. "Even if she's Lollobrigida, the meet's on my turf."

Monteleone says, Gino does. I tell you God's honest truth, this babe's a looker ten times better than Lollobrigida. In my time I fucked some real beauties but never any ever come close to this Maria. Gino told her I speak English, so I show off and say real fast, "Newark is in New Jersey, Tren-ton is the capital of New Jersey, New Jersey is in the United States, how's that?"

Well, this Maria chick says, "How is it you speak English so well?"

I say, "How come you speak English so bad?"

This Maria, fire in her eye, looks me up and down like nobody told her who I am. I say to her, "You speak limey English. I speak genuine U.S.A. English."

I can't tell if she's smiling happy to meet me or smiling to put me down, it's that kind of expression, you know what I mean? Very exciting when a woman does that. She starts telling me how she studied English four years in Milan, one year Rome. Believe you me I've screwed every type of woman, and this Maria, she's one of them ballbusters who don't want to know God gave men the pricks and women the holes to put them in. I don't care if her smartass mouth graduated ten universities, what counts is she's built so's my eyes pop looking at her.

I figure her for twenty-six or -seven. Older than me just means a couple of years more experience, right? This babe knows what she's doing. You see nipples through her dress? She's turning the whole fucking world on. The first minute Gino introduces me to this Maria, my balls get tight as a fist. I see nipples, tits, ass, mouth, *mamma mia.* "Gino," I whisper to him so's she can't hear, "you'd make a first-class pimp."

Gino likes to make me happy. He smiles.

I whisper, "I want to own this one."

"Hey, Garibaldi," she says to me, "whispering isn't polite."

"My name's not Garibaldi, it's Giovanni."

Gino says, "Everybody calls him the lion."

"Is that so? Where does he sleep, in the zoo?"

So I says, "You want to know where I sleep, you find out real soon."

She gives me that real put-me-down ha-ha. If she wasn't so beautiful I'd give her head something to think about.

Gino says to her, "You like my American friend?"

Maria pays no attention to Gino, says to me if you're American how come you're in Rome more than ten years.

"Gino talks too much." I pull out my U.S.A. passport, shove it right in front of Maria's face. She turns pages. "That picture's me when I was age fourteen," I says.

She hands the passport back, flashes a smile worth a million bucks to a hungry man. I think, the way she's blonde, she must be from up north. The girls down here, some of them are darker than niggers. Anybody looks like Maria, what do I care she's full of university crap? She wants what every woman wants, ready or not here I come.

"Gino," I says, "go find something to do."

"Like what?"

My good friend Gino sometimes got his head up his ass. I tell him I want a map with all the Rome police stations marked.

"Where do I buy that?"

"*Stupido!* You buy a map of Rome. You mark police stations on map, *capisci?*"

That will keep Gino busy. "You see any of the others around," I says, "you tell them I got my do-not-disturb sign hanging out." What I want with this Maria is three, four hours minimum. I mean the first time with a girl is when she decides if there's a next time, right?

Goodbye Gino. Maria and me walk around the neighborhood. People see me, they go inside. Most people got enough trouble already.

"Gino says all the men in your group are Italian."

"You bet," I says.

"No French connections? No German?"

"So what? I thought you was Italian."

"I am," she says. "Gino says you don't have Libyan connections."

"Gino talks too much," I tell her.

"He says you're a big man."

"What does that mean, big man?"

"I don't know," she says. "You tell me."

"You think big education makes you big woman? If you such a big woman how come you don't know what a big man is?"

Maria laughs. First time my life I get hard-on from a girl's laugh.

"Why did you leave America?"

"What's the matter, you CIA or something?"

Out of her purse she takes this piece of paper.

"What this?" I says. I'm feeling today is a day off, no business except monkey business.

"Read it," she says.

I tell her, "Say please."

"Please read it."

"For you," I says, "I read a whole newspaper. You know something? Once a newspaper, I don't mean *Corriere della Sera*, a nothing pissass newspaper, said things about me they deserve to die. Next day the warehouse where they keep paper blows its roof like Mount Etna, fire everywhere. No paper, no newspaper."

"Who do you think you are," she says, "Mussolini?" and shoves the piece of paper at me.

"Listen," I says, "that there is nothin' compared to a lot of things I've done. What's with this?" Her finger's jabbing at the piece of paper.

All right, I open it. It says, MARIA OKAY. D. The 'D,' it's got a mustache coming from it, one piece on each side. Dominick's sign. Very interesting. "How you know Dominick?"

"How do *you* know Dominick?" she answers.

"What experience you got?" I ask Miss Smartass.

She laughs, I could kill her.

She sees my anger. "Take it easy."

"You know how to make *anything?*" I ask.

"What kind of anything?"

"A bomb."

"I thought bombs come already made."

"You ever handle a ready-made?"

She shakes her head no. I wonder why Dominick sent her to me.

"You shoot a gun?"

"You show me, yes?"

"Show you what?"

"Everything. Guns, bombs, everything you know. You teach me to make war, I teach you to make love."

"I ought to slap your face."

"You slap me, I'll slap you."

"Hey, what kind of woman are you?"

"What kind do you like?"

This time I smile.

"How many people in your group?" she asks.

"Enough."

"You have room for more?"

"With no experience?"

"I have experience."

"Experience I can use?"

"We will see." When she says this, she pinches my cheek. Nobody ever pinched my cheek since I was six years old.

I look around, we're three, four blocks away from the house I use in this part of town. The man and his wife who own this house, he's a magistrate, like a judge. This magistrate puts my friend Iggie in jail. We had to go to a lot of trouble to spring him. When we get Iggie out, one night real late Iggie and Gino and Luigi and me, we take a little visit to the magistrate's home. Real nice house. Makes me wonder what kind of money this magistrate makes on the side.

In the bedroom we find he's in one bed, his wife in the other. He's snoring. We laugh so loud they both wake up. The wife sees us, she don't know if she gonna scream or hide her buzooms first. The magistrate sees our guns, he tells her shut up. We tell them, "Out of bed!" They move like scared old dogs. We say nice night, we go for a drive. By now she got an idea who we are. Please, no, the old lady begs. I take her nose between my two fingers so she can't breathe except through her mouth. I put my other hand on her mouth. "Shut up," I say to her. We don't want to wake up half of Rome.

Like I promised, we go ninety kilometers, a real drive, come to nice woods, Iggie's in charge. He tells the magistrate and his wife they got to lie down face down on the ground.

That magistrate, he puts a handkerchief on ground so his face won't get dirty, ain't that a laugh?

Iggie puts the gun right against the back of the wife's head. We hear sissing sound, not from her. Would you believe the magistrate, his head on the handkerchief nice and clean, he's lying there, a piss stain spreading down his left pants leg?

I feel sorry for this old guy. Iggie doesn't feel sorry for nobody. He leaves the woman, goes over to the magistrate, with his right leg he steps on the magistrate's butt, takes aim, and splat. The woman is crying. "Shut up," Iggie says. "I got nothing against you, just your husband." She cries louder, so Iggie shoots her in the ass, just for laughs, but she's screaming murder so he leans over and gives her what they call a *coup de grâce*.

The two of them got to be buried in a big deep hole. Don't think this isn't work. Who wants anyone finding them and coming around to the house? No safe house is safe forever. I want to keep it for a while.

When we finish pretty exhausted, Luigi and Gino go home to sleep, but Iggie and me, we go to the magistrate's house. Interesting things there, in the closets, in the drawers. Iggie and me we stay up till nearly morning, having a good time finding things. Iggie puts the jewelry in his pocket. I shake a finger at him. He puts the jewelry in my pocket like he's supposed to. Then Iggie puts on the old lady's bathrobe, I could die laughing. Anyway, this the house I'm steering Maria to. Once Maria knows where this house is, she's got two choices, be friendly or be dead.

This is no time for me to be thinking things like that, I ain't been laid for two weeks. When I look at this Maria, it feels like two months. Man!

So she's bullshitting me, I bullshit her, we're in front of the house, I take my keyring out of my pocket, pick the right key, smile at Maria. She says, "Whose house?"

"None of your business," I tell her. I open the door, walk in, wave to her to follow me. Once she's inside I lock the door to keep out anybody else gets an idea to use this place.

"How did you get so rich?" she says.

I says. "How do you get so smart?" I pull her over so close her tits are in my chest and her hips are up against me so she can know what I've got for her. I wonder when she's going to yell stop, but I do this and that and I don't hear anything from her except her breathing, which sounds real good to me. Next thing we're upstairs in the magistrate's bedroom and I'm taking my clothes off faster than I ever did and she just stands there.

"How come you just standing there?" I says, taking my socks off.

She says, "I thought you were going to help me."

Well, it's one fucking pleasure to help. I unzip her back, I let her step out of the dress, I unhook her bra, which is one of those that got holes for the nipples, and bang, there are the most beautiful tits I ever saw anywhere. I'm ready to go at them, but she holds me off and takes her bikini-type panties down and I tell you, that is something else. You bet I'm looking. She puts her hand on my cock. That gets my attention. I got to be super careful or I'm gonna come before anything happens. I push her down on the bed where she belongs and I work on her, which gives me time, except she's reacting unbelievable. Boy does she like what I'm doing. Then she's telling me okay, come on, and I'm trying to get in, I'm so excited I can't find it, and she helps, and I find out this Maria she fucks like a wild horse. Believe you me, I forget where I am, I can't get enough. Maria laughs. She says if I keep it up I'll be a basket case. Some basket I says, and down she goes.

Well, you got to rest sometime. When we're lying back, smoking some stuff she brought, loose, she says, "Tell me about yourself."

I look at her because that's sort of my line with chicks, and she's asking me. "Nothing to tell."

"Come on, tell me about when you were in America. Before you were a big man."

I pinch her nipple. "I was always a big man." She laughs. "My father was a big man, too," I tell her. "My father Alfredo so rich he owned a Cadillac with specially installed window shades."

"You're making that up."

"So help me it's the truth. When I was six years old he even made a bank trust for me to go to college, isn't that something? Every Sunday he gave me five dollars pocket money. If any kid on that block ever gave me a hard time, my old man would come out and stare at whoever gave me trouble and the kid would run like from the evil eye. Those kids' parents were more scared of Alfredo Monteleone than of the cops. Then, something happened."

"What happened?" Maria asks.

I can feel my face get angry red.

"When I was thirteen," I tell her, "I had to go in front of a judge who says, 'Son' . . . listen to the fucker say son when he's got not one ounce of Monteleone blood. 'Where's your mother? Didn't she come to court with you?'

" 'She's busy,' I says. 'I can handle things.' Then the judge looks over at this lady who is typing away as if he wants to complain to her about me. Like he's exasperated, the judge says, 'Why didn't your father's lawyer come with you?'

" 'How should I know,' I says. 'My mother says I got to be in court, I'm in court. Now what's up, judge?'

"He looks at me like he never saw a thirteen-year-old kid before, and says, " 'Your father is ordered deported.' "

" 'What!' I shout so everybody can hear me.

"The judge says my father is ordered deported right out of the United States because he lied in his naturalization.

"That's fuckin' crazy. One lousy lie and you get kicked out of your own country, whoever heard of that? Well, I'm hearing it from this bastard sitting up there in his black dress like he's God Almighty.

"I say what about my mama? My mama's a saint. I want to hear this judge say one thing against my mama, and I'll jump up on his bench and choke him with my own hands.

"This judge says my mama, she didn't commit no crime, she's okay. 'She's going with your father voluntarily.'

" 'Go where?' I yell.

"The judge leans down to say something to this guy in the gray uniform, who comes up to where I am and says, " 'Behave yourself,' like I'm some kid in school. 'Speak quietly.'

"Okay, I speak normal and ask where my mama is going. The judge, he says she is going back to Italy. I say, 'Wait a minute, judge, she's never been to Italy, she was born here.'

"It doesn't matter. She is going with my father. For the first time in my life I learn that if you're with someone you don't want to be without, it doesn't matter if you're born here, boom you're out.

"Then the judge says, 'It is customary in these cases to talk to members of the family individually so that no one is intimidated.' This judge guy doesn't even know that an Italian family is like glue.

"I ask what about my sister? He says my sister Anna, she goes with them if she wants to or not because she is only seven. Anna doesn't even have a choice! But the judge is putting the finger on me because I'm thirteen. He butters me up, says my school record's good, you have aunts, uncles, relatives all kinds here, this judge says I can stay here and live with a relative. I say, 'Damn right I want to live with relatives, I want to live in Newark with mama and papa, not my cousins.'

"This judge is getting ready to turn me over to some kind of social worker. I tell him I don't want any social worker, I want to be with my family. He says ordered this, ordered that, and the next thing I know I'm off to Naples with the rest of the family. You think that fuck judge gave me a choice? What kid doesn't want to go with his family? Maybe a kid in lots of trouble, not me."

"Don't get so angry," Maria says.

I tell her I was angry then and I'm still angry. "My mother's scared, she won't go on an airplane even if the pilot is Italian, like on Alitalia, so we have to go on a boat to Naples in the middle of winter, everybody gets seasick. My father tries to make me feel better about getting kicked out of America. He shows me a thousand-dollar bill from his sock. I never saw one before. He says Mama has two of them in her bra. He says since I'm big boy, he'd give me five big ones to put in my jockey shorts before we get to Naples.

"Okay, in Naples we're rich but my old man he keeps saying he loves America, he misses America, he wishes we could all go back to America. Six, seven years go by, I say how can he still love America after it throws him out. I love my father like God. When I say how can he love America, I can't believe it, he spits in my face."

Maria reaches over and puts her hand on my head, kind of like brushing my hair. I take her hand off because I don't want anybody to feel sorry for me.

I get up on my elbow and I say to her, "Listen, my old man teach me before crossing a street, look right, look left. Now he crosses our own street without looking. A taxi going normal speed, they say, hits him bang, drags him halfway down the block like a sack of potatoes before it stops. Someone gets my mama. I come running. Anna comes running. Mama bends over him. My father, oil dripping on his face like he was a dead mechanic, has no more answers for anybody.

"At the funeral, as the coffin goes down, I try watching the face of the priest so I don't have to look at my mama. The priest suddenly looks like he's seen the devil. I look where he's looking, my mama is on her hands and knees. Before anybody can stop her she's sliding into the grave on top of the casket. My uncle and I jump in to pull her out. People are screaming all around, thinking maybe we're trying to be buried with him like Mama. Maybe we should have just let her die there. Two months later she writes a long letter to Anna and me and sticks her head in the oven."

I wish I hadn't told Maria. It's no good to feel like sorry for anything. But she leans over and kisses me right on the mouth and pretty soon I'm forgetting all of my troubles. That Maria has got one helluva machine for forgetting.

Afterwards, we're having another joint, Maria says she'd like to introduce me to some of her friends.

"What friends?" Someone you don't know says he is a friend and you better make sure your wallet's in a pocket with a button on it.

Maria says her friends they're a group with a purpose.

"What purpose?" My suspicion is up there like a hard-on. "Does Dominick know about these friends of yours?" Christ, this woman knows about this house. Am I gonna have to kill her?

I want to meet her friends. Any time, she says. Right now, today, I says.

She sees I'm serious, so she makes a couple of phone calls. The meet is set for Friday. That gives Maria and me three days to get better acquainted, you know what I mean? I do her, she does me, vice versa, she tells me her life, I tell her more about mine.

Then it's Friday. We go to meet her friends. They sound like they come from all over, not just Italy. One guy I swear is German. His girl is some kind of Scandinavian, blonde like Maria but not so good-looking and nothing in the tits department. Also Hugo, maybe he's German too, who knows. One thing for sure, this high-class limey Chadbourne talks like a red. These friends of Maria, especially the chicks, their heads are full of Russia, workers' rights, shit like that. They say I'm not political. "Fuck that," I say to them, "I got one politics. Screw the U.S.A."

Then all these university types want to know how come I got such a hate hard-on for America.

Hugo, he says, "How zoo vee know you are really American?"

I show Hugo the same passport I showed Maria. That shithead says, "Anyone can get a passport for money. That's a kid's passport."

"Listen, smartass," I says to him, "you name any street in Newark and I'll tell you what neighborhood it's in."

This fucker Hugo doesn't even know what Newark is. "Newark, New Jersey, U.S.A.," I says to him, looking over at Maria so she can be proud of me. "I was born there, dig?"

They are all ears. "Go on," Maria says, "tell them."

So I tell them real quick some of what I told her. "Listen, man," I said to Maria's friends, "if I live to be a hundred years, I'll never forget what America did. Sure, I can go back there. For what? To kill everybody? Plenty of Americans to kill right here."

I can see Maria's friends, they understand me. I tell them after my father got run over and my mother killed herself, I went through our apartment, every inch, to find every shoebox, any place my father kept his lire. What I find is U.S. hundred-dollar bills, lots, some are in a Bible hollowed out in the middle, some in a box of spaghetti I could have thrown out for being old if I wasn't careful. And in the bottom of my mama's filled-up jewelry box, what do you think I found? That's right, more jewelry, diamonds, the works.

"I want to give the jewelry to my sister. No, she goes off with this guy Paolo from up north, near Genoa. Paolo is blond, doesn't even look Italian, works like a dog in some bakery I think. I ask Anna what the fuck is she doing with her life, she says what am I doing with mine, and she marries Paolo the blond because she's already got his bun in her oven. I know Paolo's kind. He has the mind of a snitch. I'm not going to end up in some judgefucker's courtroom in a cage like some animal because Paolo decides to rat on me. I forget Anna.

"What's the first thing I buy, a Fiat?

All Maria's friends laugh. I tell them the first thing I buy is two guns, one for the apartment, one always on me. I am so full of hate anybody sees me in the street they walk around me.

I says to them, "You want to see something real nice?" I show them a knife. The handle is like ivory with a drawing on it, both sides, scrim-something, a real beaut. You don't have to open the knife, I say, you spring the spring, the blade jumps out like it was alive. They all jump. It's my turn to laugh. "This," I tell them, "is my father's knife. Don't be scared. I never use the knife on people. On people, I use a gun."

My turn to laugh. I tell everybody, "Relax. We all friends, right?" To Maria I say, "My throat's dry." Maria get me a glass of water. I say to her, "This the best you can do?"

She says she can do better later. Everybody laughs because they know we're not talking about a glass of water.

Hugo says I should go on with my story. "It's not a story," I say. "It's true."

I tell Maria's buddies dough is one thing I've got plenty of. What I'm looking for is revenge. Deals don't mean anything to me if the target isn't America.

Maria is proud of me. She comes over and right in front of everybody kisses me. And all of them clap hands like they're watching a movie.

I'm so crazy happy, Maria says I'm a walking hard-on. I tell her I'd rather be that than a talking machine. Pretty soon I get the drift of what Maria's group is up to. I like it, I like it. I tell them mine's a speciality. The Arabs machine-gun people standing in line in the airport, Swiss people, Italian people, some Americans sure, Jews, whatever, but what the crazy fuck good is that? My specialty is Uncle Sam. He's got a white beard because he is old and half dead. I want all Americans scared what is Monteleone going to do next.

Maria says that maybe I'm getting political.

"Fuck that," I says. "I'm getting international like a conglomerate."

Couple of years later the people say like after Carlos there is only me. And nobody calls me "the American" who wants to live.

When Iggie puts the bomb on the general's car and zips away, I'm so proud I could kiss him. I tell him bravo, the best job he ever pulled. We're gonna celebrate, and what happens? Iggie doesn't have one day to enjoy life before that bastard who wears a wig. . . . It makes me crazy just to think. Iggie was my brother. His religion was me. I hope they got TV in heaven and Iggie saw that casket blow. *That was for you, Iggie, capisci?* Revenge is the sweetest fruit on earth.

CHAPTER 21

David

When you've eaten gluey army rations for weeks on end in the jungle, you get pretty good at avoiding the insects swarming over the food. The conditions for eating airline food off a tray aren't really as bad as most civilians make them out to be.

"This isn't bad," said the businessman sitting on my right.

"No insects," I said.

"How's that?"

"No competition from insects."

He went back to sawing his beef fillet with a white plastic knife as if he were alone in the cabin.

Susan, who'd turned around to look at me, was trying not to laugh. I was glad. I wished I could distract Mrs. Whitcomb, too. One thing I learned in Nam was that you don't edge into someone's grief by playing up to it and telling them how sorry you are. You enter through the funnybone.

After the stewardess cleared the trays away, Mrs. Whitcomb volunteered to change seats with me, "So you and Susan can talk."

Mrs. Whitcomb took my seat and I took hers, both of us nodding thanks to each other as if we were Japanese.

I settled in next to Susan. Her breath in my right ear, she whispered, "You are a merciless game player."

"With you?"

"I meant with the man behind me."

I looked at him over Susan's right shoulder. He'd been watching us. When my eyes met his, his gaze flicked back to his copy of *Business Week*.

"Just my way of keeping adjacent busybodies from invading my turf," I said.

"Does that include me?"

"I elected to sit next to you."

"I think my mother got you elected."

I said, "Hold still, I've got an idea worth trying."

I unbuckled and went forward to business class, where a very pretty dark-haired stewardess was supervising a section of seats that was two-thirds empty.

"Not much business in business class," I said. "Is it usually like this?"

"Sometimes," she said, distancing me. I decided to put her at ease.

"I just got married," I told her. "In Rome."

"Congratulations," she said, looking in the direction I'd come from. "Is that the bride?" I turned. Susan, next to the one empty seat in tourist, was watching us.

"That's her," I said, flashing my pride. "We keep trying to talk, you know, about our plans, and that guy next to us keeps listening in. Any chance we could upgrade to a couple of spare seats up here?"

She seemed uncertain.

"As a wedding present?" I said.

"If anyone asks, don't lay it on me."

"Hell no, it was my own idea. I'll get her. And thanks."

Back in tourist I leaned over Susan, my lips almost touching her ear, and whispered, "Take your handbag. We're moving."

"What about Mom? What if there's trouble?"

I looked up. Mrs. Whitcomb was asleep.

"If anybody was going to hijack this plane, they'd have done it already."

"And how would you know?"

"They'd want to be close enough to be able to land on this side of the ocean, not in New York. Your mother'll be okay. I'll come back once in a while to check."

* * *

"This feels good," said Susan, stretching her legs. "What did you tell that stewardess?"

"That's our little secret. Hers and mine."

"You're a handy fellow to have around," she said.

"Why, thank you. If I were ever in a bad jam stateside, would you defend me?"

"You're defending me, aren't you?" Susan said.

"I get paid for doing it."

She said, "I'd get paid more than you get paid. What are you thinking?"

I was thinking about her body. "Nothing," I said. "A mindless blank."

"You don't lie well."

"I'm just not used to mind readers."

"Not mind readers. Clever women."

"What I—" I stopped. What I really wanted was to drop walls around us.

We were a tolerable distance from the nearest passengers, but it wasn't private enough. I wanted to put my hand out and touch her belly. The belly's a safe place to start. Makes it fifty-fifty. She can remove your hand. If not, you can move it up or down, depending on how much consent you think you're getting. Here the stewardess could come by. Anybody could come by. Is that what made the temptation so interesting?

"You are having x-rated thoughts," Susan said.

I was at a loss for a quick lie.

"When we get to New York," she said, "do you stay or go back?"

"Only till you and your mother are safely home."

"I live in the city. Her place is in the suburbs."

"I know."

"Now how the hell do you know that?"

"I've been briefed."

"Jesus, when do I get to cross-examine?"

"Will you stay with your mother?" The minute I said it I knew she'd misinterpret it. "That's not a personal question," I said quickly. "It's a security question."

"I don't mind personal questions. It's you who do."

"Right. Now, will you stay with your mother?"

"I'll try to be with her as much as I can the first few days, but I've got to get back to work. How soon do you go back?"

"We'll have to see, won't we?"

"David?" She touched my sleeve.

"Yes?"

"Never mind."

I hate it when someone starts to tell you something, then changes their mind. I could feel the heat in my face. When I was a kid my father used to say to me, "You'd better learn to control that. Folks don't know how to deal with someone who gets madder'n hell over nothing."

Susan was scribbling something on a slip of paper. She folded it once and handed it over.

I opened it. *Who the fuck are you?*

I laughed and crumpled the paper into a ball. From the pocket on the chairback in front of me I took the barf bag and dropped Susan's message into it.

"Please talk," she said. "Tell me who you are. Trust me."

"Oh, I have no trouble trusting you. It's just the rest of the world."

"You work for the government. Start there."

She was making my nerves dance. For years I'd trained myself not to talk.

I didn't want to lose her before there was something to lose.

"There are days," I said, "when I hate the government the way some people hate their parents."

"David, I don't want your rank or serial number, I want to know what you do. I've prosecuted two men who killed under orders. And I would have prosecuted the man who gave them the orders if we'd had enough on him to convict at trial."

"Sam would appreciate that."

"Who's Sam?"

"The guy who gives me my orders."

"Orders to do what?"

"Whatever it is I do. Like watch over you and your mother."

"I don't believe for a minute that you're a bodyguard."

"I'll tell Sam I've lost my credibility. He's a very sweet fellow. You'd like him. I hope you never meet."

"Don't you do things of your own volition ever?"

"Sure, and it always gets me into trouble. With women."

"Well, you're in trouble with me at the moment." She swallowed. "Maybe I'm in trouble with myself. The man who killed my father, if I had a way to get even, I would—"

"You'd do what?"

"David," she said, "what was it like the first time you killed somebody and knew it?"

My temper began to ease out of the bottle. "Never ask a soldier that question. Did you ever ask your father if he'd killed anybody?"

Susan looked away.

"I'm sorry," I said quickly. "I didn't mean to remind you."

"It's okay."

"Nothing important comes easy the first time, not even riding a bicycle."

Susan looked up from her lap. Her face couldn't have been more than inches away from mine. She said, "Who taught you to ride a bicycle?"

"My father. He taught me to ride a tractor first, then a bicycle, only it was a motorbike. We skipped the bicycle stage."

"How old were you?"

"Fifteen, give or take."

"Where was the farm? The one the tractor was on."

"Scaville, North Dakota. Ever hear of it?"

She shook her head.

"Outside of town it's sort of a landscape without people. Silos, of course, and occasionally a barn or a house a few hundred yards from the road. You might spot a man on a tractor. Or a boy. The trouble with tractors is once you learn to handle one, they don't fight back. I used to wish we had a ranch instead of a farm so I could ride horses that didn't want to be ridden. I kind of like a little resistance in a mattress, too."

The dark-haired stewardess came by just then with a small tray on which she was balancing two plastic champagne glasses. To Susan she said "Congratulations," then handed each of us one of the glasses filled almost to the brim.

As soon as the stewardess was out of earshot, Susan said, "Champagne?"

"I told her we were just hitched. That's how we got these seats."

"Very clever," Susan said. "I'd hate to have you as a client. You let loose lies as if they were balloons. You better get back to safe territory."

"Like?"

"Like North Dakota."

"It isn't all that safe either. If you get off the main roads back home, you get to see two kinds of silos. The kind you store fodder in, and the kind that go straight down into the ground. All that farmland is no man's land. The only way you can live there," I said, "is to put the fact that you're in the middle of a priority one target out of your mind the same way you know that you're descended from an ape but you don't like to think about it. Ever been on a farm?"

"No."

"Never?"

"I think I've been in every European capital at least once."

"But never on an American farm?"

"Right."

"Well, that tells a lot about you, doesn't it?"

"There are all kinds of ways to be square. When I was a kid I played with dolls and skipped rope. What kind of games did you play?"

There were games I played I wouldn't tell anyone about.

"Come on," she said. "Don't be bashful."

"I don't know if I'd call them games. I had a weird way of showing off."

"Like what?"

"Oh, on my own I'd go out and test the electric fence that kept the cattle in, touching it to get the jolt and see if I could take it. Once I lured some of the kids over after school and took them out to the field and showed them I could touch the fence. They wouldn't do it. I got respect from their eyes. So I rolled up my sleeve and swept my forearm across the barbed wire until I was running blood down into my palm and said, 'Anybody want to try it?' They just stared at me, some of them backing away a step or two. Then I just flung my arm out at the nearest boy, splattering the blood at him, and they all ran. What's wrong?"

"You were really a crazy kid."

"You haven't heard the half. One of those kids, a sissy named Randy, told our homeroom teacher, Mr. Beane, what I'd done. I'd always gotten high marks from Mr. Beane because I could get my thoughts in line better than most. He called me up front and said, 'You didn't do what Randy said you did, did you?'

" 'He must be making it up,' I said.

"Randy said, 'Make him roll up his right sleeve.'

" 'Mr. Beane, sir,' I said, 'make Randy take his pants down so he can show you he doesn't have one.'

"Mr. Bean couldn't keep from laughing and I never did have to show my right forearm."

Susan put her hand on my arm. "Roll up your sleeve," she said.

"You make it sound like an order."

Susan nodded. I rolled up my right sleeve and slowly turned my arm so she could see the long scar.

"Are you going to tell me what you do or do I have to sub-poena you?"

"You can't subpoena me. You don't even know my real name."

"I'm very persistent."

"I see that."

"If you won't tell what you do, will you at least tell me how you got into such an offbeat line of work?"

"Okay," I said. "But you realize, after you know my secrets I'll have to kill you."

From Susan, silence.

"I'm kidding," I said.

From Susan, not a word. Any experienced interrogator can tell you it's a great way to make someone talk.

"I was eighteen in 1967."

"I'm waiting," she said, so I let it roll.

"The bad days of Vietnam," I said, "trapped people my age. Ever see an animal caught in a trap? Guess not. Dad used to call family meetings after church every Sunday. One Sunday he told us—us was my mother, my two kid sisters and me—he'd had a dream that if I went to Vietnam something horrible would happen. I would come back paralyzed from the neck down, with no use of my arms or legs—he didn't say pecker but I knew he meant that, too—and end up in a wheelchair for the rest of my days.

"Nowadays I think he said that out of love, to keep me from volunteering. But then all I needed was that speech. I was off to Fargo like a shot, to join up long before I would have been drafted. Says something about eighteen-year-olds."

Susan nodded, waiting for me.

"Over there it wasn't like touching an electrified fence. At the farm I controlled the show. In Nam it was all Dick and Jane."

"What does that mean?"

"Dick is a soldier away from home, sighting for people instead of squirrels. Jane is a too-young girl walking along the road with a basket and Dick doesn't know if she's got food in it or a grenade. Mr. Beane never prepared me or anyone else for that kind of Dick and Jane."

I couldn't read Susan's expression. "What are you thinking?" I asked.

"Just go on," she ordered.

"Yes ma'am, sir," I said. "Back home you'd meet up with an Indian or a colored person, you'd notice cause folks were mostly white. In Nam they mostly weren't. It was like a war between Africa and Asia, a whole other world, our side mostly black, the other side all skinny and slant-eyed. For a time Lester and I were the only white boys in our squad, and the other grunts would say to us, 'Hey man, you look pale. You sick or something?'

"Lester was was from North Dakota, and in the twitch of a tail we were strong friends. When it was his turn to take point on a patrol . . . the point man goes first to flush out whoever's up ahead."

"I know."

"Forgot you're an army brat."

Her eyes were truly beautiful.

"You're staring."

"Sorry."

"Go on with your patrol story."

"It's not a story!"

"I didn't mean you were making it up. You get angry too quickly. Come on, tell it."

Her convincer hand touched my arm, just for a second.

"Well, this day I was telling you about, Lester was moved up to point. I was as scared for Lester as I'd be for myself when I was up there. When the point man's fired at, you've had your warning. We thought we were lucky, because after a couple of hours the lieutenant relieved Lester of being a human target and sent some other jerk up front.

"Lester came back to where I was. We were reconnoitering in two files down both sides of a dirt road, fifteen feet between men so no machine gun could catch a bunch of us in a burst. Lester was up ahead of me and slowed a bit to pass me a stick of chewing gum. He was holding it out behind him but keeping walking, searching the trees on either side. His hand with the chewing gum froze. I knew he spotted something a second before the crack zinged smack into the bridge of his nose.

"Everyone in the squad hit the ditches, firing up into the trees in the direction we thought the shot had come from, except me. I was down on the road next to Lester. His face didn't look like his face. I shouted 'Medic!' so loud you could have heard me in Saigon. I held Lester's head. His eyes were still alive, looking at me, scared shitless. The medic made his way through the ditch, glancing up, hoping the sniper had tied himself in the tree, which is what we all hoped, and dead from the fusillade, not getting set to take a potshot again.

"The medic was going bananas. What do you do, put a tourniquet around the man's neck? Put a hand-sized bandage on his wrecked nose and mouth? How would he breathe? Lester answered all the questions. His open eyes stopped moving. I put Lester's head down gently, and looked around in the dirt for the stick of gum, which I was going to save. When I picked it up, I realized I had blood all over my hands. I wiped them off on my fatigues. I didn't want to get any on Lester's wallet, which I took. The medic protested but he didn't get through my fog. I just wanted to make sure that the pictures in it were censored by me before the rest got shipped back to his parents. When the medic put his hand on my arm, just like you've got your hand on my arm, I gave him a look I had that made people think twice about messing with me. He let go. I don't want you to let go."

She let go.

"I kind of realized I never had a friend till Lester, and he got took, as they used to say."

"Do you have friends now?"

"My kind of work, the only friends you can have are the ones you work with."

"Doesn't give me a chance."

I thought I misheard her.

"Go on," she said. "I didn't mean to stop you."

"Nothing more to tell, really. After Lester was gone, I was like a madman high on uppers. I was getting a rep. Once the lieutenant had a Cong who wouldn't tell us what was up ahead. Most of them chicken-chatter a bunch of lies because they think we're stupid, but this one refused to talk."

"So?"

"So I'm like you. I did something to make him talk, something the lieutenant didn't have the guts to do, and we ended up ambushing the ambushers."

"If you'd let yourself walk into the ambush, would that have made you a hero?"

"A dead one."

"I don't know what you did, but if I was in that situation, I would have done something to make that man talk."

"I believe you. You sure as hell made *me* talk."

"Not really. You still haven't told me how you got from there to here."

"Well, whatever I did got me pulled out of my battalion for special training. What they put us through made basic training seem like kindergarten. If you couldn't go twenty-four hours without food or water you were out. If you couldn't wade through a waist-deep pond filled with cattle guts, you were out. If you couldn't make a thirty-mile forced march with five minutes rest per hour, you were out."

"That must have been awful."

"To tell the truth, I loved it. Those of us who didn't get washed out got sent on missions you never saw on home TV." I lowered my voice. "Everyone on this plane can probably hear me."

"No one can hear you," she said. "Except me."

I wanted her to know me. I'd have to take the chance.

"On one of our expeditions," I said, "Kissinger knew where we were, and maybe two generals and a colonel. That was when I first learned that our missions were deniable. If we failed, nobody would know for months. Back home, they'd get a missing-in-action telegram eventually, and then more eventually they'd start to collect insurance. If we succeeded, meaning we stayed alive, we didn't come back to medals. As far as the rest of the world was concerned, we hadn't been anywhere or done anything. We got some R and R and were off again.

"It was on mission five I learned that two of the guys with us were civilians—how about that!—and were earning umpteen times what I was getting as a soldier for doing the same thing they were doing, maybe better. I saw the light. When my time was up, I wasn't of a mind to go back home and start pumping gas. My officers all said I was college material, but I wasn't about to sit still for seven or eight years to become a doctor or a lawyer. My mom kept writing saying how much everyone missed me and other bullshit, and when was I coming home? I thought if I paid a visit, they'd press me on what I was doing. And then when I left it would be worse than before. It's better if they just forgot me. I did write once when I was on assignment in the Middle East, the other side of the world, and I wrote to say that the stamp would tell them not where I was but where I'd been, and that I was no longer in the army."

"What were you in?"

"I was at war. Permanently."

"With whom?"

"Well," I let her see my smile, "not with my old man any more. I guess I ended up at war with the real terrorists. Every last one in the world."

She sat there, staring straight ahead.

"You've never told this to anyone?"

"Never had anyone to tell it to."

"I'm flattered. I'm even getting to like your wig."

"I've got another one in the suitcase. Lend it to you, if you like. It might fit. You've got a big head."

"Thanks a lot."

"Tell you something. If there are a lot of crazies looking to get you and you want some protection, a wig is a lot lighter than a bullet-proof vest and sometimes keeps you from getting shot in the first place."

"David?"

"Present and accounted for."

"Do you know any more about what my father was up to?"

"Sort of. Not in detail."

"Will you tell me?"

"It's not up to me to tell. It's safer to remember him from what you know."

"He wasn't a tin soldier?"

"He was a brave man."

"He didn't talk about it."

"He had a lot more discipline than I've had. You turned me into a blabber."

My right hand was on the armrest. Susan put her hand on my arm right on that scar.

"I'm glad you talked."

She unbuckled and stood up. The back of her legs brushed my knees as she moved sideways past me. "I'm going to check on Mom."

"I'll come with you."

CHAPTER 22

Susan

As the plane lost altitude descending over the water toward Kennedy, the idea of coming home had a hollowness. Mom and I were an incomplete family.

"David," I said, "I don't know if I'm up to handling the press right now."

"Not to worry. No press."

"They must know about the casket blowing."

"They've been advised that you and your mother are coming back on a military plane heading into Andrews Air Force Base."

"Very clever."

"Very routine."

At the plane's door I held David back so Mom could walk through the slightly uphill exit tunnel ahead of us. Her sprightly tennis-shoe walk seemed to have declined into slow motion.

As we came into the terminal proper, she stopped. David and I came quickly up to her. One side of her lower lip was spastic, out of control.

"What is it?" I asked.

She drew both of her hands to her chest.

Anxiety pitched my voice into an unfamiliar register. "Mom?"

"No, no, no," she said. "I'm perfectly all right. For a second, I thought I saw your father waiting for us."

* * *

We sat on three attached plastic chairs, David on one side, I on the other, and Mom between us until her heart's pounding subsided. "What I wonder . . ." she said.

"Yes, Mom?"

". . . is where you bury someone when there's nothing left to bury."

"Arlington," said David. "His won't be the only grave marker with nothing under it."

Mom said, "Not Arlington. I have decided that I want the tombstone in our back yard."

Ever the lawyer, I asked, "Not literally?"

"I do mean it literally."

"Burials aren't allowed on private land. I thought you planned to bury him in Sleepy Hollow instead of Arlington."

I deserved the look I got from her. "He'll be buried on the grounds of our own home. Don't worry," she said, "we won't be violating anybody's ordinance. It'll only be a headstone."

In the baggage claim area Mom sat down on the edge of a nonmoving conveyor. She said, "Hamlet got some conversation out of his ghost. Mine just went poof the second I saw him."

"Hamlet," I said, "also had a murder to avenge."

"Look at him," said Mom.

"Who?"

"David. Over there."

He was collecting our luggage onto two carts with dispatch. He signaled us to follow him to the customs inspectors waiting for the mob to descend on them.

I insisted on pushing one of the carts. David went scooting ahead with the other one. He had his wallet out, flashed something at the rotund customs inspector in the line he'd picked, and said a few words I wasn't close enough to hear. The customs inspector nodded, put his chalk mark on each bag and motioned us through. As Mom passed, he said, "I'm sorry, ma'am."

Death is a marvelous passport. If the casket had arrived with us, would we have been met by another honor guard, or would the customs people have jimmied it open to check for cocaine?

In what seemed like a porterless hall David had snagged a porter with a trolley. Mom and I were hard put to keep up with them as they went through the swinging doors.

There, behind the barrier, among the small horde of other people's welcomers, conspicuously waving his hand up and down like a semaphore, stood Farlan Adams.

"David! David!" I yelled to stop his headlong march with the porter.

Before I could say *How did you know to meet us?* Farlan put his arms around me and held my body against his.

"Did you get my message?" he said happily in a low voice.

"I certainly did."

"Do I get my answer?" he asked, his face beaming.

Near one of the support pillars stood David and Mom, watching us.

"We'll talk later . . ." I said and squeezed his hand, which was the only invisible thing I could do.

"I can't hear you with all this noise," he said. "Or didn't you say anything?"

"I said we'll talk later. We mustn't keep everyone waiting."

I managed the introductions as best I could and very nearly introduced the puzzled porter into the bargain.

"I'm so pleased to meet you, Mrs. Whitcomb," Farlan was saying, but his eyes were on David and David's were on him, the message each to the other being *Who the hell are you?*

"I'm so sorry about your loss," Farlan said to Mom, nodding in my direction to include me in his message. I watched him as if through a scrim. He seemed so urbane. He had to be at least two inches taller than David.

"How did you know what plane we were on?" I said.

"I called your office. Your secretary couldn't have been more helpful."

"Jesus!" David said. "You let your office know? There could have been a tap on the line. Anyone," he said, looking at Farlan, "could have asked her, and she would have given your arrival away."

"David," I said as gently as I could, "I appreciate your cautions but we're back home now."

"That's what I was afraid of. Back home and caution's out the window."

"Mr. Smith," Farlan said, "is something wrong?"

"Professor Adams," David said, "didn't TV and radio carry the news?"

"I haven't read today's paper yet. I seldom watch TV. I was listening to music on the car radio on the way down. Have I missed something?"

Dear beloved Farlan, A.W.O.L. from the world.

"The general's casket," David said quietly, "was rigged with a bomb."

Farlan stood speechless, as if the idea, so real to us, was incomprehensible to him.

"The people who killed the general," David said, "are trying to make a point by killing the rest of the family. Everyone managed to get away from the casket before it exploded. We were lucky."

It wasn't luck, David. It was you.

"It is absolutely essential," David said, "that their exposure to hazard be minimized."

David's language turned abstract when speaking officially. Or was he just putting it on because the professor was a professor?

"Are you some sort of *bodyguard*?" Farlan asked, as if bodyguarding was something just slightly obscene.

I wasn't about to chance David's reply to that. "David is a friend," I said. I might as well have said David was my lover.

The hurt in Farlan's eyes stung me.

"I suggest we get to a taxi," David said, more to the restless porter than to us.

"I brought my car," Farlan said. "I suggest we can all fit."

"Mom's going up to Scarborough," I said. "It's a good hour and ten minutes from here."

"I don't mind," Farlan said. "I canceled all my appointments for your homecoming."

I said, "Well then, Professor Adams can get his car." Saying *Professor Adams* made me feel as if I were making a speech in someone else's dream. They were all waiting for me to continue. "The porter can drop our bags at the curb and we'll stand guard."

"Perhaps you'd like to accompany me to the car," Farlan said.

I caught one glance from David and thought *Bloody murder*. "Come on then." I put my arm through Farlan's triangle and walked away feeling that I was going to be shot in the back.

At the striped pedestrian crossing, the taxis and limos didn't even try to stop. *Come on*, they seemed to be saying, *we dare you*. Farlan took hold of my elbow with his right hand and held up his left like a traffic cop. The vehicles screeched to a stop to let the madman who didn't understand the imperatives of traffic get across unharmed.

"Farlan!" was all I was capable of saying.

"They would have hit me first," he said. "Now answer my question."

"What question?"

"In my letter. Don't make me seem obtuse. I've never proposed to anyone before."

He looked so like an eager boy.

"I love you," he said.

I thought of Farlan holding court in his office, his books down one wall, the photos of important people down the other, answering every question I ever had of him as if the answer had been stored and waiting for retrieval. About my work he knew more than I could ever learn. To have him as a husband would be like living in a library full of more books than one could read in a lifetime.

"I hope you heard me despite the din."

We were both breathless from walking fast.

"I heard you."

"And?"

"Look," I said, "I've never been proposed to. We need to talk everything over in peace and quiet. I didn't have a chance to really think straight about your letter. Won't you give me a few days?"

"Take all the time you need," Farlan said, pointing me toward his car, "as long as the answer is yes."

With his unfailing courtesy he unlocked the passenger side door first and opened it for me, adding the merest suggestion of a bow.

I slid into the seat.

I thought of Farlan as I had first seen him at the lectern, surveying us. Annie had said once, "The only way to get through Columbia without losing your mind is to imagine what every one of these fuddy-duddies looks like naked with his equipment showing." We'd laughed until tears came to our eyes, as Annie rattled off name after name, each one sending us into a spasm of guffawing. When she came to Farlan Adams she said, "Now that one, he's got balls." "Just balls?" I said, and Annie said, "Who knows, maybe a banana, too," and I laughed so loud I thought I'd pop a blood vessel. *Annie, Annie, Annie, what would you say now?*

Farlan turned the key in the ignition, beaming one of those classroom smiles in my direction. My friend, my mentor had a body that he'd pressed against me. *Like when Al died.*

I smiled back the way I'd learned to smile back at a juror who seemed to be agreeing with me. Had Farlan taught me that, or had I learned it on my own? *Will you be as clever a lover as you are about the law?*

Farlan had to swing nearly halfway around the airport to get onto the proper arrivals ramp. I spotted the odd couple, Mom and her alleged bodyguard, chatting away. Why was David paying zero attention to arriving vehicles? Had he really come along just to be with me?

Farlan honked for their attention. There was no way he could pull up to the curb crowded with cars, trunks sprung open like mouths awaiting luggage.

Farlan double-parked, pressed the trunk release button under the dashboard. David started slinging each piece of our good luggage in as if it were a duffel bag, then at the very last second he stopped and lowered each gently onto the floor of the trunk. Our hero would make a fantastic bellhop.

My thoughts were interrupted by horn-honking and the approach of an overweight traffic cop. Farlan wanted me in front next to him. I said, "Mom deserves the leg room up front," and got in back just as the traffic cop came over to Farlan's open window. "Come on, mister, move."

"In a moment," Farlan said, as if the policeman were a waiter.

David had not yet gotten into the car on his side.

"You, you're blocking traffic," the cop bellowed at David.

"Come get in," I said to David's reddening face. "You'll get nowhere talking back to a New York City cop."

The cop heard me, but Farlan, bless him, inched the car forward, giving David no alternative except to hop in or lose a leg.

For the next fifteen minutes we drove as if we were caught in the long silence before thunder. Then the deluge, a sudden torrential downpour that caused Farlan to cantilever his face closer to the windshield, where the imperfect wipers performed their half-circle race against the rain.

The voice needed to break the silence came from Mom. "Professor Adams," she said, "there's a kind of liquid that comes in a yellow plastic bottle one can use to coat the windows with an invisible film that makes the rain bead and roll off. My husband took some of it to Italy with him, for our driver, Audley, the one who died."

If there was something someone could say after that, they didn't. I just watched the sheeted rain, wondering what Mom might be thinking of this homecoming.

We arrived in Scarborough a half hour later than we'd expected. Mom and Dad's red brick, two-story imitation Federal house had a clear view across the wide expanse of the Hudson River. I could hear a train on the Metro North tracks that lined the shore and remembered how all of us learned to put that sound out of our minds and make believe that the sound of the railroad was a sound of nature, like the chirp of finches or the west wind riffling leaves.

A family, Dad had said, must have a place where you'd known the neighbors for a long time. If he was going to be stationed anywhere in the East, he'd want to have his "spot of earth" available on short notice, even if he and Mom could only get to it for an occasional weekend to make sure it was intact, the driveway cleared of snow in winter, the grass mowed in summer, everything in readiness for the soon-to-come days of his retirement.

Damn death. He'd been in the safe part of soldiering and drew a short straw. What about David's end of the business? What were the odds against premature dying if you were other people's soldier boy?

Hearing our arrival on the gravel driveway, the Websters, Don and Marjorie, were out front to greet us in force. That included a ten-year-old boy and a shy girl just a year older called Susan, a name I was not likely to forget. Don Webster had one of those huge doormen's umbrellas hooked over his arm just in case it started to rain again.

Marjorie Webster ran to put her arms around the new widow. I wondered whether the Websters had clipped the obituaries.

Mom introduced everybody with characteristic care. Then Marjorie Webster said, "Why don't we find our way inside and get some refreshment."

David had already carried our luggage to the doorstep, where Don Webster disengaged himself from his oversize umbrella and took charge.

"Susan," Farlan was calling to me, "shouldn't we be getting back to the city?"

I told Farlan I intended to stay with my mother for at least the one night to see how she got on. "Why don't you drop David off in the city," I said. "I'm sure he'd appreciate it."

What Farlan would really appreciate is not leaving David behind.

David said, "Sounds like a good arrangement if Professor Adams doesn't mind."

"Of course I wouldn't mind," Farlan said with the kind of sincerity that in the witness box advertises a liar.

By this time we were all crowding the front hallway. David said, "I'd like a word with the Whitcombs before I go," and without waiting for a response steered Mom and me to the far end of the adjacent living room.

"I'm certain we have the same intention," he said, "which is not to alarm the family you're staying with. But I'd appreciate it, Mrs. Whitcomb, if you'd find some excuse for making your way around the house to be sure that the windows are all latched. I'm sure the outside door is locked for the night but please check anyway. Blame it on your nerves, or that you've been living in Rome. Whatever seems plausible. I'd rather you did it than Susan, so you'll get used to doing it when Susan's in the city."

"Dear David Smith," Mom said, "I do appreciate everything you've done for us. Now that we're back home, I intend to put that whole European nightmare behind me."

"It's not just Europe, Mrs. Whitcomb. This—"

"I won't live in a jail. Or a fortress."

"Mrs. Whitcomb, I—"

"Please. I just won't have it. I don't need a bodyguard and Susan is quite capable of taking care of herself."

"I have a responsibility to—"

"That's final," Mom said.

I could see that David was not used to arguing with a strong-minded woman. Expelling breath to vent his anger, he scratched out a number on a card and handed it to me.

"This is where you can reach me if I'm needed. In a few days someone from the service will be in touch with each of you."

I looked at the number he had written down. "If you're returning to Rome, what's the point of having a number in New York?"

"That number is always answered if you let it ring." He wrote the number on a second card and handed that one to Mom. "The number is picked up not in New York but elsewhere on this side of the Atlantic. It's like an 800 number, it won't show up on your bill. They'll patch you in to me or have me get back to you quickly."

"So we can't even tell where your cut-out is located, much less you," I said.

"Very clever," said David. "What I want you applying your cleverness to is playing it safe."

"Until Monteleone forgets about us."

"He won't forget. The best cure is prevention."

Mom was looking at the card David had given her. For a moment I thought she was going to tear it up. "I must spend a few minutes with my hosts," she said. "Please excuse me."

When she was out of earshot, David said, "Now, mind telling me who this professor fellow is?"

"Well," I said, "he's very secretive. Can't get him to talk about his past at all."

"I did, didn't I?"

"Against all your rules."

"Yes, dammit! Now who is Mr. Fusspot?"

"My lord and master at Columbia, great teacher of courtroom tricks and tactics, an aspiring lawyer's dream resource."

"Bullshit. You've been out of school for years."

"That I have. But Professor Adams and I still see each other."

"Fully dressed?"

I could see Farlan in the hallway looking at us.

"I'm rapidly coming to the conclusion," I said, "that men, as a subspecies, are capable of instant jealousy to the point of madness.

Professor Adams and I liked each other when I was a student and we've never gotten over it."

"I suppose you find him useful."

"You bet I do. He's a brilliant tactician."

"I suppose you'll tell him you found me useful?"

"What makes you think I'll talk about you?"

"Susan, why are we fighting?"

"We're not."

"Well, we're quarreling, aren't we?"

"We could quarrel about whether we're quarreling, couldn't we?"

That finally drew a flicker of a smile from him. "Listen," he said, "why don't you join me for lunch tomorrow so we can talk all this over without eavesdroppers?"

"I'm working tomorrow."

"You eat lunch, don't you?"

"A lot of young lawyers eat in these days."

"I don't expect you to adopt all the bad habits of your profession."

"What restaurant?"

That earned me the three-point smile. "Something between the Four Seasons and Chock Full o' Nuts."

On a card he wrote the name of a restaurant in midtown that I'd never heard of.

"This where unsung heroes meet to eat?"

"We'll see, won't we?"

"Sounds intriguing. Captain, please show me to David Smith's table."

"He won't know what you're talking about. You'll have to ask for Frank Barton's table. Doesn't matter. I'll get there a few seconds early and spot you at the door."

"Yes, Mr. Barton. Is that your real name?"

"No. Call me Smith."

"But not in the restaurant."

"Once we're at the table and can't be overheard, you can call me anything you like."

"That will be a pleasure."

The humming was not in the air. It was in me. We'd just been squabbling. Is this the way love starts?

We both looked up to see Farlan Adams heading for us.

CHAPTER 23

David

Susan stood alone by the bronze-leaved Japanese maple on the Websters' lawn, waving to us as the car pulled away. I responded with a nod she probably didn't see. Adams took his eyes off the isolated road and waved back like a teenager zonked on beer.

I was ready to grab the wheel if another car showed up. I didn't have to. Adams stopped waving, and returned to driving.

I said, "Good of you to give me a lift, Professor Adams."

"Entirely welcome."

I was used to small European cars. The Buick, emptied of its other passengers, seemed enormous. The last time I'd been in a big car was three months ago, a chauffeur-driven Citroën owned by Reza Nezhad, one of those pompous Iranian traders who got rich under the Shah and flourished again when Holy Ayatollah got his thumbscrews on Persia. These merchants think they're Talleyrand adjusting to a new regime. Talleyrand had class to go with his arrogance. What Nezhad had were connections and more money than anyone can spend usefully in a lifetime. It cost him certain favors, such as funneling hard currency to two Beirut-based terrorist groups and a particular one in Europe.

Nezhad and I had been properly introduced. That meant a man of influence had said he'd better talk to me. When I phoned him for an appointment, Nezhad put me off. He was just on his way to catch a plane at Orly.

I asked could I ride along with him? Perhaps his chauffeur would drop me off on the way back?

Couldn't I wait until he returned? Of course I could wait, but the man of influence who had called him might feel insulted should an urgently arranged appointment of great business promise be postponed. Now, when could we reschedule—

No, no, Nezhad now insisted, I was to come along at once.

On the way to meet him, pleased that I was able to turn his no into a yes, it occurred to me that had my father not filled my head with his war stories, I might have ended up as a supersalesman of some kind. Instead I had been drawn by whatever magnet causes sons to best their fathers. It turned out that in at least one respect my father bested me. When his war was over, it was over. The war against the terrorists has its lulls, but it is never over. When I finish an assignment, there always seems to be another waiting. When I was given Nezhad, I was also handed a rhinestone-bedecked cigarette case that might have been owned by a *nouveau riche* with especially bad taste. Nezhad's Beirut beneficiaries were on somebody else's agenda. My mission was to try to persuade this Iranian pariah to stop funneling funds to Monteleone. If I succeeded, fine. If not, I was to use the cigarette case.

Riding in the back seat of his Citroën, with Nezhad on my left, I complimented him on the splendid leather of the interior of his car. That pleased him. And then, as planned, I asked him if he was interested in a shipment of laser printers.

"What use could they possibly be to me?"

"They have the remarkable ability," I said, "to preserve a copy of everything reproduced on them. The machines look perfectly ordinary, just off the production line. Their interiors, however, have had some refinements made."

His expression was that of a fat man standing in front of an ice cream parlor.

"These machines are very expensive, I'm afraid."

With a wave of his hand, Nezhad dismissed, for the moment, the vulgar issue of price. "Where are they fabricated?" he asked. "Japan?"

I smiled. "These particular adaptations are made in San Jose, California."

"How much?"

At last. I had to pick a number carefully. Too little would arouse suspicion. Too much would lead to bargaining, which I wanted to avoid.

"Seven thousand dollars each in quantity," I said.

"What quantity?"

"Ten or more to one pick-up place."

"Cash?"

"Half on order. Half on satisfactory delivery. There is a delivery charge of a thousand per machine."

"Five hundred."

"Seven fifty," I said.

"Five hundred."

"Done," I said. Having invented the machines just hours ago, I could afford to give him the pleasure of a successful negotiation. He shook my hand warmly.

"By the way," I said, "do you know a man by the name of Monteleone?"

Nezhad's face was suddenly expressionless.

"No," he said.

"Never met him?"

"I assure you, never."

"Never heard of him?"

"Never."

I passed Nezhad a snapshot showing him with Monteleone in a Rome restaurant.

He looked up from the photo and stared at the back of the driver's head.

"Very sad," Nezhad said.

"Why sad?"

"You have made me lie."

"Mr. Nezhad, nobody has made you lie."

"I thought we had a deal for some equipment," he said.

"Our deal is that you cut off Monteleone's source of hard currency. I assure you the most important thing you can do in life right now is stop that flow."

"I don't see how—"

"I'm certain that you will see how." Then I made a mistake. I asked for my photo back.

Nezhad said he would like to keep the photo as a souvenir of our friendship.

"Of course," I said. "Please keep it. Some day, perhaps when our friendship is older, I might even give you the negative."

That did it. Nezhad leaned over the back of the driver's seat and issued several sentences of instruction. I didn't have to know Farsi well to understand that when the driver dropped me off on the way back, I was not to be alive.

I slipped the rhinestone-bedecked cigarette case out of my right pocket and wedged it into the cleft between the seat back and cushion. Then I leaned over to tie my left shoelace and, in a much-used maneuver, whipped the .38 out of my ankle holster and shoved the muzzle into Nezhad's crotch. God knows what he would have done had I merely pointed it at him, but Iranians are like men everywhere, more protective of the family jewels than of their hearts or brains.

"Have him stop the car." As the Citroën pulled over near a rest-stop, I eased the pressure on his crotch and transferred the .38 to my left hand. Then, sliding over to the right, I came up with the cigarette case, which gave me a chance to press the latch, and said, "I believe one of your lady friends may have left this behind." I handed Nezhad the cigarette case and got out of the car.

"You Americans are stupid idiots," he said, waving the cigarette case.

I watched the Citroën roar off, spewing a trail of dust and road grime. It was perhaps a quarter of a mile away and still in view when a roaring explosion shattered the side and rear windows of Nezhad's car. It seemed to lurch sideways for a second, and then, still at speed, it careened off the road and slammed into a retaining wall.

All along the road cars screeched to a stop. Drivers and passengers scrambled out of their cars and ran in the direction of the shattered Citroën. I didn't go. The cigarette case, I had been assured, was fabricated by a perfectionist in a small Virginia laboratory. If Nezhad had still been holding the case, he would have been dead before the car hit the wall. Holy Islam would need a new conduit to Monteleone. What we had gained was time. In war, in which so much is wasted, that is enough.

* * *

Professor Adams didn't say a word all the way to the city. A psychologist would say I had thought of the Iranian because the idea of leaving a cigarette case in *this* car would quench my jealousy. Civilians have thoughts like that, why shouldn't I?

Because in my line outcomes like that aren't fantasies. The explosive on General Whitcomb's car was no fantasy. The exploding casket was no fantasy. The airport massacres, the 241 dead marines in the Beirut barracks . . . I stopped the escalation.

Professor Adams was saying, "Where can I drop you?"

"Anywhere you see a taxi stand."

"I'll take you to your hotel if you like."

"No reason to go out of your way," I said. "Just have the one bag." I never let anyone take me to the door of where I'm staying.

"As you wish." Then he said, "I hope they catch whoever killed Susan's father."

"Oh, I don't think he'll be caught."

"I'm sure he will," Adams said. "In many years of studying the criminal justice system," he said, "I've found the statistics very clear. The vast majority of murderers are caught sooner or later. If the victim is a prominent person, the odds are even better."

"I'm sure you're right," I said. "Have you known the Whitcomb family for a long time?"

"No, no, just Susan. She was a student of mine in law school. Quite brilliant. We became friends. Quite good friends, after a time. I've asked her to marry me."

CHAPTER 24

Susan

Watching Farlan and David drive away together made me feel as if I'd sent two friends off to talk about a movie they'd just seen that was in a language neither of them understood very well. Farlan would gab about the law and me. David the outsider would talk about terrorists, the army, Europe, anything to excommunicate Farlan from our experience. Or they would nettle each other with silence. I liked them both. Suppose they liked each other?

I turned back into the house just as the Websters were coming out.

"We're off to do a little supplementary shopping," said Marjorie. "Don's coming along to help carry bags. Back in a jiff."

"I hope you're not doing that for us."

"Oh no," Marjorie said, "we're out of all sorts of things really, and anyway we were planning to shop today."

I envy people who can go through life armored in politenesses. "Mother downstairs?" I asked.

"She's gone up to unpack and rest a while."

The house felt familiar and comfortable for the first time. The Webster kids had vanished. I had the downstairs to myself.

Bushed, I let myself scrunch into a soft armchair. How business-men can fly the Atlantic and immediately go on to their offices is something I never understood. Maybe it wasn't jet lag but the strain of that ride from the airport with both sets of balls in the same car.

All the women I went to school with who didn't get married fast complained that as far as their eyes could see the field of eligibles had dried up like the desert. To most of them eligible meant not married, not gay, not constantly morose or hopelessly addicted, and above all, not broke. I'd always thought of eligibility as vitality, a sense of now, energy to find, grab, stoke whatever came your way. Here I was with two exotics who met most of my own criteria, yet could I imagine daily life with either of them?

Two years ago when I visited Mom and Dad in Paris, we ended up driving south to Les Baux in Provence. Dad paid tribute to the limestone cliffs, and that wonderful moonscape of a plateau where you could feel the blast of the *mistral*. When we got there I climbed up quicker than they did, loving the way the fierce wind pulled at my hair. I held on to each iron grab-bar embedded in the limestone as if my life depended on it, because it did. When I got to the top I was alone on the deserted moon.

Trying to peer down over the edge made me dizzy. Weren't there any other people here, even tourists? I was absolutely, thoroughly, completely alone, and I panicked, as if I were the last person living on earth.

It was only minutes before Mom and Dad appeared, puffing and smiling, Dad saying, "Didn't I tell you it was wonderful?"

I can't believe that anybody voluntarily elects to spend life alone. How would Mom manage? Take up with general what's-his-name because he came from the same milieu as Dad and happens to be a widower, or would she stoic it out? If Dad were alive he'd say, *Go on, Heather, marry him, have some fun.* And to me he'd say, *Meet any interesting young lawyers lately?* Meaning someone younger than Farlan Adams.

Dad, there are so damn many advantages to an older man who's smart and cares. It's like having someone up in the prow of your boat who's a terrific navigator.

What about this David? Your mother seems to like him.

Of course. She's a woman. David makes our engines vibrate. But his turf is Europe. My work is here. I'm not going to sink into a once-in-a-blue-moon arrangement.

"Susan!" someone called.

"Yes," I answered, but it was only a neighborhood girl shouting for the Websters' Susan. I'd better go see how Mom was making out.

She was awake, and pleased that I'd come up. "Look, the Websters have rearranged the room so you can stay here too. I do so appreciate them taking me in."

"It'll make them the envy of the neighborhood."

"I want to see everyone. Not immediately. Perhaps in a few days. . . . There goes the phone ringing downstairs. I always told your father it would be a courtesy to have an extension installed in the guest room."

"I'll get it," I said, clattering down the stairs.

It sounded like phones ringing all over the house. Had the Websters put in more extensions? I spied the nearest demanding instrument in the hallway and picked the receiver up before it could ring again.

"Hello," I said, breathless. "Hello?"

Maybe they were expecting a familiar Webster voice. "This is Susan Whitcomb," I said. "The Websters are out at the moment."

Whoever was on the line hung up.

With a sudden thump of alarm I realized that despite all David's warnings to be careful I had stupidly and forgetfully done the civil thing and failed us.

I hurried back up the stairs to tell Mom not to settle in, that because I'd just been a damn fool she'd have to find someplace else to stay.

"Yes, maybe it was careless of you to say who you were without knowing who was on the other end of the phone," Mom said, "but I am not about to move from here. It's bad enough I have to be a guest in my own house. I'm not going to let you put me into a hotel in town."

"I'd be able to see you every day."

". . . and I'm not about to start calling friends to see who can put me up when I have my own house and everybody knows it."

"Please, Mom."

"Don't please-Mom me now, I won't be patronized. And I'm not calling people up and saying *My daughter thinks it's dangerous for me to stay in my own house. She thinks the maniacs who killed Hal are after me now and I'd feel much more comfortable in the safety of your house.* Susan?"

"Yes, Mom."

"Hasn't a dab of danger sometimes spiced up your life a little?"

And so Mom remained with the Websters. I consoled myself with the fact that Dad had installed an excellent alarm system in the house. There were panic buttons in the master bedroom and at both front and rear doors. I suddenly thought *Were we always in danger before because of Dad's work and we just didn't know it?* I had thought the alarm system was to protect against burglars!

That first night I stayed with Mom. Of course nothing happened. That phone call had probably been a wrong number.

I promised Mom I'd be up for the weekend. Don Webster was good enough to give me a ride to the train station. From Grand Central I went straight to my office, with the first order of business to call Judge Ballin's clerk to say I was back, to apologize, to spell out what had happened if they hadn't read it all in the newspapers.

It turned out that I didn't have to explain anything. The priority mail Betty had sorted out for me included a letter from Judge Ballin expressing his sympathy and clarifying what he had done so that I needn't be concerned. Even judges could be sweet. There were several condolence letters, but I skipped to messages that demanded my immediate attention by phone or letter. Hours seemed minutes. It was noon, time for me to find that restaurant, what was its name? And what was I supposed to call David? I found the card in my purse. Frank Barton. I liked David Smith better.

Betty had the habit of looking over my appointment book to see what I'd added.

"Who's D?" she asked. "New client?"

My secret life was beginning.

"Someone who's helping mother and me straighten out my father's affairs." Betty stifled a laugh. I thought it'd be easier if I laughed too. "I'm sorry," I said. "That sounded awful. I'll be back as soon as I can."

And I was off like an experienced New York City quarterback, left a little, right a little, through the crowd, trying to make the next crossing on the "Walk" signal even if the taxis were honking ready to go. The city's pace could still speed my adrenalin, or was it the prospect of seeing David? Either or both, I made it to the address

David had given me in record time. I was exactly two minutes late as I went down the three concrete steps to the carved wooden door with the brass handle.

Inside, the world was transformed into an underground garden. In the center of the room a tree grew straight up through the plexiglas ceiling. Overhead and out-of-doors, the top of the tree fanned its leaved branches in an almost perfect circle, speckling the sunlight that came through onto the bright red tablecloths and marbled floor. There were potted plants throughout the place. On every table a small vase held up a single flower.

I'd hardly had the words "Frank Barton" out of my mouth when the maître d' turned because David was striding up to the front. David nodded to him and took me by a willing elbow to a row of curtained cubicles in the rear.

I looked at David. He just smiled a three-point smile of pure fraudulent innocence.

The maître d' parted the curtain enough for me to enter ducking. David handed some folded bills to the man and slipped into the banquette as the maître d' with a slight flourish let the curtain drop back into place. In a restaurant full of people we were suddenly alone.

"Where did you ever find a set-up like this?"

"It's a copy of one in Paris in l'Hôtel, on the rue des Beaux Arts. I swear they actually call these alcoves the sin rooms. I find it convenient not to have to watch the other diners to see if they are watching me."

"Aren't you bothered by the waiter bouncing in and out?"

"See this?" David lifted the vase. Beneath it was a brass tit with a button at its center. "After the main course is served, you push that, you get a waiter. You don't push it, you're left alone for as long as you like."

"You rogue."

David chuckled. "I've been called many things in my life but never a rogue."

"That's what you get from mixing with the unwashed and undereducated."

"My lady is a snob."

"Guilty," I said.

"Does your lawyer let you admit to guilt without trying a bit of plea bargaining first?"

For a moment the banter made me feel as if we were lovers in danger, guarded by all those other folks lunching in the open. David, ever the mind reader, said, "The only dangerous eating places in New York are Mafia hangouts. And certain restaurants in Chinatown."

I was startled to see a waiter suddenly standing before us.

"Anything from the bar before lunch?"

"Why not?" I said. "Something long and cold."

"Gin and tonic?"

"I'd rather have a white wine spritzer."

David held two fingers up. The waiter nodded and was gone. It seemed scarcely a minute before he was back with the drinks and two menus hand-lettered in calligraphy. Each dish, in French, was followed by a not-quite-accurate translation into English that I could have done without. I ordered a hot artichoke to keep my hands busy, then poached salmon as a main course. When the waiter had vanished, I said to David, "And how was your ride back to the city with Professor Adams?"

"Long."

"You didn't talk to each other?"

"We trashed each other like gentlemen. I went easy on him because he was driving. Seriously, what the hell gives between you two?"

"Space. David, he was a marvelous find in law school."

"A real chum."

"He knows courtroom tactics like he invented them."

"Light bulbs, like Thomas Edison."

"You're jealous."

"I never wanted to invent a light bulb."

"Farlan knows everybody a start-up lawyer needs to know. He helped me land a job. He's advised me on cases I've handled, all on the cuff. I swear there is not now and never has been anything . . . physical . . . between us."

"Except that he's proposed to you. How did he do that if it wasn't physical? Telepathy?"

When caught by surprise, say nothing. Most people blurt out the first lame thing that comes to mind. I provided silence. The word was out. *David cares.*

"You're supposed to guard me," I said, "not be my guardian."

The waiter startled me. With a flourish he placed the artichoke in front of me, a shrimp cocktail in front of David, and was gone. *If I'm being unfair to David, am I also being unfair to myself?*

"I'd better explain something about Farlan Adams," I said. "It's all in his head. He hasn't had any experience in the courtroom as far as I know. But his stuff works, and it makes life a lot easier for those of us who don't want to use our early courtroom years for trial and error at our clients' expense. Farlan's like a master chess strategist who advises players but doesn't play himself. He's like that about . . . women. He was a lifetime flirt until I came along, then something hit his circuitry. Maybe mine, too. He developed a crush. Our relationship turned into something much more personal than either he or I intended it to be. I swear he's never laid a hand on me."

"Quite a trick to do it without hands."

"David, stop it."

The sounds of the restaurant seeped in, unclear voices from nearby tables outside the curtain, the swinging of the in and out doors to the kitchen, the occasional muffled command of the maître d' letting everyone else know he was the man in charge, and, of course, the clinking of silverware on plates, including our own.

When I turned to catch a glimpse of David I saw more than I had suspected. The hard man, the veteran of tractors, arm-wrestling contests, and jungle war, the man who protected innocents from terrorists, who carried a gun at his left ankle as if it were a detachable part of his body, had at this moment the face of a boy from the farm who saw something in the big city and was totally baffled by how to go about getting it.

"What are you thinking?" David asked.

"I couldn't tell you that for the world."

"I'm a very good interrogator, as you know."

"You'd have to humiliate me. You wouldn't do that."

"No, I wouldn't," David said. "But I'll tell you what I was thinking."

"Shoot."

He laughed. "Watch that kind of language around a fellow like me."

"I'm watching your hands."

They were good, strong hands. One held a knife, the other a fork. He put the utensils down gently on the side of the plate.

"You are the first woman I've met that made me wish I hadn't run away from home. That I'd finished school, gone to a good college somewhere. I feel I can never catch up now."

"To what?"

"To you."

I wanted to trace the vein on the back of his right hand with my forefinger. "You don't have any catching up to do except with civil life. The army was Dad's hideaway, too. I wonder what you'd be like as a free man."

Truly, I hadn't intended to hurt him. I hoped the pain that flickered in his eyes wouldn't erupt into anger. He was trying to control his reaction. I was rooting for his success.

Finally he said, "Do you know how much I get paid?"

I shook my head. "Not a clue."

"Year before last was a busy year. I earned more than the president."

"I'll bet you took more risks."

"With my life? No. The President's got all those nuts out there waiting to take a potshot at him."

"David?"

"Yep."

"Risking your neck is not the height of achievement."

"It's the only thing I know how to do well."

"If you stand on a busy highway you're bound to get hit by a truck sooner or later."

"I don't stand on highways. I plan my work carefully."

"What are the odds?"

"I've got to be right a hundred percent of the time."

"Nobody ever is."

"Why do you care?" he said.

I wanted to touch him.

Then he said, "I'm no burden to anyone. I'm expendable."

"That's no way to think. Or to live."

"You depend on me to live that way."

"What are you talking about?"

"I'm returning to Europe."

There was an unexpected shift in David's voice. In that moment David reminded me of my father when he was young and I was very small. *How can it be that I am in a restaurant in the middle of New York and my father is dead in Rome!*

"David, will that man on the motorcycle ever be caught?"

"No."

"Why not?"

"I've dealt with the man on the motorcycle."

"What is that supposed to mean?"

"The evening of the assassination, when he came to his girlfriend's flat I was waiting for him."

"Did you arrest him? Is he in jail?"

"I'm not a policeman."

"You could have told the police!"

His voice a mere whisper, David said, "The motorcyclist is dead."

The door to another world opened a crack.

"Dead?"

"Dead."

"Killed?"

"Yes."

"By?"

"Of course."

"You killed him?"

I'd asked this question of someone on the witness stand, but never of someone I cared about.

David nodded.

"How did you know it was the right man?"

"Susan, it's my business to know."

"Business?"

"Not money. Competence. In a just cause. Or don't you think it was a just cause?"

"I suppose you want to kill Monteleone too?"

"Before he does something to you or your mother or some anonymous person I don't even know? You bet. Monteleone's a terror junkie. He likes to kill."

So do you. I couldn't keep it back. "I suppose you'd actually like to kill him," I said.

David's face stiffened like a mask. "You talking about me?"

"I'm talking about whoever kills."

David hesitated only a moment. "In your goddamn lawful world, if you kill someone in a premeditated way that's first-class murder, isn't it?"

"First-degree," I said, but I don't think he heard me.

"If you kill someone in the heat of an argument, that's second-class, right?"

"It could be manslaughter."

"But if you kill someone who's trying to kill you that's self-defense, isn't it?"

I nodded.

"Well, the killing of your old man was premeditated, planned to a T, and executed with precision. When I killed his killer it was self-defense for his next victim and the ones after that."

"Sounds more like self-offense than defense, and even the self part is wrong. You're our side's executioner, right?"

"No, I'm our side's preventer of executions."

"It didn't prevent my father's death."

"I'd have risked my life trying if we'd had a clue. Other lives are on the line now. Yours. Your mother's. God knows who else."

"And you're gearing up for a preventive strike?"

"Make it sound as ugly as you can. I do what I do."

I moved my hands to his face.

"What are you doing?" he asked, making no move to stop me. With my fingers on the sidepieces I slowly pulled his oversized eyeglasses away from his face. How wonderfully different he seemed.

I looked through the spectacles. Plain glass.

Quietly David said, "You're doing something very dangerous."

"I'm not finished," I said. I put my hands on the sides of his face again. I could feel heat from his cheeks. I couldn't tell if the rhythmic sound I heard was his breathing or mine. Carefully, I started to remove his wig. I expected resistance. Instead he helped me pull it off. His real hair was in disarray. I looked at the wig in my hands. Removed from him it was without life. I put it on the banquette between us, then reached up to smooth down his real hair with my hands.

"I feel naked," he said.

"Yes, I know."

"Stripped."

"Naked is better."

His kiss caught me by surprise. I hadn't expected the tenderness. He kissed my earlobe, my ear, my cheek, my mouth. I was afraid the curtains of our cubicle would be pulled apart and everyone in the restaurant would be staring at us.

The curtains stayed closed.

I was breathing as if I'd been running. He said, "I'm not good with words the way you are. I guess I've let you put my life in your hands."

"Your face isn't dangerous. It's very . . . attractive."

"I shouldn't have let you do what you did. I mean the glasses and the wig. None of the groups I've worked against know for certain what I look like. They know my height, they know I've got a bad scar on my right arm, that's all. The exit wound in my right side doesn't show through clothes. If they thought anyone knew what I looked like undisguised, they'd grab that person off the street and shove photographs in front of them and say 'Which one is David Smith?'"

"They have a photo of you?"

"If we've got one of Abu Nidal, they could very well have gotten one of me some way. Maybe not. But they sure know how to squeeze a description out of someone."

"Squeeze?"

"That's the wrong word for what they do," David said. "When you don't want to leave evidence, the best place to beat someone is on the soles of the feet. Do you know how sensitive feet are?" He opened and closed his hands as if trying to keep them under control.

I said, "If they're after me already, it doesn't matter that I know what you look like. I'm glad to know. And I'm glad you trusted me."

"I hate that facial paraphernalia. But these days I wear it so goddamn much when I take it off I feel undressed."

"As in exposed?"

"As in undressed. Do you feel exposed when you take your clothes off?"

I thought of dates in adolescence, the back seat of a car parked somewhere removed from the eyes of the world, the come-ons in-experienced boys use. David wasn't inexperienced. He must sense how he looked to a woman undisguised.

"You know," he said, "if you want to extract information from an enemy sworn to silence, strip them naked. Saves hours of interro-gation time. And it works quicker with men. I think they feel more vulnerable naked than women do."

"How can you be so sure?" I said. "Have you interrogated women as well as men?"

"You're grubbing for information."

"I'm asking. You don't have to answer."

"Actually, you have all the information on which to base an as-sumption that might just be correct."

"That's a British expression."

"What is?"

"Beginning a sentence with actually."

"I guess it's what you pick up if you hang around with the S.A.S."

"Who's that?"

"I'm glad you don't know."

"My father talked about the S.A.S. They're special forces of some kind, aren't they?"

"British. Not American."

"Then how come you get to hang around them?"

"I'm a civilian. I can work with whoever I please whenever I please."

"Don't be angry with me, David, if I guess correctly . . ."

"Go on."

"You're a mercenary."

"So the hell are you. We all work for money. I only work for us and for any close ally who needs whatever special skill I might have for a specific task. I'm telling you too much. I'd better stop."

I took a sip of water, buying a second's time. "My father and you couldn't have been more different."

"I never got close to being a general."

"That's not what I meant. He always said he was engaged to Mom first and the army second. The fact is he never left either of them. I suspect you and my father never thought about becoming veterans, giving it up. You enjoy playing full-time soldier too much to quit. You both sacrificed your life to the game."

"It isn't a game. And I have not sacrificed my life. I've been living on the cliffhanging edge instead of dying of boredom the way you civilians do much of the time."

"I thought you were a civilian."

"That's what we call the rest of you."

"A term of derogation." I couldn't stop myself. "You ought to read Shakespeare some time," I said.

"For my health?"

"For your brain. It's full of heroes who don't know when enough is enough. David, have you ever really given thought to doing something else just to have a better chance of staying alive?"

"That matters to you?"

"It matters now to me."

"The truth is," he said, fire in his face, "I wouldn't know what to do with myself. War is the only thing I know."

"You could try so many things."

"I can't stand to fail. In this damn job when I fail I'll never know about it because I'll be dead."

"There must be a way out."

"There is," said David. "I just told you. Death." He hesitated for a long second. Then he very carefully put his hands on the sides of my arms and gently swung me slightly around to face him. Was he was preparing to kiss me again?

I said, "I find it strange to be touched by a man who kills people."

Still holding my arms, he said, "It would be kinder if you just thought of me as a soldier. Like your father."

I was about to answer that my father didn't kill people when I remembered the team in Czechoslovakia.

As David let go of me I felt a rush of regret.

In a barely audible voice he said, "I want to ask something."

"Well ask it."

"I'm not used to asking."

"You just give orders."

"Something like that."

"Ask."

"Will you go to bed with me?"

We both heard the sounds just outside the curtain. "Not in the restaurant."

"I wasn't thinking the restaurant."

He leaned toward me. His lips touched my neck. Just as suddenly he pulled away. "I've got something for you," David said, producing a small snap-case no larger than a pillbox. I felt a moment's alarm. I hadn't dealt with Farlan's proposal yet. "It's not a ring," he said, opening the lid.

I recognized it as a military emblem, crossed rifles on a blue background, and in small gold letters the words FOLLOW ME.

"It's the infantry school motto," he said. "Keep it in a drawer somewhere. Remember who gave it to you."

I could tell that he wanted to kiss me again. I sure as hell wanted to kiss him.

"It's academic," he said.

"What?"

"My question about going to bed. I feel like a quarterback who specializes in incomplete passes. My gear's in the checkroom. I have to grab a cab in less than five minutes. I've got a plane to catch."

"Postponable?"

"Not anymore."

I put my hand down on the settee we shared. He put his on mine.

"You know where to reach me," he said.

"In emergencies."

"I hope there aren't any. Got to go. My assignment shouldn't last more than a week. That phone number, don't wait for emergencies. It's okay to use for an ordinary message like 'Everything under control.'"

"That's one thing it's not."

"Me, too," he said, and he was putting his wig on, smoothing it, fitting his glasses on his face, and standing up, pulling the table away from me with the greatest care in order not to knock over the vase with the flower. I lifted the vase an inch off the table, slid out, and put the vase down. Everything seemed in slow motion. I wanted it to slow down even more. "You don't have a check yet," I said.

"It's all right."

The waiter was in his path. David glanced at the bill and peeled off cash. He couldn't live in the credit card world. He let me go ahead of him, but I could feel his need for pace behind me. At the cloakroom, he got his carry-all.

In the street, he put two fingers in his mouth and whistled for a cab, something I hadn't seen anybody do for years, and never as well.

As one pulled over to the curb, David said, "Normally I'd let you have the first one, but I'm running behind. Forgive?"

"I could ride with you for a few blocks."

"No." The three-point smile was gone.

"I know you're going to the airport, what's the secret?"

"You don't know which airport."

He waved to me from inside the cab. I stood with my hands at my side, my left one clutching the small jewel box with the pin that said FOLLOW ME. It was a pin I could never wear and never explain. If I said my father left it to me, Mom would know I was lying.

I don't know what David told his taxi driver in addition to his destination, but the cab raced away as if it were a sirenless ambulance.

CHAPTER 25

David

Through the scratched plastic window I could see cloud cover drifting beneath us. The DC-10 was pulling me away from Susan at better than 500 miles per hour. The engine throbbed the way a wound throbs till the first shot of morphine starts to work.

I ordered a couple of those one-tenth-of-nothing bottles and poured them over the three ice cubes the stew handed me in a plastic glass. I swished the bourbon around the ice, trying to get it to melt faster.

For pain, this was kid stuff compared to the shot of morphine you'd get if you were wounded. I swallowed a slug. Nothing. I finished it off and put my temple against the side of the window where I could feel the vibration of the engine, an old trick for putting myself to sleep on a plane. I opened one eye just enough to see my left hand holding the plastic glass with its melting ice cubes at a dangerous angle. I put the seat-back tray down, set the glass on it, shut the left eye, and started to count, one-o-one, one-o-two, one-o-three, and vroom I was off flying a Learjet with Susan in the co-pilot's seat. "Susan!" I yelled at her, "you don't know how to fly. Get your damn hands off the controls!" Susan said, "Why don't you put the autopilot on?" and like a schmuck I said, "What for?" and Susan said "Guess what for?" as she wrapped her arms around me. "Hey cut that out," I yelled, "I'm trying to fly this thing." She let go and started sucking two of my fingers at the same time, the forefinger and the middle finger.

The next thing I know we're on the floor. I forgot to put on the autopilot and the plane is sashaying in a dangerous yaw. I'm yelling "Let me up!" and I hear Susan protesting "Where you going?" I'm struggling to get to the controls and all of a sudden *Bam!* I woke up and the stewardess with the tray was saying, "Sorry, sir, I didn't realize you were asleep." Hell, I wasn't asleep, I was wide awake in my dream!

I ate every last bit of that meal. Two minutes after the trays were collected I couldn't remember what the hell it was I ate. My sick brain was into self-flagellation with questions like how many hundred miles was I further from Susan from the beginning to the end of that so-called meal.

I hadn't realized how much solid sleep I'd missed in the last few days until, back in my quarters in Rome, I saw my sacking place. The white sheets were an invitation. I was all set for seven uninterrupted hours.

A haunted brain has no tolerance for deep sleep. The minute I dozed off, I was in some theater and Susan was up there on the stage by herself. She was on some kind of production ramp that jutted out into the audience, dressed in something skin-colored and walking —that was some walk—straight toward where I was sitting till she was towering above me. My eyes were on a level with her ankles. When I looked up I was unnerved to see that her skin-tone tights weren't tights—she was stark naked. Her body, which I'd never seen before, cried out for touching and kissing. She was looking down at me looking up at her as if she might be thinking what I was thinking. What must all those other people watching her be thinking? I swiveled my head around. Nobody. Hell, we were alone! It was more than a fellow can stand. I reached up to touch her ankle, and my fingers were just brushing her skin when I realized that she was losing her balance and falling toward me and the next thing I knew I was gasping for breath, awake in my own bed, empty except for myself.

I turned off my enemy the alarm clock, put my arms around one of my two pillows and said to it, "Susan, you get some rest too."

CHAPTER 26

Susan

I hated needing Farlan's help. I'd been whisked away to Rome in the middle of my trial—listen to that, *my* trial, it was Jim and Judy Flegelmans' trial. All that we'd had time for was opening arguments. Like a dumbbell I'd played it straight. In his opening, Tammus's lawyer, Bill Corzini, had made it seem like we were all gathered for an unnecessary exercise that would waste the Court's time and the taxpayers' money.

I was torn as to which of the Flegelmans to put on the stand first. During rehearsals, Judy had shown a clearer understanding of the case. But if I put her on, the jurors who live in a male chauvinist world would wonder why I had skipped him. So Jim was it.

"Mr. Flegelman," I'd said, "why don't you tell the jury in your own words what happened, beginning with the signing of the contract between your record label and Mr. Tammus's distribution company."

Jim looked at the palm of his left hand as if there was something in it. I'd tried like hell to break him of the habit. He'd promised faithfully that he wouldn't do it in the courtroom, and here he was, at the very first question, looking at his palm instead of at me.

"It was like this," he said.

Come on.

"When we were on our own, we had commission reps covering the key accounts, but not in depth. We were very excited about the possibility of real national distribution through Tammus. They told us they could get out forty to fifty thousand units a month. We'd been getting out maybe sixteen thousand tops."

"Go on, Mr. Flegelman."

"Judy and—Mrs. Flegelman and me were a little leery of the production costs for so many disks but Tammus Distribution advanced the money, so it was okay. The problem was we were laying out the money for the artists, the recording sessions, the artwork for the jackets, all of that plus the overhead, and we were really looking forward to when the payments from Tammus would start flowing to us so we could catch up on the bills."

"And then what happened?"

That was his cue.

"What do you mean what happened?

"Did you receive the payments called for in the contract?"

"No."

Like pulling teeth. Go on.

"Did you complain to Mr. Tammus about his company's failure to pay?"

Corzini was on his feet. "Objection. Leading the witness."

Judge Ballin leaned forward. "Mr. Corzini," he said, "Mr. Flegelman is testifying for the first time in his life, as we heard earlier. Why don't we try to be patient while he tells his story? If counsel leads him a little, that's okay. If she starts to lead too much, I'll accept your objections. Meanwhile, counsel, if you'll rephrase your question, perhaps Mr. Corzini will enjoy his day better. Please proceed."

You are a doll, Judge Ballin. "Mr. Flegelman, did there come a time when you complained to Mr. Tammus about the payments?"

"That's right."

Is that all you're going to say? "Would you like the question read back to you?"

"Nah."

Sweet man, don't say nah in a courtroom. "Is that your entire answer?"

"Oh, I called Mr. Tammus's secretary and asked her to remind the boss about the two payments that were overdue. When nothing happened, I called again and was put through to Tammus's comptroller, Henry Zatz, who said that the news was not good, that the projections showed the records weren't selling at all well and they were reserving the account. Hey, I said, if I don't get the money, all my suppliers are going to come down on my head. Besides, I had called some of the accounts and they said the line was moving okay. I want to talk to Tammus, I said. I don't care if he's in Bermuda, I want a meeting right away."

"And was there such a meeting?"

"Eventually, when he brought his suntan back to New York."

"Mr. Flegelman, I show you these spread sheets. Are these the spread sheets that Mr. Tammus and Mr. Wood gave you at that meeting?"

Jim nodded.

"Please answer so the court reporter can hear you, Mr. Flegelman."

"Yes. These are those."

"Your Honor, I want to have these marked as Plaintiff's Exhibit One."

As soon as we got through the necessaries, I asked Jim Flegelman to identify and comment on each line in the top sheet.

"Judy does that better than I do," he said. "Actually our bookkeeper does it better than either of us."

I could hear Farlan's voice as if he was in back of my head. *Get rid of him fast. Use his wife and the bookkeeper to deal with the projections.*

"Was there anything you said to Mr. Tammus at that meeting that you thought was of special importance?"

"Oh sure. I said if the records were selling so lousy, why didn't he stop distributing them and just wind up the contract. That's when Tammus jumped in and said that if we'd jazz up the record jackets and offer some promotional money to the retailers he was confident things would pick up."

"And what did you say to that?"

"I said if they didn't pick up yesterday he'd have to wipe us off the floor. We just couldn't carry all those extra costs without getting the cash flow that was due us."

"But you said Mr. Zatz maintained that the records weren't selling well enough."

"He's a goddamn liar. I know, because I talk to the dealers!"

Judge Ballin leaned over. "Counselor, do caution the witness to keep the expletives to himself."

I cut the rest of my questions short. The more I had Jim answer, the more openings I would leave for Corzini on cross.

When his turn came, Corzini, beneath those lovely Italian eyelashes, gave me a look that could only mean *pity*. I hoped he would trip and break his neck on the way to the witness stand, where Jim Flegelman sat like a long, limp doll.

"Mr. Flegelman," Corzini said, "you testified that before the Tammus firm started distributing your disks, your commission reps got out sixteen thousand a month. Was that for an average month?"

"No, sir. I said it was our best month."

"What would your average have been then?"

"Maybe ten to twelve thousand."

"Were those gross sales?"

"Well, no," Flegelman said. "We got returns."

"Then what would be your average sales after returns?"

"Maybe eight to ten thousand units a month."

"Can you translate that into dollars for the Court?"

"About $35,000 a month."

"And were you able to meet your payroll and other expenses on time at that level of income?"

Jim hesitated. "Usually."

"And when you couldn't?"

"Well, Judy and I often didn't cash our paychecks on time."

"Was any of your cash flow difficulty attributable to your having to pay production costs promptly?"

I objected. "There's been no testimony on cash flow difficulty prior to the Flegelmans' involvement with the Tammus company."

Judge Ballin said, "I'll allow it."

I sat down. *Never grasp at straws*, Farlan would say. *It makes your whole case look weak.*

The question was read back to Jim.

"Well, yeah, it was tough getting up the scratch for production."

"But when Tammus started distributing your label, didn't they pay your production costs?"

"Sure, but we never saw any of that money."

"Mr. Flegelman, is it possible that the eight to ten thousand disks a month that you testified were your average net sales might have meant that that was all the customers you had for your particular label?"

"I don't believe that for a minute. Our distribution was lousy. With good distribution you should sell a lot more."

"But you didn't?"

"According to Mr. Tammus we didn't, but I don't—"

Corzini roared. "Answer the question I asked. Yes or no."

"Yes or no what?"

"You didn't sell more when you got widespread distribution."

"I was trying—"

"Yes or no!"

I was on my feet. "Your Honor," I aid, "my colleague is badgering the witness."

"Sustained."

That didn't stop Corzini. "When you distributed your own recordings, was your business profitable?"

"So-so."

"What does so-so mean? Was it profitable or not?"

"Sometimes."

"And sometimes not profitable?"

"Uh-huh."

"Did Mr. Tammus know that?"

"I told him."

"And yet he was willing to take your line on, give you a chance to go from a maximum of sixteen thousand a month to forty to fifty thousand a month, *and* to lay out the money for your production, and you've brought him and his company into court because despite his help your record sales were as lousy as they were before he distributed them, is that not true?"

"Your Honor," I said, "that is not a question."

The judge told the jury to disregard it, but I could bet that none of them did. Corzini had given part of his closing argument in the process of demolishing Jim Flegelman.

Before the day was out I managed to get Judy and their bookkeeper on the stand, but it was an anti-climax. I would have bet the jury had already come to the conclusion that Jim Flegelman wasn't much of a businessman and was just whining because his records hadn't sold well enough. Case closed.

And Corzini had not even called his witnesses yet when I got the phone call from Mom and had to dash to Rome. Now that I was back I wanted more than ever to get even a small slice of justice for Jim and Judy. Or was it a chance to beat Corzini without Farlan's help?

Betty normally manages to maintain the piles of paper on my desk so that I can put my hands on what I need in a hurry. But even she was having trouble locating things because the disarray on my desk reflected the jumble inside my head.

David's being away didn't put him out of my mind. I kept remembering every moment of those two hours in the restaurant.

Farlan called every day. I put him off with excuses that became less and less tenable. He was hurting so. And I hadn't intended to hurt him. I tried to get lost in work. Instead I'd find myself holding conversations with Farlan in my head.

You're a great teacher. A friend in need. A networker second to none. I want to please you. Suppose I didn't please you? Suppose we went to bed and you went limp? I'd have to pretend. Oh Farlan, I wouldn't want to pretend, I'd want it to be whatever connects a man and a woman to each other and excludes the rest of the world.

Instead of the absent Farlan, I heard a devilish voice inside my own head saying *Try it. You might like it. If he doesn't like it, that will be the end of it.*

I answered *I'm in love with the inside of his head. It's my security blanket, my legal encyclopedia. . . .*

Bullshit! answered that devilish other voice. *Any woman wants to go to bed with an encyclopedia is nuts.*

You just don't understand!

The trouble is I do.

My generation was the one that said going to bed with someone wasn't exactly a holy act, it could be experiment, recreation, it didn't mean you were signing a pledge to donate your life to the affair.

I rehearsed it with the voice I liked. *Okay, Farlan, let's try it, see how it goes.*

"See how what goes?"

It was Betty, her head past the slightly open door. She let the rest of herself in. "I hope I didn't interrupt, but we're in court tomorrow," she said, "and we are not prepared."

Someone like Betty is priceless to someone like me.

"Unless," she said, "you're going to wing it without notes."

"Please get Professor Adams on the phone," I said.

"Your desk needs sorting."

"You can sort it while I'm getting my fix at Professor Adams's."

Betty shot me one of those crazy-lady looks. *Are you sure you want to do whatever you're going to do?*

"Hello, mentor," I said when Farlan answered, hoping to establish the basis of my call without ambiguity.

"Susan. What a change, your calling me."

"I need to see you."

"I need to see you. By all means. When?"

"As soon as possible."

"I've got two students scheduled, at two and at three."

"Would it be asking too much to reschedule them? Farlan, I have a damn trial continuing tomorrow, the Flegelman case I was on before I left. The distribution company is putting their CEO on the stand, a man named Harry Tammus, remember?"

"Vaguely." He sounded as if I'd scratched his face. "I thought the topic might be my question to you," he said.

"That too."

He suggested we meet over lunch at a wine bar. When he gave me the address I realized it was only a block or so from where he lived. Had I set sail for D-Day?

The wine bar was called Babs'. It wasn't a student kind of place. The walls were mirrored, the lighting reminded me of the lounge at Radio City Music Hall, and the tables were filled mainly by women lunching with women. I was ushered to a table set for one. Did I look like someone who doesn't have a date?

I studied the wine menu. It started with plonk at two dollars a glass and went all the way to a California Cabernet Sauvignon at four-fifty, pricier than the French. The Japanese weren't the only ones who could intrude successfully on somebody else's turf.

"Have you decided?"

I looked up and it was Farlan, dapper, handsome, a touch weary under eyes that locked on mine and wouldn't let go.

"I meant have you decided on the wine," Farlan said, pulling his chair as close to the marble-topped table as he could.

"We haven't shaken hands," I said.

He took mine in his and whisked it up to his lips.

"You seem a bit nervous," he said. "Anything wrong?"

"Here comes the waiter," I said.

Farlan ordered a half-bottle of Soave Bolla. "Reliable," he said. "I don't want either of us to be disappointed. . . . Were you surprised by my proposal? Angry?"

"No anger. Complimented. Concerned."

"I know all the problems. You needn't recite them. Let's just have a pleasant lunch."

If that was all, why this place so close to his place?

"Tell me your worries about tomorrow."

I summed it up. Tammus was an impressive bullshitter, white collar and cuffs on a colored shirt with a paisley tie, a quick answer for everything as if he was telling the truth. I had to destroy his credibility in cross-examination.

"You'd think it would be easy with an habitual liar," I said. "Wrong. He's had a lot of practice memorizing invented facts. By now he may even believe them."

"You don't need me," Farlan said. "You're perfectly capable of handling someone like that."

If that's true, why am I here?

"Farlan," I said, "that record company is just an amateur label grown up and undercapitalized. It's got a total of thirteen employees, all overworked. If the distributor doesn't pay them what he owes, they'll never get their knees off the ground again. They're nice, talented young people. The distribution company has been milking their cash flow for four years. Everybody said they'd settle the day before the trial, but they haven't. They're cocky-sure they're going to win. I can't let them."

"I find your determination erotic."

"I don't feel confident, Farlan," I said. "I just can't let these people down."

I shouldn't have lowered my eyes. I raised them and looked straight at Farlan's. Look at him, he's in love, he's bleeding to death, and all my merciful instincts are for a client I didn't know a few months ago. He wanted me and I was giving myself to them.

"I'd like you to look at something you might find useful," he said.

"What?"

"You'll see."

"Where?"

"In my apartment. It's right around the corner."

What went through my head were scenes straight out of silent-screen shorts, the lady proclaiming no, no, while the mustachioed villain held her arms and tried to pull her closer. *He is not a villain. You are the villain.* If you didn't always need his help, you could break off the relationship any time. Or don't you want to? Maybe it's the other way around. Maybe you don't go it alone in the courtroom because you don't want to cut the cord with Farlan.

How do you fire a voice that's inside your own head?

I expected Farlan's bachelor apartment to be small because all the bachelors I had known were students or young lawyers living in their first pad away from home, tight little places to remind them of tuition loans. Even my late, sedate, unlamented boyfriend Woody, who'd gone straight from law school into the second biggest of the large law firms at a salary that embarrassed him, had a studio with the sleeping quarters up seven stairs to a loft under the ceiling. That was the biggest difference between us and the Wall Streeters. We were scared it would vanish, they spent it before it could be snatched away in a crash.

Farlan had been a bachelor all his adult life. His pad was like nothing I'd seen before, a spacious, high-ceilinged apartment in an older building with a doorman, and a live operator in the elevator.

When we were let off, I was surprised to see a single door in the hallway. Was his the only apartment on the entire floor?

The entrance foyer had a floor of what looked like handmade tiles from some Mediterranean country. The half-round table under the mirror had taken someone weeks to carve the legs. On it sat a crystal vase with fresh flowers. And over it was a Chagall. I don't mean a print, I mean an original.

Farlan led me into the long living room, the other end of which seemed half a block away. Midway on the right, in front of the fireplace, were two overstuffed chairs that looked as if they'd been planted there for this special occasion. Farlan waved me into one of them.

"I'll get what you need," he said. The minute he left, I got up and rushed all the way down to the other end of the living room. Between the two windows was either a Mondrian or an illusion.

I heard his voice.

"Here we are."

I turned. We were the length of the room apart. "You have good taste," I said.

"Thank you."

"And a great deal of money."

"I spent a lot of it on the pictures."

Still at a distance, he held out a sheaf of papers. "What you need starts on page three," he said.

We walked toward each other as if in some unrehearsed ceremony. I had the urge to run to him, hug him, kiss him on both cheeks, because what he had proposed was to share all this. I took the papers.

"You'll find that a comfortable place to read," he said, gesturing at one of the armchairs. "I'll put coffee on."

I watched him leave the room. I could be very comfortable in this room.

What he'd handed me were about two dozen pages that had come out of a three-ringed notebook. The first page was headed: DESTROYING THE CREDIBILITY OF A WITNESS. When Farlan came back in with a tray, I hardly noticed, for in these pages was exactly what I needed for court the next day, a brilliant exposition of how a witness of high station could be brought low.

When I finished I wanted to read through the pages again. I looked up to see Farlan sitting eight or ten feet away on the half-round sofa, gazing at me. "You are beautiful," he said.

"Thank you. Farlan, what is this from?"

He touched his left earlobe, saw me observing, and quickly took his hand away as if an absent-minded gesture was somehow obscene. "Once upon a time," he said, "when I was just about your age, I was tempted to turn to the practice of law instead of teaching it. And so I wrote for myself something the size of an unpublished book, a point-by-point instruction manual for a trial lawyer, with citations where needed, but mainly, as you've seen, focusing on method, technique, timing, tricks. It took me more than several months to complete, and when I did I read it through in one sitting, all two hundred and ninety pages. I decided that whoever wrote it ought to teach others because in a lifetime one can train hundreds of practitioners, while if I went into practice I would have educated only myself."

Can you love someone for what they believe? For what they teach you? I knew all about the mentor-student trap. Had Farlan fallen in love with his ideal student? Had this absolutely brilliant man created an illusion for himself? Wasn't that what we all do, illusionists practicing sleight-of-tongue in the courtroom, lovers practicing sleight-of-hand in the bedroom, and the better we are at it the more of a mystery it becomes to others?

"Think you can handle tomorrow?" Farlan said.

I waited till he finished pouring the coffee into the cup and handed it to me. "I feel more confident about tomorrow than about handling today."

"Meaning?"

"Being here."

"Do you want me to withdraw my application?"

I had to start giving Farlan answers. And before I could tell him the absolute truth, I had to know it myself.

"No," I said. "Don't withdraw it."

"Do you mean not yet?"

"I mean exactly what I said. Would you like me to read the record back?"

Farlan smiled with an openness I had not witnessed before.

"Would you like to see the rest of the apartment?"

"Can I take these with me?" I held the papers up.

"Sure. Copy them if you like. Just please do return the originals. I take it you don't want to see the rest of the apartment."

"Not this time."

"Then next time?"

"Yes," I said.

For a moment I thought he was going to kiss me. I wanted him to. More than that, I wanted to kiss him. But he was already walking to the door.

As he said good-bye, I could see that the skin beneath his eyes was still smudged with sadness. I stole a glance at the Chagall as if I might never have another chance.

In the hallway, as a whirring sound announced the arrival of the elevator, I blew a kiss to Farlan standing in the doorway of his apartment. He seemed lightstruck with joy. How little he wanted. How much he gave. How many men in the world are like that?

"I want to see all of them again soon," I said as the elevator gate opened. "And you."

I suddenly felt as if I had stepped into the shaft and there was no elevator there, just Alice tumbling into the darkness.

CHAPTER 27

Susan

This afternoon's talk with Farlan had given me heart to return to what had seemed a losing battle. I felt as if I'd been given a second chance.

I had stayed in my office late, away from my desk, in the one comfortable armchair, my feet up on the hassock, making notes for the trial. Then I reread Farlan's pages on destroying a witness. Unbelievable! It was as if I were watching a sadomasochistic movie. To know what people can do to each other is one thing, to see them do it another. Farlan's examples were so vivid that I felt I could reach out and touch the squirming witnesses.

Publicly cornering a person in the confinement of the witness box, exploiting his contradictions, challenging his memory, ridiculing his lapses, cutting off his retreat, bringing his brain to a boil, has the same damn goal as physical torture: getting the captive witness to destroy his cause with his own words.

Maybe I was still too young, too inexperienced, too idealistic to take human nature on the rocks without soda. My God, a clever lawyer can go a long way before the judge stops him. *You mean to sit there and tell this court you remember Willy Mays's batting average and you can't remember whether or not you purchased a .38-caliber Smith and Wesson before or after the day your business partner of twenty years Jerry Michaels was shot at his desk two hours after the office was officially closed for the day? You want this jury to believe*

*that you can remember baseball scores and you can't remember set-
tling a score of your own?* Oh your opponent will move to strike,
but the jury will have gotten the point.

David said the torturer beats the bottoms of your feet. The trial
lawyer uses a needle to the brain. How different are they, the man
who asks questions with a fingernail puller on the table, and the
three-piece-suiter who says to a witness under penalty of perjury and
the threat of contempt, *You were in that room, the victim was in that
room, you've admitted that no one else was in that room, do you
expect anyone in this room to believe that you came there to have what
you call a quiet discussion and that after you left your partner shot
himself with a gun that you bought?*

Farlan says the purpose of the lawyer's jabbing at the witness is
to convince the jury that black is black or black is white, depending
on which he is trying to prove. But, Farlan observes, one has to
exercise care in tormenting an answer out of a fidgeting human under
duress on the witness stand. Judges, like surgeons, become anesthe-
tized to the pain of people under their jurisdiction. The reality, Farlan
says, is that if you don't work a witness that way, opposing counsel
will, and your *politesse* may result in your client losing. Winning is
the thrust of the game, not just for the ecstatic high of triumph in
the courtroom but the unblinkable fact that fees go up and business
piles in for lawyers who can be counted on to mutilate a hostile
witness's memory until he trips and destroys his credibility in his
own words, to which the ban on self-incrimination does not apply.

If you rely on the fairness of jurists to govern the outcome, Farlan
says, you are making a fundamental error in theology. The religion
of the courtroom is overseen by a man serving *in loco dei*. He is as
fallible as the hundred Italian priests who, when hearing one at a
time the same confession from a clever sociologist armed with a tape
recorder, gave a hundred different answers for the One True Church.
The law, Farlan says, is a lottery that depends both on chance and
on the whims of human nature. Precedents are as usable—or as
ignorable—as the Ten Commandments. Use them, use witnesses, use
the judge, but don't rely on them. Rely on your preparation. Rely on
your skill.

I suddenly realized that Farlan was not "just a teacher," as he
once put it. If a judge is a poor simulacrum of the Deity, Farlan was

the shadow of Lucifer. His cleverness is diabolical. He conceives the battle, presents the strategy and tactics, and then lets others carry the result into courtroom combat. I was merely the general's bright soldier. Like David.

I quickly skimmed for a third time the twenty-four-page extract from Farlan's unholy bible. His brain was a buzzsaw that could cut through all the crap to uncover the one secret you needed to pull a rabbit out of a hat in the courtroom. With his coaching I could override the remnants of my adolescent conscience and win every courtroom battle I'd ever have to face. Why not marry him? Or at least live with him?

Some men say they love a woman and mean they like her tits and ass and legs and everything in between. Some women want an escort who looks good to other women and privately gives good head. Farlan gives good head of a different kind, in these papers, in the classroom, and in private. Any man that wily about how to handle sin would have to be clever between the sheets, right? What did I have to lose?

You are using Farlan. Why shouldn't he use you?

I argued Farlan's case. Suppose he hadn't been my teacher? Suppose I'd met him at some dinner party and heard him being his clever self, would I be thinking differently about him? Was I succumbing? To what? Did Farlan, master teacher, have cloven hooves I didn't want between my legs? Was I to be his succubus? I knew what I wanted from him. What did he want from me?

I swung my feet off the hassock and went back to my desk. Whatever pulled me there made me look at the brass double picture frame, the general on the right side, my mother on the left. When I was very young, her advice came unsolicited. The first time I got my period she helped me see the marvel of its clockwork, that it was a nuisance which, if understood, you could cope with. I carried that lesson into a life that was full of handleable nuisances. Mother taught me to live *past* annoyances. Life was the web, she said. Think of the difficult moments as interstices. The image was hers. She *is* a clever woman. If she'd been born a generation later, if I'd been the mother and she'd been the daughter, maybe she would have been the general in the family. Growing up I often saw her hand on the throttle of whatever was happening. Why didn't I talk to her about Farlan? Maybe she could see things without the clutter in my head. I'll be with her on the weekend anyway. Why not?

That settled, I shoved Farlan's ghost aside and concentrated on what he'd written. I scribbled notes fast. Just beginning that process turned me on. I'll bet Farlan didn't feel guilty about others doing the dirty work he conceived. *Anything I could do to win for Jim and Judy Flegelman was good, not bad.*

That thought stopped me. The eleventh commandment in every civilized book was *Thou shall not use a bad means toward a good end.* That could be the biggest lie of all. Didn't anybody ever stop to really think about it? All the classic examples came to mind. The rapist is attacking your daughter. You come upon the scene, gun in hand. Do you shoot? Of course! Do you shoot to merely wound? The man has a knife at your daughter's throat. If you merely wound him, he can still stab her. And so you, brought up to believe *Thou shall not kill,* shoot to kill. If your children are hungry, and you are without money, of course you steal! And if it were filmed, every audience in the world would applaud as they watched you steal. We are trained hypocrites, daily practicing foul means to good ends. A woman can't afford to be queasy about tough tactics while they're still looking at us as female lawyers. Female warriors is what what we are. Geronimo, here I come!

I boiled everything down to essentials on three-by-five cards, ruthlessly cutting out all the extrinsic stuff I couldn't use. My aggressive juices percolated with anticipation of that delicious moment when Bill Corzini, Tammus's lawyer, finished with his client and it was my turn to cross-examine.

At ten the next morning, I was ready. But Corzini had other plans.

"Your Honor," Corzini said, "may we approach the bench?"

I stood next to Corzini. I could have guessed what was coming.

"Your Honor," he said, "I move for a mistrial. I have the deepest personal sympathy for the reasons behind Ms. Whitcomb's absence, but with respect, the jurors have had five days in which to let the testimony they heard, including the cross-examination, grow dim. It is my—"

Ballin cut him off. "Mr. Corzini, I have a high regard for your professional skill, but not at this moment. The government has already expended good funds in the time taken to impanel a jury and to hear the plaintiff's case. If I conceded a mistrial because of Miss Whitcomb's necessary absence, where would it stop? Lawyers get sick, defendants get sick, sometimes somebody close dies." He looked at me for a split second. "If we start granting mistrials every time there is a continuance, the present clogged-up calendar would seem like nirvana compared to the chaos that would ensue. If the jurors have trouble remembering anything that they think is important, we can have the record read back. Motion denied. Proceed with your witness, Mr. Corzini."

Through questions as carefully planned as mine were, Corzini made Tammus sound like a kindly distributor, always willing to take on a neophyte recording company and give them a chance.

"Mr. Tammus," Corzini said, "did you intend to harm the Flegelmans?"

"On the contrary. I tried to help them by distributing their records in markets they couldn't otherwise reach."

"Did there come a time when you realized that the Flegelmans' records weren't selling well?"

"We found that out pretty soon."

"Did you report that to the Flegelmans?"

"Right away."

"But you continued to distribute their records for four years?"

"Yes. They were nice young people. I thought that if they jazzed up the record jackets to compete visually with other product, it might turn around."

"Did it?"

"Unfortunately not."

"But it was they and not you who terminated the contract?"

"Correct."

I had to admit Corzini was good. Better than good. He managed to insert into his questions a comment about business always being somewhat of a gamble. If a man had business problems, he could take them to a priest or a rabbi, or better yet, he could try to solve them, but the proper forum for discussing business problems was not a courtroom. I could have objected, but not without calling attention to what he was saying. He left the jury with the impression that this case was an unnecessary nuisance and that Harry Tammus always meant well. Well, we'd see.

I got up and walked toward the witness stand.

Tammus had one of those mustaches that come in two parts like Charlie Chaplin's, separated by the cleft above his lip. I thought of the mustache as pasted on. I planned to reduce his appearance to comedy, to put the meanness of his eyes into a frame that looked ridiculous.

I noticed that the eyes were taking a good long look at me. During his deposition I had soft-pedaled my questions, getting what I wanted onto the sworn record as if I were a clerk taking notes. *Just a girl, right? Easy pickings, right?* When our faces were six feet apart, he smiled.

I looked right at Tammus's mustache. He touched it, as if something might be wrong with it.

I turned my back on him. That always makes a witness anxious, Farlan says, especially up close. I looked at Jim and Judy Flegelman, who had put their hopes and savings into a record label that spoke to my generation and who were about to go broke because of Tammus's fiddles. *Trust me, you're in good hands.*

I turned around to Tammus and asked some innocuous questions so that he would relax his guard. Then I went for the question that Farlan said was like picking up a piece of rotten food with tweezers from a pile of garbage and laying it in front of the witness.

"Mr. Tammus," I said. "When your counsel asked about your education, you said you were a graduate of Iona College, is that correct?"

"Correct."

"You sure it was Iona?"

"Absolutely sure."

"You are under oath, Mr. Tammus."

"I know I am."

To the judge I said, "Your Honor, I would like to put into evidence plaintiff's Exhibit Four, a photostat of the witness's college record."

Corzini came up quickly to take a look. "Your Honor, I don't see the relevance of a thirty-year-old college record to the plaintiff's case."

"Mr. Corzini will see the relevance within one minute flat."

The exhibit was marked. When it was back in my hand, I passed it to the witness. "Mr. Tammus, does this refresh your recollection of your time at Iona?"

"Indeed it does."

"Is Iona a four-year college?"

He didn't answer.

"I can't hear you," I said. "Please speak up so that the jury can hear. Is Iona a four-year college?"

"Yes."

"And what does that record indicate as to the length of your attendance?"

He looked over at the jury.

You weren't properly coached, Mr. Tammus, or you'd avoid looking at the jury when caught.

Tammus said, "Two years."

"You attended Iona for two years?"

"Yes."

"And did you not say under oath that you were a graduate of Iona College?"

"In those days not everyone went to college, and two years was better than most."

"But you invented the second two years, didn't you? You said you were a graduate. That wasn't true, was it?"

Tammus touched his mustache. "No."

"You lied to this court, did you not?"

Corzini was on his feet. "Objection! The document speaks for itself. Your Honor, this is a trivial matter of long ago and hardly bears any relevance—"

"Your Honor," I interrupted, "Mr. Corzini on direct tried to give the jury a picture of an honest person, a well-educated person, because we tend to place a certain weight on education, and the fact is that the witness is a college drop-out and not a graduate and my line of questioning goes directly to the witness's credibility."

The judge had a nice way of sighing. "Objection overruled. But will counsel please get to the heart of the matter. Quickly."

"Yes, Your Honor." I took the photostat from Tammus and passed it to the clerk. "Mr. Tammus, you said that when you first withheld payments from the plaintiff's company your projections indicated that a high percentage of the records would be returned, is that correct?"

"That was our estimate."

"And so you withheld a payment that you testified would have amounted to $163,000?"

Tammus looked to Corzini for help. Corzini kept his seat. He nodded to Tammus.

"Yes," Tammus said.

"Now that we're dealing with actuality instead of projections, do you admit that your projections were wrong?"

"They were projections."

"Have they been proved wrong?"

"Yes."

"And did the money you withheld constitute a float?"

"You could say that."

"And did you make a profit on that float, did that money earn interest for you?"

Tammus nodded.

"The court reporter can't record a nod, Mr. Tammus. Please speak up."

"Yes!" he said, nearly shouting.

"And is that float still earning money for you?"

"Yes."

"And did the money you misappropriated and earned interest on—"

"Objection! Counsel is harassing the witness."

"Your Honor," I said, "the record company owned by the plaintiffs has been decimated by the withholding of cash flow to which they were entitled."

"Sustained. Misappropriation has not been proven."

Damn! All the jury would take away from that exchange was that I was doing something wrong.

I asked my next question from the front of the jury box, looking not at Tammus but at the jurors. "Mr. Tammus," I said, "did there come a time when your company's own auditors questioned your understated liabilities to the plaintiffs?"

"They were just doing their job."

I whirled around and headed straight for Tammus. "And wasn't part of their job to see if your books of account were kept accurately?"

"Of course."

"And, according to your auditors, were those accounts accurate when it came to the amount recorded that was due the plaintiffs?"

"I'm not going to waste time fighting my auditors. I—"

"We're not talking about wasting time, Mr. Tammus. The money that was withheld, according to your own auditors' depositions, belonged not to you but to Jim and Judy Flegelman, isn't that correct?"

"All right."

"Wasn't that misappropriation?"

"Objection!" bellowed Corzini.

"Wasn't it theft?" I shouted at the witness.

The judge's gavel came down hard. He summoned Corzini and me to the bench. Corzini, getting a bit red in the face, went on about self-incrimination and my hectoring of the witness. When he was finished, the judge told us just to get on with it.

"Mr. Tammus," I said, "If the $163,000 now admittedly withheld had been paid to the plaintiffs, do you have any idea as to what they would have done with the money?"

"How should I know?"

I deserved that. If you frame a question stupidly, you're wide open to backfire.

"Mr. Tammus, Mr. Flegelman testified that because the monies due his company were not paid, he fell behind in his royalty payments to recording artists, he was unable to pay for the record covers, the typesetters, and in fact had trouble meeting his payroll and was forced to reduce staff drastically. That is his testimony. Was that deplorable situation attributable to poor record sales or to inaccurate projections of those sales by your company?"

"My company has distributed for literally dozens of small producers over the years and our system of estimating is based on extrapolations from those figures, which have proved to be reliable time and again."

"Will the witness please answer the question."

"We get our percentages on sales, not on gross shipments."

"Mr. Tammus, I didn't ask you for your history. I want to know if your projections proved to be right."

"I don't have a crystal ball. Projections are projections."

"But the effect of those projections was to withhold money that wasn't yours, is that not true?"

Tammus didn't answer. I let it go unanswered because as far as the jury was concerned, his silence was answer enough.

"Mr. Tammus," I continued, "your distribution contract with the Flegelmans, was it designed for you to make money if the Flegelmans' records sold well and they made money?"

"Of course."

"Is it also true that if the Flegelmans' records allegedly sold poorly and had high returns and they lost money, your company nevertheless would make money?"

"My company is in business to make money." Tammus looked at the jurors and then at the judge. "That's what everybody in business tries to do, make money. What's wrong with that?"

I wanted to answer him, to say that the way he ran his business didn't give the Flegelmans a shake at making any money, but I had to convert it into a question and my mind went blank.

"Counselor?" It was the judge. I turned. Everybody in the damned courtroom was looking at me.

"Is something wrong? Would you like a recess?"

"No, Your Honor. I'm prepared to continue."

When I turned back to Tammus, he seemed to be exulting over my discomfort. *Watch out for the anger of the client if you err in court.* I looked over at the Flegelmans. Each of them nodded to give me strength.

"Mr. Tammus," I said quietly, "Did you or did you not know of the grave financial difficulties the Flegelmans were having as a result of the funds being withheld from them?"

While Tammus was deciding whether to lie, I walked over to the table where the Flegelmans were sitting and picked up three sheets of paper held together with a paper clip. Jim Flegelman had mailed a long letter to Tammus detailing the huge difficulties he was experiencing. Tammus, during discovery, denied ever having seen it. I'd asked Jim why he hadn't sent it certified mail return receipt requested and he'd told me they were trying to save on postage, things were so bad.

Tammus didn't know what the papers I was holding were. Farlan taught me that trick. Did I have some proof that Tammus had gotten the letter that he'd said he hadn't got? He decided he'd better tell the truth.

"I was aware. After a time I was aware."

"Mr. Tammus, did there come a time when you were aware that three of Mr. Flegelman's creditors got together for the purpose of putting his firm into involuntary bankruptcy?"

I knew raising the issue hurt Jim and Judy, but it couldn't be helped.

Tammus hesitated a long time. I was hoping he would lie. I could prove his knowledge of the fact.

"Yes," he said, "I knew about it."

"Can you tell the court the circumstances in which you found out about this plan?"

Tammus shifted his weight, glancing over at Corzini for help. There was no way Corzini could help him without theatrics that would get the judge angry.

"The principals of the three creditors asked to meet with me."

"And did you meet with them?"

"Yes."

"Will you please tell us what they said to you and what you said to them."

"They said that if I worked with them, they'd see to it that I—I mean my company—would have a chance to buy Flegelmans' firm out of bankruptcy."

"Would that entail a big investment?"

"No."

"A small investment?"

"Sure."

"How small?"

"I don't remember the figures."

"Under a hundred thousand dollars?"

"Yes."

"Under ten thousand dollars?"

Tammus looked over at his lawyer. There was nothing Corzini could object to.

"Shall I repeat the question?"

"No. It was under that amount."

"Was it under five thousand dollars?"

"Of course not."

"And what would owning the Flegelmans' record company do for you?"

Corzini was on his feet. "Objection! Counsel is asking the witness to speculate."

"I will rephrase," I said before the judge could say anything. "Mr. Tammus, at your meeting, did the three creditors say how your firm might benefit from your cooperation?"

"They said there would be an advantage for a distributor to have his own label."

"Would that be more profitable than distributing somebody else's product?"

"It ought to be. It means taking a greater risk."

"You mean in addition to taking your normal risk you would be assuming the risk that the Flegelmans took also?"

"Yes, of course."

"If you took over the Flegelmans' business, would your risk be the same as their risk, or would you treat yourself more honestly than you treated their company when it belonged to them?"

Corzini was on his feet.

Before the judge could reply to his objection, I said, "I withdraw the question." *Thank you, Farlan. Some questions don't need an answer to make their point.*

"Did you have anyone in your firm draw up comparative figures showing what your company earned as a distributor on a given record line and what your company would earn if you were both the record producer and the distributor?"

He knew we'd found *that* piece of paper in discovery.

"Yes."

"And so is it fair to say that in addition to withholding funds from Jim and Judy Flegelman that were legally, lawfully theirs and causing them to fall into such serious debt that they could be pushed by hostile creditors into bankruptcy, you discussed a way in which your firm might end up owning the Flegelman firm for practically nothing?"

Corzini was on his feet shouting "Objection!" but it really didn't matter. The jury had heard what was in effect a one-paragraph summation of our case.

On Friday when I called Farlan from a phone booth in the courthouse, he said, "You sound exhilarated."

"Oh I am, I am. Three million will go a long way towards making the Flegelmans whole."

"I assume Tammus will take an appeal?"

"Sure, but they'll have to post a bond for three million and with that verdict behind them the Flegelmans will get credit and be able to function. How long do you think the appeals process will take?"

"Three, four months if you're lucky. However, don't be surprised if they don't appeal."

"What have they got to lose?" I asked.

"The legal fees and something much more important. There are criminal aspects to Tammus's conduct. The judge could recommend that the District Attorney look at the transcript. Or the D.A. could pick up on his own. You've been there, you know how it works. A little bird at an assistant D.A.'s ear? Tammus might settle now just to get the whole thing behind him."

"Wouldn't that be wonderful!"

"Susan, you're thinking like a human being and not a commercial advocate. An appeal gets your firm fees, remember?"

"I just want this over with for Jim and Judy's sake."

"You still have a kind heart, my dear. I wonder how long it will take before you view clients primarily as a source of income."

"I hadn't noticed that you'd become a mercenary, Farlan."

"I teach."

"And very well. The Flegelmans asked me to thank you."

"What's this?"

"I told them you'd been of enormous help to me. And you have been, Farlan, more than you know."

He put the gift aside without opening it. "Now you listen to me, Susan. You're not to tell a client where your tactics come from. They'll value your services to the extent they think all of it is yours. That's rule one. Rule two is that you can show a modest amount of gratitude by being my guest at dinner tonight. Nicola Paone's on Thirty-fourth Street. You can't say no to Nicola Paone's."

"You certainly know how to organize your temptations, Farlan. I can't. I promised Mother I'd come up for the weekend."

"I won't keep you from your mother's. Dinner with me and I'll drive you up there."

"But she's expecting me for dinner," I lied. "And besides, I'll need my car up there to get back."

I didn't like his silence on the phone. *Susan, you are an ungrateful son-of-a-bitch.* He would never say that. Even if he thought it.

"Susan?"

"Yes?"

"Dinner?"

Farlan was a clever tactician on his own behalf. He had let me rebuke myself.

"Yes," I said, "dinner."

When I hung up, I was startled by the sharp knock on the phone booth's accordion door. A short, dark man was gesturing to me through the glass. I opened the doors and stepped out as if in a daze. "Come on, lady," he said, and shoved me aside.

The barbarians were everywhere.

CHAPTER 28

Farlan

Lathering my face, I thought what an extraordinary thing to be doing. I'd shaved in the morning, of course. I almost never shaved again in the evening.

Clearly I was as nervous as a high school senior readying himself for a prom. I hoped Susan hadn't accepted entirely out of gratitude. She wouldn't, that's one of her strong points, isn't it?

I ran the razor carefully over my cheeks. This was no time to cut myself. Stray thoughts kept intruding. The very idea of a taboo attracts man. The injunction *not to arouse* itself arouses. Patients fall in love with their physician-touchers more often than either patients or doctors admit. Isn't that akin to the mentor complex, where the naked yearning of Shaw's Eliza Doolittle touches the naked arrogance of the lust to teach what one knows to perfection? It is perfectly normal for a student's libido to entwine itself with her teacher's. The relationship is not as physical as the doctor's, with his hands on the patient's back or waist or breasts, feeling and pinching and stroking. But if the brain is the true erogenous source, in the mentor relationship each brain is exciting the other's almost all the time. Still, with so many students within my reach over so many years, why this ferocity of feeling for Susan?

I quickly washed the remaining lather off my face and was about to slap some lime aftershave on my cheeks when a sudden rush of feeling hit me. I must sit down or I would fall.

I couldn't bring myself to sit on the lid of the commode, so I sat down—hard, I may say—on the edge of the tub. If I keeled over in a faint, who would know? Susan might guess when I failed to appear at the restaurant. She wouldn't just dash off to her mother's like a young woman stood up, she'd be worried. She would phone. And if the phone wasn't answered, would she drive up here to see what was wrong? Or might she suspect a trap? God knows I've taught her to be suspicious of other people's moves.

I decided that feeling faint was a message. It is time I shared my life.

Susan arrived at the cloakroom of Nicola Paone's just as I was taking the check from the attendant. I insisted that her coat join mine on the same hanger.

I was stunned by the light in her face as she offered her cheek to me and thanked me once again for my help with her case.

As we were being led to our table, she said to me, "Dr. Frankenstein, you've made me into a courtroom menace."

"I'd like to have been there."

"Believe me, you were."

At the table, when the white wine had filled our glasses Susan proposed a toast.

"To Jim and Judy Flegelman."

"May all just causes have good lawyers," I said.

I'm not quite sure why I laughed at my own remark, euphoric as I was—over what? Susan's extraordinary ability to pick up on tactics and put them to her own use? The truth is that in my chest beat the heart of a young man, bouncing with bliss at being in her presence. "I love you," I said quietly.

She smiled at me. And said nothing.

"Truly, Susan, it is as impossible as one hand clapping."

"What?"

"One person being engaged."

This time she laughed.

"Please," I said.

"Please what?"

"Please me by responding. I have proposed to you. In writing and in person. If you have no feeling for me . . ."

"Stop it."

I had stopped. Then, softly, she said, "Of course I have enormous feeling for you, Farlan. I am happy when I'm with you. I'm grateful for every blessed wicked lesson you've taught me. I would like to be your student forever."

"School's over," I said. "It's not a teacher-student relationship anymore, is it?"

"No," she said.

"There now. What holds you back?"

"I always hated contract law."

"We could live together. I don't need a contract. My need is for you."

I found her silence as unbearable as the supposition that one is alone on this earth. Finally I said, "Is it that David Smith person?"

"Our bodyguard?"

"Susan, whatever my faults, I'm not a stupid person. He's not just a bodyguard."

"Of course not. Somebody's got to deal with the terrorists."

"That's not what I meant. Something personal has developed between the two of you."

"Protecting us from my father's murderers is not exactly impersonal."

"You're avoiding the issue," I said. "Again." I could not rest my case. "It says something about our society, doesn't it, Susan, that we spawn killers and those who kill killers?"

When I saw a butterfly of color spread on her cheeks, I instantly wanted to pull my words back.

She said, "Name one society that hasn't spawned killers and called them soldiers!"

"Please, Susan." It didn't stop her.

"That makes my father a killer, doesn't it? Except he got killed and it's people like David Smith who see to it that at least those particular killers stop killing. Look at what you've taught me, Farlan, to dissect people while they're still alive."

"In a good cause!"

"And do you think protecting me or avenging my father's death *isn't* a good cause?"

"It's a sad world that resolves its disputes by having many more soldiers than lawyers."

"Well, the lawyers are catching up."

"It will not advantage you in your work to despise your profession."

"I don't despise anything, Farlan, except hypocrisy. If I'm going to spend my professional life being a courtroom torturer, I'm not going to try to pass my conscience off as if it belonged to Florence Nightingale."

And so it went. We talked at each other without concluding anything about my proposal. When the check came, I said, "I am a poor advocate for my most important cause." I waited, trying to use the hush of pausing as I had advised Susan to do in the courtroom.

And what I got again was the din of her silence.

Speak to me, I wanted to cry out. "Speak to me," I said in as normal a voice as I could muster under the circumstances.

"We've been speaking all evening, Farlan."

"You've been avoiding my proposal all evening." I was surprised to find myself flushed with anger, a largely useless emotion. And so I said, "It is that David Smith person, isn't it?"

"You are both friends, Farlan. You've been one a very long time. He's a new friend."

"I don't believe that either he or I are just friends, as you put it. If you hate hypocrisy, at least be consistent. We are both men who are interested in you as a woman."

"How do you know what he thinks?"

"Susan, I am not blind."

And as my eyes found Susan's I was blinded by a rush of love.

That was when Susan said, "Farlan, I swear there is no reason for you to be jealous."

I held her coat out for her as she inserted first her left arm, then her right. I would have put both my arms around her if I had dared.

Outside, as I expected, she announced that she'd brought her own car and it was parked just two blocks away. I walked her to her car, the pain of my love for her tumbling inside me. If I said to her *I'm going to faint* she would not leave for Scarborough. Would she insist on accompanying me home? Not Susan. She would take me to Bellevue.

"Good night," she said. She didn't offer me her cheek. She offered her mouth. I leaned down and kissed her, gently, gently.

As she drove away I was sure my heart would burst right there on Thirty-second Street and I would be rushed to Bellevue anyway by strangers.

I decided that a walk in the brisk night air would do me good. Half a mile meant ten blocks. Five blocks up and five blocks down. *I swear there is no reason for you to be jealous.* Had she lied to me? Her kiss wasn't a lie.

I had hardly walked two of my self-assigned blocks, my eyes to the fore like a soldier's, when my right foot suddenly tripped on something. The something moved, gathering the surrounding things to her—yes, it was a woman—and growled, "Watch where you're going, mister. Who the hell do you think you are?"

"Sorry," I said. "I didn't see you."

Three absolutely villainous-looking people leaning against a storefront were glaring at me.

"Sorry," I repeated and quickly walked off.

Were those three following me? I shouldn't look around. To avoid attack, one has to appear unafraid.

A hand touched my shoulder. I whirled, ready to strike.

It wasn't any of the three. It was a pitiful-looking old man, now holding out the hand that had touched my shoulder.

"A dollar for something to eat," he said.

You can't get a meal for a dollar in Manhattan. The man just wanted me to take my wallet out so he could make a grab for it and run.

I reached into my left trouser pocket where I keep my change. I felt for coins the size of quarters. In my hand were five quarters. He'd only asked for four. Before I could put one back, he'd grabbed my wrist with his dirty hand and with his other hand plucked the quarters from my palm. He grinned, then burped and farted simultaneously. I gave up the idea of a late-night stroll and headed straight for my car.

It wasn't there.

My heart racing away, I looked at the sign on a nearby pole. NO PARKING, 8 A.M. TO 7.P.M. EXCEPT SUNDAYS. It was long after 7 p.m. Had my car been towed? It had never happened to me. I don't even know where they take the cars that are hauled away or what the procedure is for reclaiming them.

I waved frantically at the taxi coming down the block. The driver would know where the car pound was. He could take me there. I waved again. The bastard clearly saw me and didn't slow down. As the yellow cab zoomed by me I saw that he had a passenger in back. I felt like a fool.

I looked around for a policeman. There were none in sight.

I headed back to Nicola Paone's. They'd recognize me and let me use their phone. Whom would I call?

Then I saw it. My car, parked where I had left it, just a few steps from the restaurant's front door. What's happening to my mind? The thought of memory loss, the sudden frightening void I'd felt from time to time even when I was young, kept me from the courtroom. I couldn't have been an actor depending on memorized lines because of my great apprehension of tumbling down the chasm of total forgetfulness. It would be worse in court, where there are no prompters. As long as I was the prompter, I was safe.

Thank God Susan had missed my lapse.

My key went into the driver's side door of the car easily. It opened not as in a nightmare but as it always opens. I slid in, locked the door against strangers, and turned the key in the ignition. The sound of that engine was like Bach to my ears. I was safe from bag ladies and beggars and bodily harm.

I drove uptown faster than I usually drive through city streets. If any of these creatures of the night dared cross my path now they'd be smashed by this automobile and it would be entirely their fault. *Beware*, I could have shouted, *beware!* And I heard Susan's voice again, *You have nothing to be jealous of.*

I saw the policeman under the street light waving me over. I hadn't done anything wrong. If I was going a bit fast it was to play it safe in an unsafe city. How did I know it was a policeman, anyway? That uniform could be the hired costume of a thief. I didn't stop. I speeded up just in case the stupid man had a notion to try to read my license plate. In my rear view mirror, nothing. I sang *Anchors aweigh, my lads* loud and louder still, to match the exhilarated, indomitable exuberance of being alive.

CHAPTER 29

Susan

Scarborough on Saturday morning seemed to me the perfect place on earth. From my second-story window the view west was green with foliage through which you could see the blue of the Hudson rippling nearly four miles wide. A monastic silence hovered over the landscape, pierced only by the chirp and cry of birds. Even when a distant lawnmower intruded its harsh cough into the air, it seemed another sound of nature. To my traveling mother and father this place was the magnet of home. I could revel in it.

On the phone Mom and I had planned to take our ritual cups of cocoa out-of-doors as we had done many years ago, to watch the orange sun sink slowly, backlighting the foliage, green turning gray, listening for the occasional Amtrak train carrying people north or south as we gazed west, mesmerized by the topmost curve of the sun disappearing behind the palisades.

After dinner with Farlan I'd arrived too late for any of that except the cocoa, taken indoors. Mom knew I had something on my mind, but she was drained. "Let's talk in the morning," she said. "Marjorie said they all sleep late on weekends. We'll have the place to ourselves."

Once early in the night I woke from a dream in which Farlan and David were riding wooden horses on a carousel, trying to catch up to my horse as we went round and round in circles. I tried to hold my horse back so one of them would reach me, but which one? I started to shout a name. That was what woke me, and I couldn't for the life of me tell whose name I had wanted to call out.

Back to sleep I went and slept without dreaming. When I woke early it was with the thrust of energy that comes with a good night's rest. I looked over at Mom in the other bed, her fine gray hair glorious against the pillow. Quietly, I slipped into blue jeans and pulled a V-neck over my head against the morning chill and went outside, taking a cold breath deep into my lungs. Orange juice and coffee could wait. I wanted to see the giant silver maple etched by early light against the sky.

The lawn slopes sharply at the south, then stops just where the ground plunges fifty feet or more to a stream fed by a small waterfall of ground water. Neighbors sometimes come just to observe this mini-canyon, holding tightly to the hands of young children who, thinking themselves immortal, are tempted to run down the fearsome slope. Dad was always concerned that some child would slip and stumble as in a nightmare, down to the rocks in the rushing water below. "We can't put a fence around it, can't keep people from trespassing," he would say. "They'd have to sue God."

I thought I saw something move in the trees below. Sure-footed deer sometimes wander into the hollow. I remember watching them until, frightened by my presence, they stumbled for their footing as if on crutches and then, gathering grace and speed, ran uphill on the other side, safe.

What I saw in the gully wasn't a deer. A man had stepped behind a tree.

What was anyone doing down there this time of morning? Was some stranger enjoying the early morning view from our unfenced property? Dad sometimes asked picnickers to picnic elsewhere but as a rule let people be. "It won't get used up," he'd say.

Cupping my hands to my mouth I shouted "Hello-o-o-o" to whoever was down there. A thin young man in jeans stepped out from behind the tree. I waved at him to make sure he could see me.

He didn't wave back. He looked straight at where I was standing as if he knew all along that I was there.

"Can I help you?" I asked.

I expected him to shake his head and move on.

He started uphill toward me.

"Are you lost?"

He didn't answer but came steadily on.

"This is private property," I shouted, and turned back to the house.

I'd taken no more than six or seven steps when I saw a second young man—he could have been a mirror image of the first except much shorter—standing near the front door of the house.

He started toward me.

Thank God for the security system. All I had to do was run around the back of the house to get at the panic button just inside the kitchen door. It would set off a blasting siren on the roof and light a signal on the police department switchboard.

I started to run toward the rear of the house, then stopped. *The security system was set up to keep intruders out. The kitchen door, locked from the inside, will keep me out, too.*

I felt as if a panic button *had* been pushed—inside my chest. My heart was fibrillating. My lungs weren't getting enough air. *Monteleone goes after families.* If I ran downhill toward the river, I'd have to cross four railroad tracks, each with a live third rail as its power source. Even if I negotiated each track safely, what could I do, swim across the Hudson?

I ran in the opposite direction, away from the river toward the road, remembering that an occasional jogger used River Road on weekend mornings. I looked back long enough to see that the two men and I were the points of a triangle. They were moving toward me.

That was when I spotted the brown van coming down River Road. It must be the van that delivers the morning paper. I ran toward it, light-footed with relief. I could hear the men behind me breathing hard and nearing. They were saying something to each other I couldn't make out.

Up on the road, I waved my arms wildly to make sure the van stopped. It's a good thing he wasn't going fast. The driver saw me. He pulled over. Thank God, he was getting out of the cab. I ran toward him, yelling "Help! Help!"

The driver moved to rescue me, his arms outstretched as if expecting me to run into them for protection. Less than ten feet from him, I stopped in my tracks. *He was just like the others, an olive-complected man in blue jeans.* I turned. The other two had nearly caught up. Where could I escape to? I screamed as loudly as I could, over and over again, until the driver grabbed me and put a rough hand over my mouth as another caught my arms, and the third helped pull me toward the back of the van. I struggled like a caught cat to break loose. I managed to pull my right hand free and flung a fist backward into the face of the one who had his hand on my mouth. He let go long enough for me to scream again. *Help! Somebody! Please!* My nails scratched at the nearest face. I twisted my body to get away, just as I felt the rough hand back on my mouth. One of the others opened the rear doors of the van, and then all three of them pushed me into the vehicle.

As two of the men clambered into the van after me I let out one more scream through the still open door, hoping that if my earlier screams hadn't awakened Don Webster, this one would. *Come on, get the license number, call the police!* One of the men slapped me hard across the face. "No yell, you bitch," he said. I could taste sweet blood in my mouth.

He shoved both my shoulders. I stumbled back onto the hard seat. My head was spinning from the slap. "You stay sit!"

His accent brought back Rome, the airport, David. *Where are you now?*

CHAPTER 30

Heather Whitcomb

The sound of Susan's scream woke me. For a moment I thought it was part of a dream. Then I heard the second scream, more like a wailing cry, and I was wide awake and out of the room. At the stairwell I could see Don Webster down below.

"What is it?" he said. "Where is she?"

"Outside," I said. *Couldn't he tell?*

I was halfway down the stairs before I realized I was wearing only my nightgown. It didn't matter. "Call the police," I told Don Webster and opened the front door.

At the end of the driveway, near the mailbox, was a brown van. I could see the driver. Maybe he'd heard which direction the scream had come from. I started toward the van the short way, across the grass. I couldn't catch my breath. Then I knew. *She's in the van.*

"Heather!" Don Webster was in the doorway. I stopped and turned. "The police lines are busy!"

"You probably dialed the wrong number," I shouted. *Why can't men think for themselves? Hal would have known what to do.* If Susan was in the van, why wasn't it moving? I took some hesitant steps toward it. *Because they want me, too!*

I could hear sounds of commotion from inside the van. Then one of the back doors popped open, and I caught sight of a skinny-armed man trying to close it from inside. Then I heard Susan's shout, "Mom, get back to—" The van door slammed shut.

Running toward the house, I stumbled. My right slipper came off. I left it in the grass. Inside the open door, I saw Don Webster still at the phone.

"Can't get through," he said.

Like phone calls in a nightmare. I pressed the panic panel just inside the door. It touched off a loud siren on the roof and another inside at the top of the stairwell. I yelled at Don Webster above the din, "That'll get to them!"

I pulled at Don's sleeve, and motioned for him to follow me. At the open door I realized what I had done. Instead of waiting for me to be trapped, too, the van was pulling away. I should have done something to stall them, to make them think they could still nab me, too. *I shouldn't have put my hand on the panic plate.*

Poor bewildered Don Webster, there just wasn't time to fill him in. At the hall phone I dialed the police number from memory, expecting a busy signal. I got right through. "Mrs. Whitcomb on River Road," I said. "A brown van headed south has got my daughter inside."

The voice at the other end said, "Please slow down, Mrs. Whitcomb. Is your daughter with the people in the van?"

"She's their prisoner," I very nearly screamed.

"How old is she?"

Good God, it's like the hospital emergency room. They want you to fill in a form first! "She's an adult," I said. "I'm General Whitcomb's wife. She's his daughter. The terrorists who killed my husband ..."

I didn't have to say more. Everybody had read the newspapers.

"I've got a car on Route 9, ma'am," the policeman said and put me on hold.

Don Webster was looking at me, not at my face, and I felt suddenly conspicuous in my nightgown. Looking down I could see what he saw all too clearly. "I'll get your robe," he said, and was up the stairs in a jiff.

The policeman came back on the line. "They've spotted the van. They're in pursuit." I could hear him yelling something to someone. I tried to remember where I'd put the phone number David Smith had given us to use in an emergency.

Don was back with my robe, which he slipped over my shoulders.

I held on to the phone, wondering if the policeman would get back on. Images tumbled through my head, the Briarcliff Manor police car chasing the van down past the Rockefeller park toward North Tarrytown, Hal leaning over the hospital bed as I held our newborn in my arms, Hal suddenly alive and organizing the chase. *Try to think clearly.* They'd probably called the North Tarrytown police to head the van off. If the van took to the narrow side roads at that speed it would surely crash into something. With Susan inside.

Marjorie and both of her children, awakened by the blare of the alarms going off inside and out, were downstairs now. Don was trying, above the clamor, to explain what had happened.

On the phone I could hear the policemen in the station house shouting orders like the members of a large tenement family. Suddenly, all I heard was a dial tone. Just as well, someone had better stop those sirens. Hadn't we taught the Websters what to do? Why were they just standing there? I took my one slipper off and, barefoot, went up the stairs to the hall closet where the control box for the security system was located. I pushed the square red button. Both sirens stopped instantly, leaving a huge hole of silence in which I could now hear the phone ringing. Quickly I slipped my feet into a pair of scuffs I'd brought, and went back down.

Don was at the phone, thanking the caller. The second he hung up I said, "Was that the police?"

Don nodded.

"What is it?"

Don just stood there like a zombie.

"Did they catch the van?"

Don's mouth moved oddly, as if he had trouble parting stuck-together lips. "They didn't say."

CHAPTER 31

Susan

They'd tied my wrists together with strong rope. The other end was secured to my ankles, leaving no slack, and bending me forward painfully. In that scrunched-up position, my muscles were strained to the screaming point.

Each jounce of the van erased every thought except *stop the pain*. How quickly one's mind dissolves into that of a wailing animal caught in a trap. What did these people plan to do to me?

I heard the distinct whoop-whoop of the police siren behind us. My heart leaped with hope. Whoop-whoop. The siren sounded closer. The police car must be gaining on us. We had to be near the built-up area of the Tarrytowns. The van would have to slow down.

The taller of my captors pushed open one of the rear doors. Twisting around, I could just see the pursuing police car thirty yards behind us, and gaining. The tall one darted a look of pure hatred at me, as if the pursuing car were my fault. For a second I thought he was going to grab me, trussed up as I was, and shove me out on the road in the police car's path. Instead, he reached into the navy-blue duffel bag he'd been sitting on and slid out a rifle. He yelled *Rallenta!* at the driver of the van.

The van slowed, causing the police car to slow also. The tall one got down into a prone position, his feet nearly touching mine, his head toward the open door. He had his left elbow directly under the barrel of the rifle, steadying it like a trained soldier. He aimed carefully through the open door. The other man, the short one with the dancing eyes of a moron, gazed at him admiringly.

The sound of the shot exploded like a jai-alai pelota ricocheting off the metal of the van's interior walls. I opened my eyes just in time to see the police car, its windshield crazed by the bullet, careen off the road and slam into one of the thick-trunked trees that line Route 9. I felt the crunch inside my chest as if I'd been in the crashing car.

My kidnaper, now a murderer, turned to grin at me. He pulled the metal door shut with a clang. The short one clapped his hands like a gleeful kid, yelling to share the event with the driver up front. The tall one patted the rifle and looked at me as if he wanted me to give him a medal for being such a terrific shot.

Out loud, in my best street-manner Italian, I yelled *U caz!* The marksman seemed more startled than angry at my insult. Stupid of me! If they knew I knew some Italian, they wouldn't talk in front of me. Or was Italian the only language they could communicate in? Would they have to use it anyway?

Questions kept bobbing in my brain. Why hadn't they just killed me right there on the lawn? *Because they want to use you, stupid.*

The sound of sirens cut through my thoughts. Why weren't the police shooting at the van? Because, moron, they didn't want to hit you by accident. Or was it because they were afraid of being shot themselves? If it looked like the police were about to catch us, would these people kill me? I looked at the sharpshooter. *He* wouldn't hesitate a second.

The van suddenly lurched, swerving hard right. What the hell was the driver trying to do?

We picked up speed. If we were coming to the Thruway, he'd have to turn left to head to New York City, or else cross the Tappan Zee Bridge to the right. The two men in the back of the van with me were laughing like kids on a roller coaster ride.

The van picked up speed. We had to be crossing the Tappan Zee. My insides jounced. *Please untie me* I wanted to say to the laughing men. If I asked to be untied they'd only laugh harder.

Why wasn't I hearing the sirens any more?

I needed desperately to go to the bathroom. What bathroom? I peed when I woke up this morning. I hadn't had anything to drink.

Was it nerves? Whatever it was was fierce enough for me to shout *Please stop, please pull over to the side somewhere.*

The tall one said, "No stop."

"As soon as we're off the bridge, please!" I said.

"No stop!" he yelled at me.

"I have to go to the bathroom."

He looked puzzled. Of course, they were Europeans. "Toilet," I shouted. *"Gabinetto."*

They both laughed. I wished them both dead.

"Please . . ." I said. They paid no attention. All I could make out from their chatter was that one was named Guido and the short one something like Poco.

After a while it was the tall one, Guido, who slithered over close enough so that I could smell his fetid breath. He said, "All dead people shit their pants."

Inch by inch I squirmed to get myself back against the side of the van so that I would jounce less. Guido kept looking at my body, first one place, then another. I tried not to lock eyes with him. Was I right that this Guido didn't just kill me because he was planning to send a different kind of message? Where was I being taken? What were they planning to do with me? My mind buzzed with questions I couldn't answer.

The first acid nibble of hunger came like some animal instinct I couldn't control. Even as a kid any delay in breakfast peeled the skin off my nerves. Is there any point in asking them? . . . *They don't have to do anything unless it's part of their plan.*

I rebuked myself for my food thoughts. People are able to go without food for days, even weeks, I told myself. Concentrate on how to keep alive. Know where you're being taken. Use every second.

I never understood people who want time to pass unnoticed, ticking off the hours between now and death. Every minute was to be savored. How do you savor the pain of being trussed up like an animal? As an animal you forget that every passing moment brings you closer to death.

The van came to a sudden stop. I pitched sideways. Poco, the short one with the face of an idiot, pulled me back up to a sitting position. Guido opened the van doors, glanced around, nodded to

Poco, then leaped back into the van and seized my bound legs while Poco lifted me under the armpits. Together they dragged me out of the van. Guido and the short one held me as someone—was it the driver?—backed a four-door metallic gray sedan up to the van. The driver opened the trunk.

"No!" I screamed. "No!"

"Shut up!" said Guido. His hand hit across my face hard.

The driver pulled a folded navy blue blanket out of the trunk.

Stupid flaming idiot!. Your yelling could give them the idea of stuffing you in there. Don't react spontaneously. What you should have done is get a glimpse of the license plate. You could have seen it. You muffed it. *I didn't muff anything. What the hell good would it do me to know the license plate number?*

The back door of the gray sedan was held open by the idiot. It took him and Guido both to get their tied bundle in. I tried to keep my legs as well as my bottom on the seat so that the rig would hurt less. Poco pushed my legs off. I tried to swing them back on. The idiot nearly shoved me off the seat when Guido commanded, "*Smettila! Lascia stare!*"

Poco dutifully covered all of me except my head with the blue blanket. To anyone seeing me I'd look like a passenger with a chill, not like a trussed-up turkey.

The driver of the sedan had longer sideburns than the others and a mass of uncombed curly black hair that needed washing. He didn't say one word. Was he a mute? I swung my head around to see the van.

The van was gone. I hadn't heard it leave. Who drove the van away? There must be more than three of them. Are there others where they're taking me?

Poco started to get in back with me. Guido stopped him with a hard hand on his shoulder. With a thumb Guido motioned him to the front passenger seat. Then Guido slid in beside me. At least I had the blanket.

Guido must have read my mind. He lifted the edge of the blanket and stared at my breasts.

"Please leave me alone," I said.

He smiled at me, a tough teenager about to do something he's been forbidden to do.

His hand found my right breast.

I wanted to yell *Stop it!* but knew my resistance would encourage rather than deter him.

His forefinger felt around my right breast for the nipple. When he found it, he said in his accented English, "Very nice." I tried to ignore his busy fingers, to think about something, anything except what Guido was doing.

From the sun I could tell that we were bearing south. Across the Tappan Zee and south meant we were headed for New Jersey. I always took the Garden State Parkway when I went this way. They were staying off toll roads.

It was impossible to ignore Guido's hand now that it had moved down. In a very quiet voice I said, "Please stop that."

"Hey," Guido said, "where you like to have it?"

I squirmed. What was the point?

"Hey, hey, you like to move around? Where you like to have it? Here, there, where?"

In court, jammed by my adversary, I could always think of something.

"Hey, your father is a general, yes?"

I didn't say anything.

"A big shot, yes?"

Better say nothing.

"He come help you?"

His hand had stopped moving.

"He bring whole army to help you? Hey, Poco," he shouted, "her father gonna bring whole army to wipe us out."

His face was very close to mine. I couldn't move my head back any further.

"Your father is dead," he said. His hand was active again.

"Please leave me alone."

"Soon you dead, too. So whatsa matter what I do, hey?"

"Stop that or I'll piss all over you!"

Guido laughed. "No speak English."

Poco turned around to look at what Guido was doing.

"Turn around!" Guido snapped, then said something in Italian.

"You speak English," I said. "I just heard you."

"No speak English," Guido repeated, laughing. "Also deaf." I clenched my teeth and started counting to a thousand. Somewhere between 150 and 160 I wondered why they hadn't blindfolded me. *Because,* David would have said, *it doesn't matter what you see if they're going to kill you afterwards.*

CHAPTER 32

Heather Whitcomb

I recognized the police sergeant as one of the Briarcliff policemen who many years ago came around to collect for a dog license a year after our dog had died. He was a very tall man, whose heavy paunch made him seem altogether gigantic, or else I was feeling suddenly small.

All four of the Websters and I sat facing him in the living room. Don Webster asked the sergeant to sit down in the fragile chair Hal had inherited from his mother. That worried me. I was afraid that the chair Hal cared for so much would split under the sergeant's weight. I didn't want anything that belonged to Hal to break.

The sergeant cleared his throat like a schoolboy about to recite. "The policeman who was shot from the van," he said, "died on the way to Phelps. The hospital's only a couple of minutes away from the scene of the crash."

Why wasn't he saying anything about Susan? Had the van gotten away? "I'm so sorry," I said, "about the policeman."

"Thirty-four years old," the sergeant went on. "Left a widow with three kids. One more than you have here."

Don Webster said, "I'm sorry."

The sergeant was looking at some point in the carpet between Don and me when he said, "First line-of-duty death we've had on the force."

"What about my daughter in the van?"

"It was going like crazy, ma'am," the sergeant said, "it was endangering all other traffic. A police vehicle isn't allowed to do that, even in pursuit. The Tarrytown police lost the van on the bridge."

The Briarcliff police were exonerated. The Tarrytown police were at fault. Better yet, the ordinary people constituting traffic on the bridge were at fault.

"We don't have helicopters in our force, ma'am. We sent out an all-points. The state troopers will let New Jersey know if they head south. Since it's a kidnapping, we let the FBI know. Someone's bound to spot the van if they don't switch vehicles. We'll find your daughter sooner or later."

He didn't say dead or alive. I excused myself and went upstairs.

I'd copied David's number from the card he had given me onto the back of one of Hal's calling cards that I always carried with me. I dialed very carefully so as not to make a mistake.

Hal had never had calling cards in the States. In Europe you had to have cards even if your uniform said it all. The card said REWARD FOR RETURN in Hal's handwriting. He put one of those inside every piece of luggage we had. I looked at those familiar words. REWARD FOR RETURN. I looked up. Out-of-doors I would have seen the sky. In my bedroom all I saw was the ceiling. "Dear God," I said anyway, "Reward for Return." Even if Hal could be brought back by a miracle, what about all those pieces he'd been blown to? I have to stop thinking like a superstitious savage and get on with life.

I really should be keeping a record of my calls so I can reimburse the Websters. They probably wouldn't let me, they're not like some people who always take money that's coming to them regardless of the circumstances. Nothing was happening. Maybe I had misdialed. I tried again, carefully. David said his number was like an 800 number so you couldn't tell where you were calling. Those ads that say the 800 number was good anywhere but in Nebraska are a dead giveaway that your call is going to Nebraska.

On the fourth ring a man's voice said, "Please leave your name and number when you hear the tone." *An answering machine!* It wasn't even David's voice. Had I reached the right number? "This . . . is . . . Heather . . . Whitcomb," I said, pronouncing each word as if I was speaking to a foreigner. "Please . . . notify . . . David . . . Smith . . . that . . . Susan . . . has . . . been . . . kidnapped."

I was about to leave our phone number when I stopped. Suppose I had reached the wrong party? Besides, David had our number.

As soon as I put the receiver down I picked it up again and dialed zero and then the country code for Italy, while I quickly thumbed through my little address book, found the number I was looking for, and tapped it in. I imagined switches switching, instructions darting along long lines, up to a satellite, down to Rome. In less than five seconds, I could hear the phone ringing at the other end.

It rang burp-burp, burp-burp, until I remembered it was Saturday in Italy also. I disconnected, then started all over again with the country code followed by General Milburn's private number.

"Hello."

Thank God. He was home.

"It's me, Heather."

"How marvelous to hear your voice,' he said. "How are you?"

"I'm sorry to trouble you on a weekend, Millie, but—"

"No trouble at all. I was just relaxing with the newspaper and—"

"Susan's been kidnapped."

I thought the connection had been cut. Finally, he said the one stupid word we say so often. "No."

"I need your help, Millie. The local police are . . . well, local. They chased the van and lost it. To be fair, a policeman was killed chasing the van."

"What van?"

"A brown one, the one the kidnappers took Susan away in."

"What nationality?"

"How should I know?"

"I mean were the men like Arabs?"

"The one I saw clearly was dark like some Italians. He was skinny as an Arab, but I don't think he was. Oh Millie, what can the army do to help? Anything?"

I heard nothing except the hum of the telephone line.

"I don't have Hal to turn to," I said.

"I'll see what's possible, Heather. I suspect this is something for local law enforcement."

"I don't want laws enforced. I want Susan found!"

"Of course, of course. Have you notified the FBI?"

"I've left word for David Smith."

A moment passed, then Milford Burns said, "I see," which is what people who have to think out loud say out loud.

"Millie," I said, "if Hal had given his life to a private firm a fraction of the size of the U.S. Army, they'd be doing something about the kidnapping of his daughter. I know I'm not being reasonable. I will call the FBI. Good-bye, Millie."

"Before you hang up, Heather, let me have your number."

"You have my number."

"Of course. I'll see what I can do from this end."

He would do nothing, I told myself, because the army, which has regulations for everything, doesn't have a regulation for dealing with the kidnapping of a late colleague's civilian daughter.

Downstairs I was surrounded by solicitous Websters. Don shushed them and said, "Why don't we all sit back down so Heather can tell us what is really going on."

I'm going insane, that's what's really going on. Then I told them. The doorbell rang.

"I'll get it," Don said. "You all stay here."

I saw Don taking a shotgun from inside the hall closet and slowly opening the door to whoever it was.

"It's for you," said Don. At his side was a man of no more than five feet nine, holding his hat in his left hand and in his right a wallet open to a celluloid flap with an I.D. card in it.

"My name is Earl Morath," he said. "FBI. The police called us in."

I looked at the I.D. I could hardly make out the words on the card. The photograph on it resembled the man, but anyone could get a photo of himself on a fake I.D., couldn't they?

"How do I know you're who you say you are?"

My comment seemed to embarrass Don Webster more than the man. "We'll leave you two alone," Don said.

"I'd rather you didn't leave," I said. "I'm not paranoid, I simply don't think we can blindly trust just anyone."

"Mrs. Whitcomb is understandably upset," Don said.

"I can appreciate that," the man echoed. Then he held out another card. "That's the Westchester FBI phone. You can call and check."

"How do I know that's the FBI phone? It could be anyone's."

"They'll answer 'FBI.' "

"Well, that could be some friend of yours saying 'FBI,' couldn't it?"

I could tell he was getting exasperated. "Don't go," I said to the Websters, who were on the point of leaving the room.

The man said, "Well then, call any FBI number, Manhattan, call Washington, D.C., if you like and check my I.D."

"I'll call Manhattan," I said, and went to the hall phone. The thick Manhattan directory was on the shelf of the phone table.

"Look under United States," the man said.

"I know," I said. "My husband worked for the United States." I felt absolutely manic, dialing.

The main Manhattan FBI office number answered on the first ring. "FBI," said a woman's voice.

"May I speak to an agent, please."

"You may speak to me, ma'am."

"I don't want to talk to the switchboard. I want to talk to an agent."

"I am an agent, ma'am. My name is Chris Jones."

"Excuse me, but you sounded like a woman."

"I am a woman," said agent Jones. I couldn't have been more embarrassed.

"There's a man here claiming to be an FBI agent. Let me see that I.D. again, would you?"

The man flipped his wallet open and brought it close to me.

"His I.D. says he is Earl Morath."

"Have you tried calling your local FBI number?"

"He gave me a number, but how was I to know if it was legitimate?"

"It would be the same as the local number for the FBI in your book."

"I see," I said, feeling like an idiot. "Can you hold on for a minute."

"Sure."

I opened the Westchester directory and sure enough, under FBI was the number the man had given me.

"Thank you," I said to the woman.

"*De nada,*" the woman said and hung up.

"I'm sorry not to have believed you," I said to agent Morath.

"No trouble," he said.

"We'll see you later, Heather," Don Webster said, and steered his family out of sight. I gestured to Hal's mother's chair. Agent Morath nodded his head and sat down. He seemed about half the size of the police sergeant. I sat down opposite him.

Mr. Morath had his notebook out. "Can you spell your daughter's full name for me, please."

I suddenly wanted to cry. Susan was in mortal danger somewhere and here we were, wasting time, when all the world's police ought to be out there finding the van before those crazy people do something terrible again.

CHAPTER 33

David Smith

Sam told me to take a couple of days. "Monteleone will still be here when you rest up."

I told him I was okay, I preferred to keep busy. I didn't talk about Susan. If I did I sure as hell would give myself away.

I instructed Susan to stay out of my dreams. Then early Sunday morning the double-ring of the phone shattered me awake. I rolled toward the night table. As I reached for the phone, I was aware of a headache. It was still dark outside. The penalty for reaching and not looking is that I managed to pull the damn phone, base and all, off the night table. That clatter jarred my headache loose and it bounced around in my head like a handball.

When I got the handset up to my face, for a moment I thought I'd disconnected the caller.

"Hello," I said. "Hello, hello."

"This is April."

My cut-off isn't a person, it's an office manned by different people, none of whom I've ever met face to face.

"Don't sound so stern about it," I said. "April showers bring May flowers. You woke me. I have a headache."

"Sorry, sir. We've had a relay message."

"You could have waited a couple of hours," I said. This wasn't Vietnam. A man was entitled to some unbroken sleep after a mission.

"I'm sorry, sir. My instructions are to relay at once anything from Stateside."

That woke me all the way up.

"Mrs. Whitcomb reports that Miss Whitcomb is gone."

"What the hell do you mean gone?"

"She said kidnapped, sir. There's no information from any other source about a kidnapping, sir."

My mind worked the way it's been trained to work. Sort out the facts, then the options. The phone message was from her mother. That meant they'd only taken Susan. Had they tried to get the mother? What were the bastards planning? My damn instinct had been right, I should have disobeyed orders and stayed there.

"Give me a fix on the transmission time," I said.

He took a moment to look it up.

"Nine *hours* ago! What the fuck's wrong with you people?"

It was stupid of me to yell my frustration out like that. The fellow's only a bureaucrat, minding his shift. I apologized for yelling, hung up, and dialed Dracoff's home number.

No, he hadn't been asleep, he was in the middle of breakfast.

"What's up, David?"

"Have you still got a tap on Monteleone's line?"

"What the hell's suddenly wrong with you? I've never known you to be this careless."

"Careless about what?"

"This is an open line, idiot. I'll call you on your scrambler."

He hung up and in less than a minute my other phone rang. "Now you listen to me," Sam said. "The lion is smart enough to tap into my home line, or yours. And if he is, you've just told him we're recording his calls. You need a vacation."

"Do we know where he is, I mean right this minute, Sam? Don't shit me."

"Why don't you call his secretary," Sam said, "and ask for an appointment."

"Don't fuck around, Sam, or I'll throttle you with my own hands."

"Easy, David, it's early in the morning. What's eating you?"

"Someone's been taken hostage."

"I know. The general's daughter."

"Why didn't you tell me? My goddamn cutoff took nine hours."

"I was just waiting till I thought you'd be awake. They've crossed state lines. The FBI has taken charge. Relax."

"Would you relax, Sam, if your sister was kidnapped by Monteleone's hoods?"

"I didn't know you had a sister. Or have you added the general's daughter to your string of dollies?"

"Sam, you wouldn't dare say that if we were in the same room. Where is he?"

"You don't think well when you're upset. He'll kill you."

"Nobody's killed me yet. I want him alive until I can squeeze out of him where they've taken her."

"How much help do you need?"

"Come on, Sam. You know a bunch of klutzes will only get in the way."

"I wasn't thinking of klutzes. How about Anderson and Willy?"

"And if Monteleone gets the three of us, what'll you do for a living? I'll handle it on my own."

"Do you want to give me the number of your Swiss bank account now or later?" You can always tell from Sam's voice when he stops kidding. "Listen, boychick, I don't like you playing with matches when you're in heat."

"You're wasting time, Sam. You know you can't stop me, you might as well help me. I'm coming over to your place, first to fix you and then to fix Monteleone."

Sam exhaled one of his profound sighs.

"If you come here, you'll be on the wrong side of Rome for him."

"That's better."

Sam gave me an address in a middle-class suburb. "He's been staying there more often than at the other two houses. His woman is there, but he never leaves her alone for long. Maybe he's there now. Maybe you'll be lucky. You going to tell me what your convoluted brain is up to?"

"No."

"Will you call me tomorrow?"

"No."

"I meant if you're alive."

"No."

"This isn't like you, David."

"It's like me as I am now."

"Which is what?"

Crazy for a woman? Ready to squeeze Monteleone's nuts until he orders his dogs to return Susan.

"Good-bye," I said, and hung up.

Sometimes when I get ready for work, I feel silly about the preparations. Can you imagine if someone could see me taping the sheath of my working knife to the side of my right leg? Or slipping the knife in and out several times to make sure it comes easily? Or putting the ankle holster on, then checking my Biretta and putting it in snug but not too snug. I was beginning to see myself with Susan's eyes. The 9mm went into my left underarm holster, my .45 into my belt in the small of my back. She'd laugh at me. I'd have to explain to her that it's only in TV cop shows they always seem to have time to reload, that it's easier to grab another weapon than to reload the one that's empty. Would she understand there's always a chance of my being frisked? That when an idiot pats you down your sides, he'll find the underarm gun, but chances are he'll miss either the one at my ankle or the one in the small of my back?

I checked myself in the mirror. Nothing showed. It pays to have an understanding tailor.

It took me fifty-five minutes to drive to within one block of the address Sam had given me. I looked around to make sure no one had seen me park.

Staying in the shadows on the other side of the street, I approached the house.

A man peered out of a window one flight up. I stood stock still, holding my breath. The man glanced up and down the street, then disappeared. There seemed to be a number of people moving around on the floor above him.

I checked down the block. A girl was being taught to ride a bicycle by a man who was probably her father.

A full three minutes passed before the fellow on the second floor came back to the window to check right and left. As soon as he disappeared this time, I crossed over and went around the back.

A teenager was lounging at the back of the house I was interested in. He yawned. Probably out late and got too little sleep. When I walked up to him, he stood up. In my best pidgin Italian I politely asked if Monteleone was home.

You would have thought I had asked the kid if he slept with his sister. I don't know if his expression was one of horror or anger, but he turned right around and started to head toward the back door. I grabbed him, got my hands around his throat and my right knee into his back hard. He went down.

If I'd kept my hands on his throat too short a time, he'd have screamed as soon as I let go. If I kept my hands around his neck too long, he would have died.

When I was sure he was out cold, I let go. In a year or two that kid will be zapping travelers at an airline counter. Or maybe this one will drop out and get away now that I've given him a scare. *David, you are getting soft!*

The kid had left the rear door open so he could get back in. I tried it very carefully, hoping the hinges didn't squeak.

A woman's voice from a nearby room startled me. The door slipped from my grip and slammed shut.

The woman's voice from the other room cried out, *"Rocco, chi c'é?"*

I pressed myself against the kitchen cupboards. Almost immediately she was in the room, a big Italian woman of fifty or more, wiping her hands on her apron. She spotted me and froze like a rabbit.

I said, *"Dov'é* Monteleone?"

The woman took an involuntary step back.

I drew out the 9mm from under my left arm. I told her to call the others.

She nodded.

I stepped behind the side of the refrigerator, which gave me more cover than anything else in that room.

That woman could have made a terrific hog caller back home. She let loose a string of names, four or five, that could be heard in Naples. They came thundering down the stairs, into the kitchen, asking what the hell was going on, and she, reinforcements at hand, nodded in my direction. They still couldn't see me, so I stepped out from behind the refrigerator, my 9mm pointing left to right at each of them in turn. There were four young toughs and a very pretty woman.

The old lady said a fast sentence that included the name Monteleone. As if on signal, the men turned to the young woman. She took a moment, then pointed at a rotund man, the last one into the room.

I shook my head. I'd seen Monteleone's face a dozen times in classified reports. He was handsome, clean shaven, almost as tall as I was. None of the men in that room resembled him. Damn! All I'd done was alert him. Sam Dracoff had said, *You don't think well when you're upset. He'll kill you.* I'd hoped to take Monteleone with me. I knew exactly the place where we'd go. When I'd implanted all my leftover sadism in black and blue marks on his body, I'd do a little number that convinces even the toughest prisoner that you are about to kill him. That's when I'd make my offer. His life for Susan. The question was could I trust myself to let him go after Susan was freed?

In any event, I was not up to a Saint Valentine's Day massacre of half a dozen Italians, though I'd have been doing the world a favor to get rid of these. Anyone in bed with Monteleone was not an innocent, not the girl who was probably his mistress, not these men, and not Rocco's mother. *You have no proof that they're members of Monteleone's team.* Something had happened to me since Susan. Maybe I was getting old. I was certainly getting soft.

Soft means you're on the way to death, Sam says.

I carefully backed my way toward the kitchen door. A jacket hanging unevenly on a man meant he had a poor tailor or was carrying a weapon. These people didn't have tailors. I could tell that at least two of these punks were armed. I had to assume the others must be. Trying to collect that many weapons would be dangerous. Besides, given the amount of hardware I'd come in with, how the hell was I going to add to what I was carrying? If Monteleone was in the house, he would have showed by now. Sam used to say *A mission has one objective. Don't get distracted by sideshows.* I got to the back door and ran.

The Rocco kid was stirring. I headed past the back of four houses, then ducked around the corner, and, still running, hit the street intending to get to my car just as fast as I could when I crashed into someone, who started cussing me out, then stopped.

The face was Monteleone's. He'd been heading toward the front of the house, obviously knew my face, just as I knew his. He was reaching under his arm when he saw my 9mm pointed at his face and stopped. *I had him.*

"Move!" I said, pointing my gun in the direction of my car. I couldn't keep my gun in his back. If I knew how to deal with that kind of situation, he would too.

I had to disarm him.

"Put your hands on the roof of that car."

"Which car?"

"Any car. Now."

He looked around at me. I'll never forget the expression on his face, no fear, just pure hatred. I was an American. And I was probably the one who got Iggie.

He spit.

"Hands on the car," I repeated.

There were two young men in the middle of the street, watching. One of them took off in the direction of the house I'd come from. *To raise the alarm. Work fast.*

Monteleone had his hands on the car. I went for the left inside first and pulled out the gun he'd reached for. I patted the right side down, checked the back in case he was carrying another weapon in his belt. It wasn't a perfect frisk. Sam was right. I should have had another man with me. I threw his Biretta underhand as far as I could into the bushes.

"Okay," I said. "My car's the black Fiat at the end of the street. Move." As he took his hands off the roof, I realized I was standing too damn close. He was turning left in a motion that would bring his fist right around to my face. My left forearm came up to ward off the blow as I swung my 9mm hoping to catch the side of his head, but Monteleone had a ducking move that took me by surprise. My left forearm took his blow, but he was coming up from underneath to grab my gun hand. I quickly stepped back. *He's counting on my not shooting.*

I squeezed the trigger. In that split second I saw the surprise in his expression, rage flaring into fear, as the shot slammed him backward. I looked down at Monteleone writhing, a bloody black hole in his forehead. There was no way that man could live.

David, you are a stupid fuck. Alive you had a hostage to trade for their hostage. The minute they hear the lion's dead, they'll take it out on Susan with a vengeance before they kill her.

I tucked the 9mm in its holster and ran to my car. For a second I thought of driving up to where Monteleone's body was and stuffing it into the trunk, but then I saw three or four of them nearing him. One was the girl. They saw me the same second I saw them. Two of them came on the run, pulling their hardware as they went.

Do you have any idea what it's like, knowing a bullet's about to tear into you any second? I was just sliding into the driver's seat when a bullet smashed into the metal above the windshield, sending a sliver tearing into my earlobe. I kept my head low and roared away, turning the wheel violently as another shot slammed into the seat next to me. With a clear road ahead of me I accelerated to a hundred and ten kilometers, hoping nobody but nobody would come out of a side street without looking.

I slowed down when I was sure I was safe, and felt my right ear. I never knew an ear could bleed so much. What the hell, a third Oak Leaf Cluster for my Purple Heart.

I could hear Sam's voice as clearly as if he'd been sitting beside me. *So the once-perfect operator David Smith has fucked up royally.*

I had no defense. I'd condemned Susan to death.

CHAPTER 34

Sam Dracoff

David sounded terrible on the phone. When he finally showed up, I said, "What the hell do you think I'm running, a safe house for war drop-outs?"

I could see he wasn't in the mood for Jewish humor.

"Monteleone's dead." He looked lost.

"You?" I asked.

"Afraid so."

He wasn't kidding me. "Have a seat," I said. "Want some coffee?" He shook his head.

"So tell me."

After he did, I said, "Don't expect a medal from me, boychick. Alive he could have been useful in this operation. If you're going to react like a freelancer, don't count on me to cover your ass."

"Sam, I ran right into him. He recognized me. What was I supposed to do, say 'Excuse me'?"

"What are you going to do about the girl?"

"You mean Monteleone's girl?"

"I mean your goddamn girl. Susan what's-her-name?"

"She's not a girl."

"I beg your pardon. The young woman."

"I need your tapes of Monteleone's telephone calls. If I can find out where his boys have taken her, I'll do the rest."

"I sent the tapes by air courier to New York."

"To whom?" David bellowed.

"To the FBI," I said.

"You gave them to the fucking FBI and not to me? I can't believe it."

"Then believe it," I said. I may be the only person in the world who can point a finger at David Smith's nose and get away with it. "I kept a copy, schmuck. You can have the copy. David, you damn well better listen with one hundred percent of your alleged brains. You are a priest," I said. "You can be celibate or you can fuck your housekeeper, but you can't get *involved*, understand? Oh sure, some priests get attached to their housekeepers. Love can do some surprising things. I know. You know I know. Now listen. The FBI will track the kidnappers down."

"And get Susan killed!"

"You think you're the only hero in the world. There are plenty of people who can deal with a hostage situation."

"This isn't your normal hostage situation."

"And why not? Because you happen to be loony about the hostage? You know how dangerous it is to get mixed—"

"Sam, are you giving me orders?"

"You bet," I said. "Holy orders. You listen. Or you pretend to listen, and then you go off and do whatever the fuck you please. I've always tolerated you, David, because you deliver and I don't have anyone to replace you. Yet. But I'm looking. If you go to the States and get yourself knocked off, what'll I do in the meantime, give Europe to the terrorists?"

"Why don't you retire, Sam. You're getting old."

"Thanks."

David insults me and what do I do? I went to get the tapes.

When I set David up with earphones, I said, "I haven't listened to the latest ones, but I don't think it will do you any good. What you need are these."

I handed him the duplicates of Monteleone's phone bills. The Italians were very reluctant to give me American-style bills with the destination of all calls listed. They'd had to write them in by hand.

"Don't kiss me," I said when David shook my hand as if I'd just given him a present. "The neighbors will get the wrong idea."

David studied the phone bills for less than ten minutes before he turned to me with the eyes of a fanatic and said, "Where the hell is Chester, New Jersey?"

CHAPTER 35

Susan

When the sedan stopped it was in the driveway of a ranch-style house. I don't remember walking into the house. How could I walk if my legs were tied? Was I carried?

I woke up with a godawful headache on a narrow bed. The headache was all in one place. When I felt the swelling on the back of my head, it hurt to the touch. *To the touch?*

My hands were free! The rope that had trussed me was gone except for the burn marks on the inside of both of my wrists. The bastards must have hit me with something to knock me out. Why couldn't they have just put a blindfold on me like . . . and I almost laughed. I had actually been about to say *like civilized people.*

I tried the doorknob very slowly. The door was locked. Both sash windows had been nailed shut from the outside. Each half of the window had six panes, and my first thought was to break a pane and remove the jagged pieces of glass. I'd never be able to squeeze through. Besides, they'd hear the glass breaking. I put my ear against the door. I could hear breathing on the other side.

The one blessing of this place was a small bathroom off this bedroom. There was no bathtub or shower stall, but it had a wash basin with a piece of Irish Spring soap and a roll of paper towels and, best of all, a toilet. My grandmother Nelly used to tell us what it was like in rural Illinois when they no longer had to use chamber pots or go out in the middle of a freezing night to the privy. Grandpa

Edwin had arranged to have their first indoor bathroom installed while Nelly was visiting relatives. On her arrival home she was surprised and overjoyed. I felt the same way when I woke up and saw the open door of the bathroom. They had removed the spring bolt so that I couldn't lock the door from the inside. It didn't matter.

My hunger was now coming in insistent waves. How long had I been here? Or was it just nerves that made me want to fill the clamoring void in my belly? Here I was, ostensibly an educated advocate of law, waiting for a door to be opened and food to be brought to me like a creature in a zoo.

At the same time I dreaded the door opening. Millennia ago my ancestors must have huddled just like this in caves with a dark fear of anything outside.

The house was on a hillside. From one window I could see down into what looked like an uninhabited valley far below. From the window near the bed I could see uphill into rough bramble and trees. Could we be in Pennsylvania? Were we still in New Jersey?

At one point, when we'd pulled off the road, Guido and the driver had an argument in very rapid Italian over a tattered map and I'd heard the words *Chester* and *Long Valley*. I hadn't the slightest idea where those towns were, if they were towns. And when they mentioned Newark and Trenton, I got confused because from what I could see out the windows, we were nowhere near cities. Maybe I would be able to steal a glance at that map. Or any map.

The sound of the door opening was unmistakable. It was Guido, a big smile on his face.

"Everything nice?" he asked.

I did not break from the stare of his gray eyes.

"*Gabinetto*, okay?" he said.

Was he trying to be friendly?

Only one way to find out. "Something to eat?" I asked.

Guido zipped down his fly.

I backed off, my gaze flying around the room in search of something I could use as a weapon.

"No eat?" Guido said. "*Tanto peggio! Peggio così!* He zipped up his fly. "Maybe you eat later, yes?"

CHAPTER 36

Heather Whitcomb

Watching that instrument, I willed it to ring. The silence was profound. When the phone finally did ring, the noise was shattering. I nearly tripped over the corner of the rug in my hurry to answer it.

Earl Morath had already picked up. They'd installed an earpiece extension so incoming calls could be listened in on without the sound of an extension phone being lifted. In the basement, they'd also set up equipment for recording both sides of every call. Old friends who'd read about the kidnapping in the papers called to offer consolation. What was I supposed to do, tell them the call was being recorded? Morath had said *absolutely not* to that idea. All I could do was keep the conversations short, not get the line tied up with sympathy. Every false alarm eroded my reserves.

Each time I said "Hello" my heart hammered.

"Meesees Wheetcoomb?"

I held my breath. "This is she."

I could see Morath signaling. I was supposed to keep the caller on the line as long as possible.

"Your daughter will no get food until ran-some pay."

He sounded like he was reading the words. Perhaps he had written them out. I couldn't quite understand all of what he was saying. Who ran? What pay? Morath scribbled on a piece of paper: RANSOM DEMAND. KEEP HIM TALKING.

"Please speak clearly," I said, "I can barely hear you."

"Two meelyon dollar. *Capisci?* Understand?"

My chest felt ready to burst. Morath was nodding at me, encouraging me to remember my lines.

"You know I don't have that kind of money. Where can I possibly get it?"

"You get, daughter eat. You no get, daughter no eat, yes? I call tomorrow. You get money, *capisci?*"

"I can barely hear you," I said. "Could you please repeat that?"

He had already hung up. I could see Morath shaking his head. I hadn't been on long enough for them to trace the call.

CHAPTER 37

Susan

The clatter of my keepers' footsteps made me swing my legs off the bed in a hurry.

The door opened. It was Guido. His face was a fury. "Your mother *stupida*."

He looked ready to strike me.

"I don't understand," I said.

"She no get ransom."

Think before you say anything.

"How can you be sure?" I said.

He didn't seem to understand.

"I'm sure she'll try to get whatever you want."

"Try not good enough. Show me your fingers."

I held out my left hand.

"Which finger she recognize? Show other hand."

Dear God, no.

He grabbed my right hand. On my fourth finger there was a plain gold ring with a single ruby Mom and Dad had given me when I had graduated from high school.

"She recognize ring?"

"Yes," I said, starting to take the ring off.

"No, no," he said. "Keep ring on finger. We send finger, she get *denaro, moneta, rapidamente*, eh?"

One voice said *They wouldn't do that.* The other voice said *They cut off the Getty grandson's ear, why not your finger?"*

"I come back." Guido slammed the door. I could hear his footsteps—had he forgotten to lock the door? Before I could reach it, I heard the key turning in the lock. Probably Poco stuck with guard duty.

I looked at the ring on my right hand. I tried to imagine myself in courtrooms gesturing to the jury with my fourth finger missing. That's what people would see first. I would be Susan Whitcomb, that lawyer with a missing finger. Know how she got her finger cut off? She wasn't ransomed fast enough.

Count your blessings. A while back you thought they were going to kill you.

On the other hand, they could still kill you. Then a missing finger wouldn't make any difference, would it?

The door opened. Poco came right at me, shoved his dirty hand against my mouth. I scratched at his face, drawing bloodlines down his cheek. He smashed the back of his hand against my face.

That's when I saw Guido in the doorway holding a wooden tray in one hand and a large kitchen knife in the other.

CHAPTER 38

David

Sam drove me to the airport, his voice rising and falling in a familiar incantation. His uncle-like face had a mustache with uneven gray patches, and eyes that always looked as if they knew something that you didn't. Behind the wheel you saw a quiet hulk getting on to fifty-two or -three, but you knew right away this wasn't a body you'd want to tangle with physically. He had a deceptive peacefulness in his expressions. Sam once told me he came from a long line of desert warriors who didn't pick fights, but if you started one they'd beat you the first time and pre-empt you the second.

When I first met Sam, out of his earshot I used to refer to him as jewboy, which is the kind of thing we called Jews back home where there weren't any. Somebody must have snitched. One day Sam just reached over and got me in his grip and floored me, then put out a hand to pick me up and said, "How about you don't call me jewboy anymore. I'm not a boy."

I waited till the next day to say I was sorry.

"Sorry about what?" he said. "I don't remember anything."

Sam's a liar. He remembers everything.

He even remembers that once when he saved my ass, I said to him in a moment of weakness, "I wish I'd had an older brother like you."

Sam looked as if I'd insulted him. "What are you talking about? If I'm not your brother, who is?"

Once we were assigned a tough mission in Beirut, Sam, me, and a skinny fellow named Rand. I didn't learn till later that Sam had objected to Rand's being assigned, and was told to mind his business. Before the chopper picked us up in Cyprus, Sam and I were alone for a couple of minutes and I asked him why he'd come on the mission. "You could have assigned somebody," I said.

He looked at me as if he really didn't want to answer. I tried for a look that said *Answer me*.

Sam let out one of those meaningful sighs and said, "You can't count on Rand for anything that depends on having a conscience. He ought to go back home and become a politician."

"He'd never get elected."

"That's true." Sam laughed. "I guess he'll have to become a banker. I'm going to get rid of him."

Rand never came back from West Beirut. Sam's only comment was "The Shi'ites mustered him out before I could."

"You risked your neck trying to save him."

"He may be a little shit but he was an American. I got reflexes."

"You tried to save him because you would have preferred to kill him yourself."

"Something like that, boychick."

"Sam," I said, "how come a guy with a graduate degree like you gets involved in work like this? You ought to be a professor somewhere."

"Yeah, yeah." He thought for a second. "I guess I'm still worried about ovens."

"That war was over a long time ago."

"There are still a lot of oven-cookers in this world, boychick." He pinched my cheek. "You could be one of them if I don't watch you carefully while you're growing up."

In the car, Sam's voice snapped, "You're not listening to me. I'm not talking for my health."

"I'm listening," I said.

"You're a liar. What did I just say?"

"You said I'm a liar."

Sam laughed from deep in his gut. Then the right half of his mustache came up like it sometimes does when he's being Sam the Schoolteacher. "When someone else talks you can be deaf for all I care. Right now I want your ears pointed in this direction."

"Yes, sir."

"Don't give me that sir shit. Just listen. The FBI has zeroed in on Chester, too. They have a battery of people phoning every listed and unlisted number in the Long Valley area. Everyone who answered with an Italian accent got marked down for a house call."

"Nothing solid?"

"Solid? Solid? Sure solid. When Monteleone's man phoned a second time, he got hysterical about the money not being ready yet. You know something, David, my personal theory is that prick was getting together a stash for stateside operations. That could be a real headache."

"Susan'd be dead already if it wasn't for the money."

"True."

"They'll kill her the second they've got their hands on it."

"Boychick," Sam said, "psyching yourself down before a mission is bad enough. Despair is out, hear me? Besides, during that second call, your Mama Whitcomb did a fine job of keeping the son-of-a-bitch on the line. The call got traced to an outdoor phone booth in a gas station near Chester."

"Why the fuck didn't you say something right away?"

"What's with you? You want I should tell the end before the beginning?"

"Get on with it."

"Now you're listening? The FBI concentrated on phones in houses on the side of that road away from Chester. And on smaller roads branching off, the theory being a gang of foreigners could hide out in an isolated place better than in the middle of some small town. The FBI isn't dumb."

"Just not as smart as we are."

"Something like that. You know why the Bureau is always playing catch-up? Before the war they hired mainly lawyers. Never send a lawyer to do a man's job."

"You don't like lawyers, do you, Sam?"

"Lawyers' wives like lawyers. And sometimes not even then. The last one my ex-wife hired makes the Ayatollah look like a saint. Mind you, there are a few respectable—"

Sam suddenly swerved into the outside lane so hard I could feel the cut of the shoulder belt. He stepped on the gas, then cut back into the right lane.

"That bastard was slowing down because he thought I was in a hurry."

"Driving is a sport here. You got something against sport?"

"I'm too old to be playing chicken on the road. David, these people had half the geniuses in the world B.C. and in the Renaissance. You see any da Vincis around today? Anybody who calls that progress has got to be blind."

After a bit Sam said, "This Susan, she's a serious thing with you?"

"That's none of your business, Sam."

"It's my business to know what I'm dealing with. There are two kinds of people who are vulnerable in this business. Teenagers and people in love."

"I've got a question."

"If it's about love, don't bother. Nobody's got an answer."

"Did Monteleone's people come through Kennedy?"

"You're changing the subject."

"Damn right."

Sam shrugged. "Nobody provided the security people at Kennedy with their files. They've got one of Monteleone just in case he ever tries to come back home, but who'd ever have thought of his gang trying something in the States? I doubt any of them have ever been there. God knows what kind of passports and visas they came on. Maybe they didn't come through Kennedy. It could have been anywhere."

"If you were the lion, how would you send them in? Hey, keep your eyes on the road."

"And since when are you the careful driver, boychick?"

"I'm needed on the other side of the ocean, not in the Rome morgue. You haven't answered my question."

"I'm thinking, do you mind?"

I waited. Finally Sam said, "What I'd do is fly them to Montreal on French passports, have them drive down in a rented car."

"Too big a risk at the border."

"Not if they ditched on the Canadian side, walked across some-where safe, and took another car down to where the snatch took place. We shouldn't be wasting time on how they did it, David. They're there."

"Sam?"

"Oh-oh. Every time you say Sam that way, you want something. What is it this time? You want to fly the Concorde? The Concorde doesn't fly out of Rome."

I hesitated for one more second, then said, "How about if you went with me? Not later, now, on the same plane."

"When a loner like you wants company, David, something's wrong. You've got your pecker in your pocketbook."

"What's that supposed to mean?"

"You've got too much of a personal interest in the hostage."

I didn't say a word.

"A strong, personal interest doesn't just mean a loss of objectivity. It means you've cut one important option out."

"What option?"

"David, you've always got to consider the possibility of *not* res-cuing the hostage. You're supposed to be an experienced profes-sional. Look what you're costing me already."

"You're coming with me?"

"No change of clothes, no toothbrush even. You're making a slob out of me."

"I'll buy you a toothbrush. I'll even buy you some underwear, how's that?"

"Next thing it'll show up on your expense account. I might as well put it on mine."

"Sam?"

"Yeah."

"Thanks."

"Think nothing of it. What's a little transatlantic trip between friends. What are you doing for hardware?"

"Locker at Kennedy."

"David, they open up those damn lockers after twenty-four hours."

"I don't use public lockers."

"Oh?"

"I've got a full-length one in the mechanics' changing room near one of the hangars."

"I'm glad to see you sometimes still use your brains."

"Then why are you grumpy about going?"

"I had a date tonight."

"Call her from Leonardo da Vinci."

"Don't be a schmuck, David. What would I say? Hello, pussy, I'm sorry but I had an unexpected trip to America? She knows my ex will serve me with papers if she ever finds out where I am. I never go to the States if I can avoid it."

"I forgot," I said. "I'm sorry."

"S'okay, kid. Glad to go. Wouldn't want it on my conscience if something happened to you."

"Nothing has ever happened to me."

"Except falling in love, right? That day at the beach I saw you in swimming trunks, remember?"

"I didn't know you noticed."

"What I noticed, schmucko, is the exit wound in your right side. You've been lucky, that's all. I'm coming along to improve your luck."

The flight over was only one-quarter full. We had a lot of room to ourselves.

Most vets like to tell war stories. Sam tells them better than most, so I was surprised when I woke up with a start and realized I had dozed off, probably while Sam was talking.

"I'm sorry."

"Why be sorry, *bubele*. A boy needs his rest."

At Kennedy, a customs man gave Sam a hard time because he didn't have luggage.

"Sonny," Sam told the customs man as he flashed an I.D., "ask your supervisor to waddle over here."

The supervisor didn't waddle. She was a freckled redhead who looked peachy in uniform. Sam had to switch gears. I never saw him tough it with a woman. Whatever he said to her didn't stop her from taking time to make a phone call before she told the fellow at the counter that it was okay.

"Thank you," said Sam. "If I had a hat I'd tip it."

"If you had a hat," the woman said, "I wouldn't see how bald you're getting."

I had to keep from laughing. Sam grew up in a world where women didn't talk back.

Sam made a couple of phone calls while I collected my hardware. It was all in one blue and orange duffel bag with stenciled lettering that said PRINCETON. I got back just as Sam was hanging up.

"You know where this Scarborough place is?" he asked.

"Yep."

"Train?"

"From here we'd better rent a car."

A policeman was standing in front of the house, yawning. If Monteleone's people ever came driving by, they'd shoot the cop before they were out of their car. In a mean mood, they'd kneecap him.

Mrs. Whitcomb came to the door to identify us. She looked like a ghost of herself.

"Oh David," she said, "am I glad to see you." She actually kissed my cheek.

I introduced Sam Dracoff as a colleague. She barely nodded at him.

Inside, I said, "What's wrong?"

"You'll see." She led us into the living room and introduced the agent-in-charge, a fellow by the name of Earl Morath, and three others. One of them with earphones looked like a kid with a Walkman.

Sam and I were led over to a side table. On it was a small box. Mrs. Whitcomb walked away from us to the other side of the room, where she burst out crying. I wanted to go to her, but Sam grabbed my arm. The FBI man opened the box. In it was a severed finger.

"They're up to their old tricks," I said. "They've got a mortician somewhere who supplies them with things like this." Then I noticed the ring. "They could have put her ring on someone else's finger," I said.

But I looked at the fingernail. And the finger. And it wasn't just anybody's.

CHAPTER 39

David

"This is the twentieth century," Sam said. "I have to keep reminding myself."

Earl Morath said, "You guys sure it's her finger?"

"It's her ring," I said. "It's her kind of nail polish."

"Well, we'll know for sure when we find the rest of her with a finger missing," Morath said.

Sam knew I could have killed the fuck for saying that. His hands were on my shoulders, ready to hold me down in the chair if I tried to get up.

"Don't try," ordered Sam the mind reader.

There's a thing I do. It's like pulling a hood over all of me, telling myself I can feel nothing. It worked for me in combat, why isn't it working now? My face was on fire.

"Sit down." Sam Dracoff pointed to a chair.

I didn't realize I had stood up. The FBI man was looking at me. Mrs. Whitcomb was looking at me. The man who'd rented the house, Webster, was looking at me. Sam was looking at me. I wanted to say *Why are you all looking at me?*

I heard footsteps coming down the stairs. We all looked in that direction. It was Professor Adams.

"What are you doing here?" I said.

"I could say the same." Adams's bloodshot eyes glared at me as if I was the one who'd cut her finger off. We were ready to tear each other to pieces over what was left.

It was Earl Morath who said, "I think we'd better strategize in a smaller group. Mrs. Whitcomb, do you mind?"

She dabbed at her eyes with the corner of a handkerchief. "I think I'll go out back. Fresh air always restores me."

"Better stay inside," Morath said. "Upstairs."

"I'll take her up," Webster volunteered.

I turned to Adams. "I wish you'd get out of here." I hadn't expected to be that rude.

"Young man, when you've been in *Who's Who* for twenty years, you may speak to me that way, but you may not speak to me that way now. I have every right to be here. Susan is my fiancée."

Sam's puzzled expression lasted only a second. "All right," he said. "Everybody's tense. Let's use our heads." He went over to Adams. "I'm Sam Dracoff. I apologize for Mr. Smith. He's disturbed because he went back to Europe too soon and feels that if he'd remained here the abduction might have been prevented."

Sam made that up, but it was true. He shook Adam's hand. "I'm very pleased to make your acquaintance. It's an honor. Nevertheless . . ." and Sam looked around as if he despised all of us, ". . . I think this meeting better be limited to people experienced in hostage operations. Mr. Morath, please stay."

Adams had no choice but to go back upstairs. I thought of all the years he'd known Susan and the very few hours I'd had with her. I hated him.

As soon as he was gone, Sam said to me, "You better now?"

The fiery flush was gone. I wanted to do something with my hands. I could use a fist fight. Anything.

"Lost your voice?" Sam asked. "I said are you feeling better."

What the hell was I supposed to say? I nodded.

"Okay." Sam turned to Morath. "Bring us up to date."

"Do you have to leave that thing lying around?" I said, gesturing toward the box with the finger.

Morath motioned to the guy with the Walkman. "Art," he said, "put it in the freezer, will you?"

Art was a comic. He held the little box with the finger at arm's length with one hand and used the other to hold his nostrils closed.

Morath said, "Art, not the garbage, the freezer."

The funny man said, "How about the parts department?"

"Shut up!" I roared.

"Okay, okay," Art said, "I thought the family was all upstairs."

In Nam, after watching them fling the body bags on trucks as if they were filled with garbage, I thought nothing like that could ever bother me again. I could have wrung Walkman's neck and Sam knew it.

"David!" Sam snapped. "Cool it."

Morath said, "We've zeroed in on the house. It's on a hill overlooking Long Valley. Owned by an older couple name of Telson. They're probably on vacation somewhere, they haven't been seen around town for days. We've got people watching the house from a distance. If they spot the Telsons coming back, they'll hold them up. We don't want them walking in on that crew."

"Good thinking," said Sam. That's what he always said when he wanted to take control away from someone.

"I thought you fellows were trained to retake hijacked planes."

"We don't shoot the tires out," Sam said. "We leave that to the FBI."

"I thought you operated overseas exclusively."

"I don't believe in turf battles," Sam said. "Let's work together, okay?"

Morath nodded.

Damn if Sam didn't look at me, expecting me to nod too.

"We'll need a terrain map of the area," Sam said.

"Got one," said Morath. "And photos from all sides."

"Good," said Sam, always surprised when someone from some other service did things right.

"We can cut the phone to the house," Morath said. "They might go berserk if they hear Monteleone's dead."

"*We* need to be able to phone," I said impatiently. "Do they have newspapers in the house?"

"They haven't been seen going out for any," Morath said. "They've got a TV."

"If they've heard about Monteleone on TV, she's as good as dead."

Morath smiled. "We took care of that."

"Took care of what?" I said.

"The antenna on the TV's picking up pure junk. We've got a beam on it. They can't use rabbit's ears in that area. Too much high ground."

"You've thought of everything," said Sam.

"Not how to get her out of there alive," I said. "Is the army or air force in on this?"

"The air force," Morath said, "isn't about to bomb Long Valley. You two and my men are all we've got. We can co-opt any local law enforcement we need."

I wasn't listening too carefully. I was getting the kind of buzz I sometimes get when things suddenly fit into place.

"I know how we're going to do it," I said.

They both looked at me. Then the phone rang like a fire alarm, and Morath stepped quickly to the hall phone to pick it up. "Yes?"

His guy with the Walkman nodded. Then Morath said, "Now you listen a minute. We *have* the money, it's in a suitcase ready to be delivered. Two million. Dollars, not lire. We just want to be sure Miss Whitcomb is . . ." He hesitated only a second. ". . . not harmed any further."

It was frustrating hearing just one side of that conversation. I stepped up real close to Morath, pointing at myself. I mouthed the words *Hand me the fucking phone.*

Morath looked at Dracoff.

Sam nodded.

Morath said, "Put Miss Whitcomb on the phone so we can assure ourselves."

I took the phone out of Morath's hand. "Is she still alive?"

"Oh live, live, okay," the voice said.

I said, "Bring her to the phone."

Nothing. Fucking nothing.

I shouted into the mouthpiece loud enough to blast his ear. "*Porta la donna al telefono!*"

"*Un momento.*"

It wasn't a moment. It was a goddamn year till I heard some shuffling, then Susan said, "Hello, who is this?"

I can't describe what it was like to hear her voice. It wasn't just proof that she was alive. I was in love with her voice, too.

"Who is this?"

"David."

That's all I said and she started crying.

"Please," I said.

"You know what they did?"

"I saw. They'll pay for it."

She cried. I guess I should have said something different. I motioned Morath to move away. There was nothing I could do about the Walkman guy. I said it anyway. "I love you."

She mumbled something I couldn't understand about her finger. What could I say—*It's only a finger?* I was afraid they would kill her. Suddenly she yelped. I could hear her in the background away from the phone yelling, "Stop pulling my hair!"

When the bastard got back on, I forced my voice down. "Where do I bring the money? Go slow. Say that again. Why don't we meet somewhere? Anywhere you say."

I listened carefully, then covered the mouthpiece and whispered to Sam, "He wants it brought to them."

"They've got a perfect field of fire from the house," Morath said. "It's on a hill."

"Okay," I said into the phone. "The money will be in the suitcase. I carry suitcase." I felt like an idiot, talking pidgin.

"What your name?"

All I could think of was the name of that hotel in Rome. "Tantillo," I said.

"*Paesano*," he said.

Sure. "I will be on foot." He didn't seem to understand about foot. "Walking," I explained. "*Camminando*. You must keep her, *donna*, standing in doorway so we know she is okay."

That was my insurance. You can't prop a standing body up to look as if it was alive. "I will stop fifty feet from the house. I will open the suitcase, *capisci?*"

He didn't say anything.

"Did you hear me?"

"I hear."

"When I open suitcase," I said, "you come down, see money, let girl come to me, take suitcase back to house, leave girl, yes?"

"No, no, no," he said. "We keep girl to airport. You have airplane to go Roma. No tricks, we let girl go."

"I'll have a plane at La Guardia."

"No, no, no, not La Guardia small plane. Kennedy big plane for overseas, yes?"

"Yes," I said. I hadn't been able to fool him about the airports. Now there was no way he would trust me.

CHAPTER 40

Guido

If suitcase is full of money, okay. But how I gonna know if suitcase have two million inside? Counting money take too much time.

Monteleone, he says give all the money to New Ark cousin so Poco can see. This way Poco can swear to Jesus Christ Mary Saints I don't keep the money. The first day we come to America I call New Ark cousin's number, tell him I am friend of Monteleone from Italy, hello. New Ark cousin hang up phone bang. Must be a mistake, yes? I call back, he don't even answer phone. I call next day, nothing. How I gonna find New Ark cousin now?

Monteleone says don't bring money to Italy, give it to New Ark cousin. So what I gonna do, bury money in a hole? I gonna try to bring money to Italy. I think if I check bag on plane, maybe it gets lost. If it don't get lost, man in Italy says what you bought in America, open the bag. Oh yeah, two million dollars. You in drugs or something? *Carabinieri* take me, *finito*. Then Monteleone gonna scream why you not leave money with New Ark cousin, hey? Next time he calls, I ask him why New Ark cousin hangs up, then never home? The lion says cops listen on phone, cousin afraid of cops. Whatsa difference? Cops know I get the money.

Monteleone wants the money with New Ark cousin so he have it when he come back to America, right? Right.

I'ma trying to think, but Poco he's waving his hands like in front of my face. I says, "Poco, whatsa matter, you scared of something, hey?"

"No scared."

"Like fuck you not scared."

"They come get woman."

"Poco, you see bad side. See good side. They coming to give money, *stupido*. They want woman, too bad. We keep woman. We take woman to Monteleone like he said."

I pray to God Monteleone telephones soon. Meantime, we study the plan, make sure everything right, we go, bang, we back, Monteleone make new plan, no waiting for nothing. Waiting is shit. This place, even the TV gotta crazy picture. Whatsamatter these people live here don't fix the picture?

Like God answer my prayer, the phone rings. Let ring five times then pick up so Monteleone know everything okay. Four. Five.

I pick up. "Allo."

It's not Monteleone. I hear a woman's voice. "Maria?" I say.

"*Si.*

"*Che c'è?*"

"The lion is dead."

I tell her you lie, you not Maria, you policewoman.

"I don't lie, Guido. He is dead."

I want to tear world to pieces. *Mamma mia*, Monteleone he is so young, impossible he gonna be dead.

To phone I say, "I kill the woman here."

"No, bring back the woman. I will kill her myself."

I want to howl like a wolf. I want to break everything. "What I do if lion dead?"

"The lioness is not dead, Guido. Do what he said to do."

"Monteleone's cousin?"

"Yes."

"He hangs up on me or he's not there."

"Try once more."

"I already try once more."

"I'll call from here. I'll tell him to be in touch, okay?"

"Police hear what we say."

"It doesn't matter. Listen. The man who killed the lion, his name is David Smith."

I say name so I remember it. "David Smith."

"Right. He is six feet. Sometimes he wears glasses. They are not real glasses. He wears wigs, sometimes brown, sometimes black. It's not his real hair. Do you understand? I can't hear you."

"I understand."

"The man with the wig who killed the lion . . ."

"Yes?"

"He's the same man who killed Iggie."

"Mother of God!"

"Remember, Guido."

"I remember."

"I'll see you in Rome."

"What I do with the money?"

"Can't talk now. Everything will be okay, we'll do everything here. Call me later."

Maria is smart woman. I figure before our plane arrives in Italy, she and the boys take some big man hostage. They let us go out of airport, maybe then we let hostage go.

"*Ciao,*" I say.

"*Ciao.*"

I go to back bedroom where Poco sits on chair outside of door. Poco looks at me. He is always worried I tell him bad news. This time he right.

I say to him, "Our lion is dead."

Poco says I lie. I hit him. I swear no lie. Dumb Poco hug me. I hug him.

I open the back bedroom door. There she is, on the bed, staring at bandaged hand. Too bad she's not a man. I cut something else off, too.

CHAPTER 41

Susan

Mom told me that when I was first brought to her hospital room by the nurse, she did what most new mothers do. She counted my toes and fingers to assure herself I was perfectly normal. *Now look.*

I stare at my bandaged right hand. There is its thumb and there are the three other fingers, with that obscene emptiness that shrieks with pain where the ring finger used to be.

If this were an accident, they would have put ice around the finger and rushed it to the hospital along with me so some microsurgeon could sew it back. *Who could believe that human beings would do a thing like this on purpose?*

Having been exposed to the human race, I believe it. I gesture to the jury with my right hand, its small stump proclaiming *I, too, have been a witness.* The melodrama in my mind founders on the simple fact that the pulsing pain in my hand has come back. The bastards won't give me anything. Not even aspirin. I'm sure it's infected. I told them the knife was dirty and they said *Good, dirty American deserve dirty knife.*

Just at that moment I hear a wail resounding from the front of the house. Then a long silence. Finally, voices outside, and my door opening. Guido is enraged. Poco looks angry, frantic, frenzied. I don't understand what Guido is saying to him, but they drag me from the room into the kitchen, open a door, and I see a set of stairs going down. Guido shoves me. I'm so afraid he'll throw me down and break my back. My feet find the stairs. I go down before they can shove me down. Guido follows me. Poco traipses after Guido. I wonder where the third man went. There's an awful smell in the dank dark. It isn't their smell, it is something else.

At the bottom, Guido shoves me toward a corner of the basement near the boiler. He picks up the end of a clothesline and ties my hands behind my back. With his open hand, he slaps me in the face with all his strength.

I howl at him like an animal.

He slaps my face again and again, until the pulsing pain in my cheek is as bad as the pain in my hand. Something has to have happened that he's taking out on me. All I can think is *Dear God, where are You?*

They abandon me in the near-darkness. The only light comes through a window well. I can barely see around me. The stench is overpowering. It's very dark in here. I try to wiggle myself closer to the boiler. The rope is rubbing my wrists raw.

I inch myself along until I'm at the side of the boiler. Every move slackens the rope a bit. Can I reach whatever the other end of the rope is tied to?

Suddenly I feel something. I swing around to see better. The other end of the rope that binds me is tied to . . . I can't believe my eyes.

In the dark I can now make out the ragbag bodies of an old woman and an older man, his mouth agape, his uppers loose on one side. He has only one eye. Where the other eye should have been, there is a black hole. I can't see the woman's eyes because her shattered spectacles are still on her face. Dark blood has dried under her nose.

No wonder Guido and his friends weren't worried about the owners of this house returning. They are already here.

CHAPTER 42

David

Sam was mapping out our plan of attack around the kitchen table when Adams decided to intrude again.

Adams's manner had changed. He was again the man I'd met at the airport, suave, urbane, in control of himself and his environment.

"I should very much like to be a part of this," he said. "It would please me greatly if I could help."

David, I said to myself, *keep your mouth shut. Let Sam handle the public relations.*

Sam put a paternal arm on the man's shoulder. "I really appreciate that, Professor Adams," he said, "I just don't want you getting hurt."

"I am not afraid."

"You can get hurt whether you're afraid or not. We're trained to deal with situations like this. If anything goes wrong, Miss Whitcomb's life would be . . ."

Sam moved a finger across his throat.

You could see that Adams thought Sam's gesture vulgar. "There need be no danger to anyone if I were to raise the ransom."

"Oh?" Sam said, "How do you propose to do that?"

"There are about thirty-five thousand people in the Columbia community if you count the graduate schools and Teachers College. I'd organize a fund drive. If only one out of ten gave . . ."

"And how long would that take?"

"Only a few days."

"And you'd expect the hostage to still be alive?"

"Perhaps I could get one of the trustees to advance the two million while I raised the money to repay it. Perhaps the university itself might consider doing that."

"If they set that kind of precedent," Sam said, "what they'd be doing is setting up all Columbia people, past and present, as especially desirable targets for any terrorists wanting to raise substantial amounts of money. Besides, to be perfectly realistic, Professor Adams, if you had two million in cash today and brought it to these people—"

"They'd take it, wouldn't they?"

"Oh yes. They'd take it and then take you as an additional hostage."

"There would have to be an agreement beforehand."

"They'll agree to anything to get the money and you or anyone else into their hands. Professor, please get it through your head that you're not dealing with student protesters."

Adams's urbanity seemed to have drained away. His words seeped out like a stain. "There . . . must be . . . something useful I could do."

You can shove it is what I would have told him. *You can get your academic ass out of the way.* Sam switched gears like a pro. He said, "I'm not sure you'd approve of what we're about to do."

"You're going to try to rescue Susan. I want to do the same."

"Of course," said Sam. "But good will isn't what we hanker for right now. How are your technical skills?"

"Such as?"

"Can you split an apple at a hundred yards? Better yet, a man's head? And most important, can you shoot someone who hasn't yet shot at you?"

"Whatever do you mean?"

"When we go into a job like this, the only way we can succeed is to move against the hostage-takers first and fast."

"I know what you mean. Shoot to kill."

"A wounded man can still target the hostage. Or one of us."

"Aren't you risking Susan being caught between two groups of men firing guns? Can't the police help?"

"We don't have a traffic problem," Sam said, his impatience finally surfacing.

"Don't the police have people trained in hostage work who try to talk hostage-takers into surrendering? Who wait them out?"

"I wish we had that luxury, professor. We know these people. They start out edgy. If there's a delay in getting the ransom, they work up a head of steam. That's when they do execute something to prove they mean business. They've already done that by sending us her finger."

Adams crossed his arms in front of his chest as if to physically defend himself against what Sam was saying.

Old Sam was unstoppable. "Professor Adams, you know much better than we do that if we fire first it can hardly be called self-defense. We don't obey the law. A long fire fight can get people killed on both sides. Including hostages. We don't do battle, we move in fast and get out faster. We know the other side's intentions and we try like hell to pre-empt them. Understood?"

Adams nodded as if a crick held his neck in an odd position. Call me a bastard, I was enjoying his discomfort.

"Professor Adams," Sam said, "the police deal with men who go berserk. Or with trapped bank robbers. Those are totally different situations. The men we're up against are not loonies, and they're not professionals figuring out how much jail time they've got coming. They are operating under orders they don't dare disobey. Once they're in, they're in. Their leaders have a mission. Their job is to carry it out, period. When they kill seemingly at random they are very clear-headed about the damage they will cause by killing a few and frightening millions. When they put the bomb on top of General Whitcomb's car, it was intended to help blow the United States out of Europe. These acts have a cumulative force."

Adams pulled himself erect. "I wish you'd come speak at Columbia, Mr. Dracoff. Our students by and large support violent dissidents."

Sam smiled. "I had my chance at trying to persuade students when I was one. I'm not in the wind business anymore. Besides, people in our line of work aren't permitted to speak in public. Plus if I showed up at Columbia, professor, I'd get hooted off the platform. People believe what they want to believe. David told me you teach the law. You're probably a master at it."

Adams, embarrassed, started to say, "Well, I don't . . ."

"Professor Adams, I don't think you want to be part of this."

"I will do anything to help rescue Susan."

"Not true. You would not fire first at her captors."

"How do you know what I am capable of?"

"No offense, professor. You're an experienced lawyer and a teacher of lawyers; please stick to the law. David and I are about to break the law, and not on a small scale. But then for everybody's convenience, we don't exist. If you feel like it, root for our success. From the sidelines."

Once Adams was shunted off, Sam got us huddled around the maps on the kitchen table, the only surface large enough to spread our plans out on except the floor.

"We shouldn't have wasted time on Adams," I said.

"Better now than later," snapped Sam. "Besides, I enjoyed it."

Earl Morath, whom Sam dealt with by pretending he didn't exist, had to get his two bits in. "Could we bring in five or six of our men with a helicopter in this flat area behind the house? We could—"

"All that generates is noise," I said. "The chopper's sound would alert them. They'd pick off your men as they deplaned. They probably picked that house because it's got a field of fire not just in front but in back, too. Your only covered approach to the house is through this thick growth here." I pointed. "I don't know if it's passable."

"If we take it slow, we can get through."

That's when I said, "Look, let's not forget. They're expecting the delivery of money by one man walking."

"Anything the Bureau can do to help?" asked Morath.

"The most important thing," Sam said, "is to find out where in the house Susan Whitcomb is being kept."

"Hold on," I said. "I want her visible at the door and standing up when I bring the money suitcase up."

"Who the hell said you're doing it! Morath's people monitored that call from Rome. They've identified you as the lion's killer. They know you killed Iggie, too. You don't stand a chance."

"They won't see me up close until it's too late," I said, raising my voice more than I meant to. "I'm more limber than you are, Sam. A local cop can't take this on."

"We've got men who've been trained in delivering ransom money," Morath said.

"Hear me." Sam was like a large pigeon gathering his patience by taking a very deep breath and puffing out his chest. "The person carrying the bag has got to be able to kill the man who comes for it. Besides," said Sam, "even if you had someone who was terrific with a handgun, Earl, and I'm sure you do, what do you want to get him in trouble for? Your guys are supposed to capture people and hold them for trial, not shoot to kill."

Morath said, "You don't have that broad a license either."

Sam said, "If we goof, Earl, you might have to arrest us."

Morath smiled. Then he said to Sam, "How about giving him a radio in his ear so we can relay any change of plan while he's carrying the money up?"

Sam said, "Oh, you mean one of those not-so-secret Secret Service things that identifies the President's bodyguard on sight? If they spotted anything like that, they'd *know* he's armed. I'd like David here to come out of this in one piece."

"Thanks," I said.

"You're very welcome," he said, "Now let's find a motel and get in some sack time. You need to be real rested tomorrow, boychick."

I was up at dawn and had to wake Sam, who was snoring away like a walrus. We breakfasted in a diner, me sipping the coffee when it was still too hot.

"Burn your tongue?" Sam asked.

"It's okay," I said. "I want to get going."

"She'll wait for you, boychick." He ducked, but I didn't swing at him.

Earl Morath drove us to Long Valley in a cortege of cars. The Feds were going to come in from up on the hill through the thick brush area, one man at a time, get as close to the house as they could without revealing their cover, and then swoop in as soon as the first shot was fired.

"That's a great way to get the hostage killed," I said.

Sam motioned me to keep quiet.

I was worried about a stray bullet hitting Susan. Ideally, I would first take out whoever came for the money and then the guy holding Susan before he shot her. I had to face it. I wasn't that fast. And suppose I couldn't get close enough to the house?

"Mr. Morath," I said. "Any of these fellows of yours a good enough marksman to be able to use a rifle from the cover of a car a hundred yards down below and hit a small target?"

"How small?"

"The size of a man's head. The man holding the hostage."

Morath said, "This is a bit embarrassing."

"What kind of embarrassing?" said Sam.

"I'm supposed to be the best marksman of the lot," Morath said. "There's a Winchester with a scope in the trunk of my car."

I looked at Sam and Sam looked at me. "This is no time for inter-service rivalry, cherub," he said to me. "If the man's a good shot, let's use him. He could fire the second you do. You can concentrate on crawling up the hill dragging the suitcase."

I looked at him. "What makes you think I'm going to crawl?"

Sam said to Morath, "You'd better arrange for two ambulances in cover down below."

"Two?" said Morath.

"One for the living," said Sam. "Just in case one of you hot shots merely wounds your target."

The ride out from New York City heading west took us from heavy traffic to lighter traffic on a road that seemed to be lined with gas stations, then finally out into open country. Morath was a good driver. I leaned my head back, and yawned.

Sam tapped me on the shoulder, saying, "We're almost there."

At the next fork in the road, a man in civvies waved us down. He wanted to see inside our car. Morath slowed. The man recognized him and motioned to take the road on the right.

The potholes in the road forced Morath to keep under twenty. Up ahead, we saw some men clustered near a hedgerow.

"That's them," said Morath. "You fellows might as well stay in the car."

He got out, leaving the engine running, and went to talk to one of the men. I could see him nodding but couldn't hear a word.

When Morath came back he leaned in the window of the car. "Here's the plan."

"Can't hear you," I said.

He reached in and turned the ignition off. "There are fifteen men in the woods up the hill from the house. As soon as Smith engages whoever comes for the money, our men will head for the back of the house, then storm it the second they hear the first shot."

Morath got back in the car and drove slowly because one of the men was running alongside the car to point the way. I had a feeling that if this was half a century ago, he'd be up on the running board.

I had to give the Feds credit. They'd studied the terrain well. We were directed to a spot just behind some trees and hedges that formed a perfect screen. Morath said he'd prefer to line up his sights from a prone position, but there just wasn't anywhere he could lie down and see. He decided to park the arm holding the rifle on the hood of the car. It was a second-best choice.

Sam warned Morath, "The men in the house might spot the muzzle blast."

"Don't worry about me," said Morath.

I was set to go. My intention was to walk slowly from the left front, far from the car, into an open patch where they could see me from a couple of hundred yards away. The quicker they spotted me, the less likely they were to be distracted by any of the Feds moving downhill toward the back of the house.

Some of the discomfort I felt came from working with men I didn't know. Sam had trained us all to function in tight groups, men who learned to trust each other's skills.

When I got a chance not to be overheard I said to Sam, "Why don't you take the head shot?"

"It's Morath's rifle," he said. "Besides, he said he was a terrific shot, didn't he? You want to know my secret, boychick? I don't see too good any more."

"This is the first time I'm going in without a contingency plan."

"You can't change your mind once you're halfway up the hill. The only contingency I can think of right now is you stay here and I take the money up."

"Fat chance."

"Remember," Sam said.

"Remember what?"

"Everything I ever taught you, boychick."

I nodded.

Everyone got set. Morath positioned his rifle on the hood of the car, looked over to where I was, nodded. Sam stood beside him. I hefted the heavy suitcase in my right hand, then switched it to my left hand.

"Good boy," said Sam. "Go."

I never felt so alone in my life.

CHAPTER 43

Susan

Once, when I was eight or nine, I woke up in the middle of the night frightened by the smell of burning.

When I tried to turn the bedside light on, the switch clicked from off to off. My feet found my slippers, and I fumbled across the darkened room to get to the wall switch. Click. Click, click, click. Nothing happened, and there was still the smell of burning.

I went to the window, fanned by panic, and couldn't see a street light anywhere. The smell was strongest at the open door of my room, and I followed it in the hallway's dark the few feet to my parents' bedroom. The door was open a crack. I knocked. I heard a shuffling and then Dad opened it, standing there, smiling, with a fat white candle stuck in an ashtray for light.

"There's a power outage, Susan," he said. "It's okay, go back to bed."

This time my dream was of a smell also. When I woke in the dark, the stench was nearby and almost unbearable. I remembered where I was: the boiler room.

I tried to pull farther away from the bodies. It was no use. The rope held.

I wanted to stop thinking. I wanted to stop smelling the stench seeping from the bodies.

Suddenly there were rapid footsteps upstairs.

I heard the door leading to the cellar open and saw the funnel of bright light moving down the steps.

It was Guido, and behind him Poco. Poco was holding his nose. Guido had a flashlight in one hand, a gun in the other.

Were they coming down to execute me, too?

Guido's flashlight stung my eyes. When I flinched, he turned it on the bodies. *Yes they are still dead. They haven't gone anywhere.*

"Get up!"

I couldn't. With the gun Guido motioned Poco to untie me.

They brought me up from the stink of the boiler room to the floor above. Guido shut the door to the cellar tight, as if that would keep out the smell that was now pervading the house.

Guido tucked the gun in his belt, then ordered me to sit at the kitchen table. Poco put a plate of pork and beans in front of me. Hungry as I'd been, I had no appetite for food. I asked for water. Guido brought me a glassful. The last time I'd asked for water, Guido had thrown it in my face and smirked. Neither of them was smirking now. I wondered what they were nervous about.

"Eat," Guido ordered.

"I'll throw up," I said.

"Eat and throw up." I took a few beans on my fork. The second I tasted the food, I had to keep myself from wolfing the glop down. *Eat slowly. You don't want to get sick now.*

Poco sliced off a piece of the dark bread they'd been eating and put it on the side of my plate with a flourish, as if it was a gift.

I got out the words "Thank you." Poco grinned. Guido nodded at him as if he'd done the right thing. The third man, the one who'd driven the van and then the car, caught my eye. He had shoved the couch over against the window and was propping up a rifle on the sill. When I looked back at Poco I noticed for the first time that he, too, had a pistol in his belt.

The barely warm beans tasted better than any I'd ever had in my life. Using a fork with my left hand was awkward. I could only get a few beans at a time. I was so hungry my instinct was to bring my mouth down to the plate. When there were only five or six beans left, I ate them one at a time to stretch things out. Then I swabbed the plate with the piece of bread.

When I was a kid, we'd put our plates down on the floor after dinner so the cat could lick them clean. I was my own cat. The plate was bare.

When I finished Guido motioned me to come along with him. He led me to the bathroom they'd been using. Clothes were hanging on hooks.

"Take a shower. Get clean."

As soon as he was out of the room I locked the door. I stepped into the bathtub so I could get close to the translucent window over it. I tried to open it. It had been nailed shut from the outside, just like the windows in the back bedroom.

There was no mirror in my small bathroom. I hadn't seen myself since I'd been shoved in the van. The mirror over the sink made me look into it. I was appalled at the dark smudges under my eyes, the dirt that had embedded itself in my pores, the jumble of my hair.

With my left hand I put my underthings in the washbasin to soak. My right hand was throbbing. *Keep the bandages dry.* I found a shower cap that must have belonged to the woman down in the basement, wrapped it around my bandaged hand as best I could, then stepped into the tub and turned the shower on. The luxury of hot water streamed over me. People go through life not ever thinking about what it would be like if they were forbidden to bathe.

Into my steamy pleasure, a thought cut like the screech of chalk on a blackboard. What was I being tidied up for? Was I to be released in exchange for ransom? Would Guido stake me out like a goat, let them see me, take the ransom, and then dispose of me? Were they preparing to shoot whoever came to the rescue? Why else the propped gun? I needed to think clearly. I hurriedly finished my shower.

I hated the idea of getting clean and then putting on what I'd worn for days. I wrapped my underthings in one of the smaller towels that looked cleaner than the rest. When I opened the bathroom door, Poco was standing there, idiot-grinning. I didn't give a damn what part of my body he could see so long as he kept his hands to himself.

He pointed the way. For a minute I thought he was making me go back down to the cellar. Then he shoved me in the direction of the back bedroom. I caught sight of Guido and the other man checking what now looked like an arsenal. Where'd they get all those weapons?

Poco was suspicious of my rolled-up towel. I unrolled it on the bed, took my still-damp underthings out, and handed him the towel. My brassiere got hung up by one of its straps in the window that had the most sun. I put the panties in the bathroom, where Poco was less likely to see them.

I heard a shout from the living room, then the three of them were all talking at once. I couldn't make out a word. The only useful thought I had was *If the shooting starts, fall to the ground.*

Poco came to get me. Guido was squatting at the second window. When I came in, he pointed. I strained to see the tiny figure in the distance, a man carrying a suitcase. I felt a snap in my chest like a guitar string breaking: *David!*

David, who strode so fast when we walked together, seemed to be moving ever so slowly. Was it caution or the weight of the suitcase? He couldn't be alone, could he? Where were the others? *I prefer to work alone,* David had said. *Fewer people to worry about.*

I turned and saw an expression of pure livid hate cross Guido's face. "It's the man," he said, and spat. Then he took the large pistol out of his belt.

CHAPTER 44

David

The suitcase was heavy, the weight of solid paper packed in tight. When I stopped and put the bag down, it wasn't because of the load. The bargain was that Susan would be clearly in view, standing.

On the porch of the house I saw exactly nobody.

Then a tall skinny guy came out the door with what looked like a .45 in his right hand. He must have spotted me from inside the house. He was staring straight at me. I stared right back. With his left hand he signaled me to come closer.

I didn't move. Taking air deep into my lungs, I bellowed one word you could hear on the wind: "Susan!"

Would they understand what I wanted? They had agreed to it, dammit.

Another deep breath, another roar. "SUSAN!"

The man yelled something in Italian. A short man came out the door, pushing Susan in front of him. Seeing her, my eyes telling me that she was alive, revved my heart's beat something awful. My instinct was to rush forward to her. My training held me back, made me do what experience had taught me to do, notice every detail first.

With a jolt I realized that the man who was holding onto Susan was no taller than she was. *His head didn't show above hers! How is Morath going to be able to take his head shot?*

The tall one with the .45 motioned at me again with his whole left arm, quickened with impatience. What would Morath do?

I picked up the suitcase and started forward again, step after step, up the grassy slope. I kept my steps shorter than they could have been, giving Morath time to think. But if he figured out something, there was no way he could tell me. Maybe I should have chanced the radio. Too late now. A pressure headache clamped both sides of my skull. I had counted on being able to shoot whoever was holding Susan if Morath missed, but the guy holding Susan was practically a midget, and nearly invisible behind her.

I was a couple of hundred feet from the house when the tall one started coming downhill toward me. I guess he felt no one would take a shot at him as long as the hostage was in their hands. He held the .45 as if he knew how to use it.

I took a few more steps. The tall one held up his left hand like a traffic cop. I sank to my right knee so that he knew I wasn't going any farther. He looked around him in all directions, then nodded his head. The boys had done a good job of hiding themselves. Nothing was visible.

Morath has nothing to aim at.

If Morath shot at the tall one, the midget would kill Susan immediately. Why the hell hadn't we taken time to work out all the contingencies? It was my fault. I'd hurried everybody.

Because I couldn't chance them seeing a weapon on me, my only hardware was my .38 in the ankle holster with the safety off. The tall one stopped maybe ten feet in front of me. I knew what a .45 could do to you at that distance. Slowly I moved my weight back and shifted my left leg forward just enough to get it into the best position for a quick draw.

I pushed the suitcase a few inches in his direction.

"Open," he said.

My first thought was to open the suitcase with my left hand so that my right hand could draw. I canceled that idea the second I thought of it. The tall one was no dope. He looked like he could smell something wrong.

Then I had a better idea. With both hands, I unlatched the suitcase, raised the lid, and swung the bag clear around so he could see that it was stuffed with bundles of bills. I expected his eyes to go nuts when he saw that much money, but he didn't even blink.

The bundles on top were real. I reached over the lid of the

suitcase, which was hiding my left leg with the ankle holster, took the rubber-banded middle batch, the only one that was real money all the way through, and threw it to him with a lob that would make him look up for a second to catch it.

He caught the bundle in his left hand. His thumb riffled it for a second, just long enough for me to draw and fire as I rose to my feet in one movement, my arm skewing my wig. Damn!

Out of the corner of my eye I saw Susan hit the deck. Immediately I heard the crack of Morath's rifle and saw the midget collapsing backward. I was so relieved I didn't notice the tall one bending forward as I shot. I had hit him not in his heart but somewhere in his gut. He was holding the .45 pointed straight at me, screaming "Wig! Wig!" In that split second I knew that Sam had been right, that no matter how good you think you are, if you are personally involved with a hostage, even a split-second distraction could cost you everything.

CHAPTER 45

Susan

David's eyes had locked in my direction for only a second. Then Guido fired that huge pistol twice. I'll never forget the surprise on David's face as the rest of him began to tumble backward like a doll.

Guido seemed to be diving at the bag—or was he falling?

Suddenly men in suits were swarming all over the place, rushing the house from the sides and back. Their shots coming from inside the house sounded more than enough to kill the third man, who'd been at the window. Then, as abruptly as it had started, the gunfire stopped. I was aware of Poco lying just a few feet from me. I didn't want to look. I looked. Part of his head was gone.

My left hip hurt where I had fallen. Trying to ignore my dizziness, I dragged myself up, looking toward David. It was as if I was on the outside of a nightmare looking in. Men were running uphill toward David from below. And then I found myself running down the sloping grass, past Guido, who wasn't moving, his face hard into the ground as if some force were holding it.

A heavy-set man with gray in his mustache got to David before I did. David was conscious, his eyes looking straight at me. The heavy-set man was soliciting answers in a very experienced way. He was asking David could he move his legs, could he move his arms, and David was trying to answer the heavy-set man accurately, as he would a doctor, his eyes still on me, and the caring man was trying to understand. I heard him say, "Don't you feel it?" and David was saying

"Negative, negative," and then I was beside David, hugging his head, kissing his face for love and for rescuing me.

I felt hands tugging at my shoulders and pulling me up. The heavy-set man said, "I'm Sam Dracoff. I'm afraid the bullet that hit our friend David may have lodged high up in his spine."

CHAPTER 46

Susan

"Look at it this way," Sam Dracoff said. "You lost one of what you had ten of. Nine fingers is a pretty good percentage."

"I think I can live with being a little freaky-looking in the hand, Sam. It's the idea of David the base-runner in a wheelchair that depresses me."

We had just left him. Sam had stepped out of the room so David and I could be alone for a few minutes. It's lousy to be with someone you want to hug hard who can't hug you back.

When I came out of the room I was shivering, though it wasn't cold. Sam said, "There's a coffee shop around the corner."

He made me order something to eat, too. I said, "You're a real Jewish mother, Sam."

"I've been called a mother before. Usually with two more syllables."

"Why couldn't David stay in the hospital for his rehab? Why'd they move him to such a lonely place?"

Sam grunted, reached across to my Danish, and broke off a piece. "Mind?"

I shook my head.

"Good," he said, munching. "My dear . . . I hope you don't mind my calling you that . . . ?"

"Not at all." I was beginning to like this friend of David's.

"People in our line of work aren't very welcome in hospitals.

You've seen them, three shifts on guard twenty-four hours a day, and none of them nurses. The nurses resent having us on their turf. Even more so when the smart ones guess why our patients need guarding. Nobody works in a hospital in order to get hurt. They complain to the supervisor that caring for a patient with a bullet wound is one thing, but worrying that someone may try to finish the job and hit you instead, that's another. We know when we're not wanted. Once the surgery's over and the patient's out of danger—healthwise, that is—we move him to one of our own facilities, here, London, Rome, wherever."

"It doesn't seem fair that David is still in danger. He's . . . he's . . ."

"Hardly David anymore," Sam finished for me. "Before the second operation, when I went back to Europe, there was still some hope that he'd eventually be able to get around with a walker or a cane. Now, there's nothing. One thing you learn in our business. If you've got a body, bury it."

"David isn't dead, Sam."

"More's the pity. Kiddo, I'm going to say something you're not going to like."

"Try me."

"One more week and David gets moved to a place we've got near Washington where the facilities are better than the crazy, isolated set-up he's in here."

Sam put his forefinger on the tip of my nose. "You're a nice kid," he said, pulling his finger away. "Take my advice. Don't move to Washington. Don't even come to visit. If you visit, he won't get over you and you won't get over him. I know David, he'd rather be dead than helpless. He might find a way of living with himself, but he'll never find a way of living with you. Know what I'm talking about?"

"I know."

"Can you accept it?"

"No."

"At least you're honest. To tell you the truth I hated the idea that David was nuts about some lawyer dame back home."

"Sam?" I put my hand on his hand the way I used to put my hand on David's. "I wake up in sweats thinking if I hadn't met David he'd still be whole."

"If, if is like junk food. Stop playing God-games. What happened

happened. There's no lesson in it except that life is full of surprises, some of them bad. You know something? The average age at which a guy gets knocked off in our kind of work is eight years younger than David is now. Considering the averages, he's had eight years borrowed time. Maybe catching a touch of love before this happened will make it easier for him not to hate the whole world. Stay away from him. It'll hurt a lot less later, for both of you."

"I thought we'd, well, get married."

"Forget it." Sam let a profound sigh shake his frame. "You can't marry someone who can't marry you for any of the many reasons people get married. I'm not heartless. I'm practical, like David. Stick to your law practice here."

"There's plenty of work for lawyers in Washington."

"That's one of the troubles with Washington," Sam said. "Last year they offered me a desk job there. I told them I'm allergic to desks. This year they're going to force me into early retirement so they can point to me as one guy who made it out the other end of this career alive."

"Sam, David is very much alive!"

Sam's sigh was epic. "That's a matter of opinion, my dear, in which your opinion is wrong." He took my good hand. "What about the professor? I was a bit rough on him. You shouldn't be. He seemed like an okay guy."

"He's been super to me for a very long time."

"Maybe it's time to be a bit super to him."

"I've got a date to see him. Tomorrow for dinner."

"Oh? It's none of my business, but what are you going to tell him?"

I reached out and removed a crumb of Danish that had nested in Sam's mustache. "I'm telling him that wherever David goes, I go."

CHAPTER 47

Farlan Adams

I gave Susan forty-eight hours to get over the shock of the news about what I now liked to think of as David's accident. Phoning first wasn't a good idea. I decided to just present myself at her apartment.

Tuesday after class I went home to put on my favorite dark blue suit, a light gray shirt, and a maroon necktie with a small paisley print. Susan had once remarked on that combination.

My pockets were full, and took something away from the shape of the suit, so I emptied them out on the bed and decided which things to leave behind. One of them was the card that had allowed me to visit David when he was still in the hospital. No danger in that. It was perfectly natural of me to visit a man I'd met through a mutual friend. Nevertheless I tore the card up and dropped the pieces into the garbage.

I checked myself once more in the mirror. This time I was not able to prevent the edge of a smile from showing. Susan had thought of me as an academic, had she? Doesn't get into the arena, eh? I had never felt more confident.

I was about to leave my apartment when the doorbell rang. I was expecting no one.

I opened the door on the chain. You can't be too careful in New York.

A chunky individual in a brown business suit was holding out a wallet. "Detective Ippolito, 17th Precinct Homicide," he said. Next to him stood a uniformed policeman whose cap didn't fit properly. If he'd been a student, I'd have advised him to cut his hair.

I undid the chain and let them in, explaining that I was just about to go out but that I could spare them a few minutes.

"How can I help you?" I asked as I led their way into the living room.

"To start with," Detective Ippolito said, "tell us about your movements Sunday morning."

I described my usual Sunday morning routine, an extra hour's sleep, browsing through the huge edition of the *Times*, a second cup of coffee, a leisurely walk.

"Mr. Adams," he said, "about what time do you begin your walk?"

"I should say about nine. Perhaps a bit earlier or later. Depends."

"That's what you did last Sunday, took a walk?"

"Every Sunday if I'm not out of town. Unless it's raining hard or snowing."

Detective Ippolito rubbed his chin as if checking to see if he had shaved that morning. Then he turned to the policeman. "It wasn't raining hard or snowing last Sunday?"

"No," said the policeman.

Ippolito leaned forward. "Mr. Adams, does that mean you took a walk last Sunday, too?"

"I do that ordinarily."

"Just a walk?"

"That's right."

"Do you ever take a walk in your car?"

"What's that supposed to mean?"

"Do you ever drive someplace and take a walk there?"

"I have done that."

"By any chance, Mr. Adams, would you have done that last Sunday?"

"Let me think."

"It was only two days ago, Mr. Adams."

"Of course. Yes, come to think of it, I did take a drive."

"Where to?"

"I'm not sure it was any place in particular. I sometimes drive about until I find a good place to park and stroll."

"Would it help if I asked was it first thing, like you say, about nine in the morning?"

"Well, that's just about my usual time."

"Mr. Adams, I'm waiting." Ippolito was scratching his groin. When he observed me noticing he stopped. "Was it first thing in the morning that you took a drive to 54 Dawnhurst Drive?"

"Should that address mean something to me?"

"Does the name Dr. Nesbit mean anything?"

"Yes, yes of course. Now I know what you're talking about."

"You mean you didn't go for a walk last Sunday?"

"I did."

"Before or after you visited Dr. Nesbit's premises?"

"Before."

"Good answer, Mr. Adams. About what time, then, did you visit Dr. Nesbit?"

"After eleven."

"Are you married, Mr. Adams?"

"Heavens, no."

"Would you mind telling me why you were visiting an obstetrician on Sunday morning?"

"Oh, I wasn't visiting an obstetrician. I was calling on a patient. By the by, how did you happen to know I was there?"

"That building is observed by one of the government services. License plates of vehicles, stuff like that. What was the name of the woman you were visiting?"

"It was a man, actually."

"Well, his name?"

"David Smith."

"Smith a friend of yours?"

"More like an acquaintance. We were introduced rather recently by a mutual friend."

"Do you mind if I ask why you visited him?"

"Why does one visit anyone in the hospital? To try to cheer them up a bit."

"Hospital?"

"Well, an institution of that sort."

"What sort, Mr. Adams?"

"I suppose Dr. Nesbit's place is a kind of rehabilitation center."

"I don't know ladies who have babies need rehabilitation."

"I'm afraid you'll have to direct any questions about the nature of that institution to others."

"Mr. Adams, when you first appeared at the premises of Dr. Nesbit, was this Mr. Smith alive?"

"Of course."

"And was he alive when you left?"

"Of course."

"He couldn't testify to that now, could he?"

"I gathered from a newspaper story that he died, poor man. Some kind of accident."

Ippolito opened his belt buckle one notch and rebuckled it. "How come you didn't tell us what happened to your friend or acquaintance right off? Was it you couldn't remember the newspaper story or what?"

I glanced at my watch. "Do you need me much longer?" I asked.

"Depends."

"I'd appreciate—"

"I'll keep it short. When you visited Mr. Smith, what did you talk about?"

"Oh this and that. The usual chitchat of a hospital visit. The man was quite incapacitated, as you know. I didn't stay long."

"How long?"

"Ten minutes."

"Was the window in Mr. Smith's room open?"

"I don't—yes, I do remember, it was open."

"Very good. Mr. Adams, you're a professor, aren't you?"

"Yes I am."

"I guess I should have been calling you professor."

"That's all right."

"Well, you being a professor, maybe you could help me understand how come when Mr. Smith fell out of the window, he ended up with a smashed forehead as well as the back of his head crushed?"

"I don't understand."

"Well, people who fall out of third-story windows don't exactly bounce. If he hit on the front of his head, the point of impact would be, well, you know. And if he landed toward the back of his head, that's where the impact would be, right?"

"I truly don't understand what you're getting at." I stood up. "Now, if you've finished your questions, perhaps you'll excuse me. I have an appointment."

Ippolito pulled himself up out of his chair. "Professor Adams, you teach at the Law School, right?"

"I see you've done your homework."

"Well, if you've done your homework, professor, you'll know what the Miranda is."

"Of course."

"Well, Professor Adams, before we go down to the station house, I'm going to read you your Miranda."

At the precinct house, despite the otherwise rude treatment I received, I was of course permitted to call a lawyer. It would be foolish to tell the booking sergeant that over the years I had trained several thousand lawyers.

I didn't need to look in my address book to call a number I knew by heart. With David dead, there would be no conflict of interest for Susan now.

Of course Susan would know my voice. I saw no need of establishing any additional connection between us in the presence of the policeman attending me. When she answered I said as calmly as I could, "Hello, this is Farlan Adams."

She said absolutely nothing.

"It will make it easier for both of us," I said, "if you think of it as my having taught you to do what, according to our canon of ethics, you now should do."

I could hear her breathing. She was listening and saying nothing.

"Susan," I said, "I have been charged with a serious offense. Will you defend me?"

I turned to the policeman. "I do believe I was disconnected."

"You're only allowed one call, mister."

"Yes, but that was an incomplete call," I said.

"You'll have to wait upstairs."

"I am allowed to complete that call."

"Who says? It ain't the law. Now move."

"Look here," I said to the officer as quietly as I could, "I know

I'm inconveniencing you, but there's a twenty in it if you'll permit me to complete that phone call."

He took my arm in a totally unfriendly way and said, "I'm not your lawyer, mister, but if I was you I wouldn't itch to get a measly bribery count on top of murder one. Move!"

CHAPTER 48 •

Susan

I hadn't intended to disconnect him. For two long days I'd hoped Farlan would call me, help me deal with this second death when I could still feel the squeeze of the black band around my heart from the first.

I went to the office to inter myself in work. *Why are you crying?* Betty wanted to know. I didn't know I'd been crying. *How can I help?* she wanted to know. *Bring him back to life, the way he was before,* I wanted to say.

I tugged myself together enough to call that number David had left with us and told the cut-off I wanted Sam Dracoff to phone me right away. I left my office number, my apartment number, mother's number. "Where will you be in the next two hours?" I was asked. "I don't know," I cried. I didn't know where I would be because I didn't know where I was.

Sam didn't phone, so I dialed the damn cut-off again and said that if Sam didn't call me, I'd talk to the newspapers.

Five minutes later Betty said, "There's a Sam on the phone, says you know who he is."

"When is the funeral?" I bellowed into the phone.

"There isn't going to be a funeral," said Sam. "You got to forget about us, my dear, as if we never existed."

"I can forget about you, Sam, but how in hell can I forget about David?"

"It's over," Sam said.

"Not for me. Aren't you people going to do anything about whoever pushed him out the window?"

I could hear Sam's breathing as he hesitated. Then he said, "Maybe he threw himself out."

"That's a lie."

"If somebody did him a favor, lovey, what do you want me to do, sue? Get even? Get locked up? Forget it. Go on with your life."

And he hung up without saying goodbye.

Not for one minute can I believe that David could hurtle himself out of the window. He always joked about being killed by a terrorist. *David, I miss you. I didn't need another death.*

Farlan must have known that David's death would tear me apart. Why didn't he phone me the minute he heard about it?

Because he knew I would suspect.

Farlan, if you had anything to do with this, I don't ever want to be in the same room with you. *I wouldn't let you touch me.*

Yes, yes, yes, I hear you, you always came to my rescue when I needed help. Yes, of course none of us is innocent, and each must still be proven guilty, right, or the whole design falls apart. Okay then, let it fall. Why in heaven's name should I care? What justice did Dad get? What justice would David get if I successfully defended you.

Betty said, "Why don't you go home?"

I shouted at her, "Why doesn't everybody go to hell!"

Betty took me down to help me get a taxi as if I were incapable of getting one myself.

I discovered myself sitting like a zombie on the chair next to the phone in my apartment. What was I waiting for?

I couldn't stand not moving. I got up to pace the room. I told myself it was to get my circulation going. What a lie! I was thinking of myself in the courtroom!

Ladies and gentlemen, here we deal with evidence. What evidence do they have?

If I decide to defend Farlan, the newspapers will surely find out I was his student as well as a friend. They'd exploit the student-defends-teacher man-bites-dog angle. Somebody will have seen me entering his apartment building. They'd find out I knew David, too.

They'd find out much too much. It would all blow up like that casket on the tarmac.

How could I spend hours of pretrial conference time alone with Farlan, in my mind's eye seeing what must have happened that Sunday morning in David's room? Will I be able to bite back my thoughts before I say them?

Can I hypothesize four convincing ways that David might have fallen from the window? *Lord, must I play the role Farlan taught me?*

You don't have to take this case.

The defendant's right to counsel, Farlan had said, *does not give him the right to specific counsel.*

Farlan knows lots of lawyers.

Would Farlan tell me the truth about what happened? *A guilty client knows better than to tell his lawyer.*

I could play up Farlan's character weaknesses, make him out to be the kind of fusty academic coward who would shrink from the use of personal violence.

The hell with it! There are tens of thousands of morally lobotom-ized lawyers in this country who'd love to defend Farlan with all the public hoopla this case is sure to attract. *You dirty rotten bastard, get someone else!*

I had a sudden vision of Farlan's spectacular apartment. What would happen to it, to those paintings, if Farlan was sent away for twenty years? He'd be in his seventies coming out. He'd never last that long. It would be a de facto life sentence however long it was.

Why was I thinking this way before I'd heard proof of anything? Am I part of a tribe of professionals so smart we *know* ahead of the evidence? Is that the real reason they keep us off other people's juries?

It wasn't true that anybody could defend Farlan. With every slip a less-than-perfect advocate would make, Farlan would hemorrhage. *What I did was a mercy, Susan. For you as well as for me.*

I am not your accomplice. You can't ask me to help you.

It will make it easier for both of us if you think of it as my having taught you to do what you must now do.

Does he think I'm his puppet? I can get him off on my own. It would be easy to get character testimony from all those faces on the wall of his office. I could show the jury how kindly Professor Adams went out of his way to help students with their careers. And boy could I squeeze the government to own up to some of David's past, portray him as the mercenary who killed as an occupation, link him to gangsters like Murder Incorporated. I could subpoena David's father and draw out of him how David got that scar, David's penchant for violence as a teenager, his aborted school career. Wait a minute, what I could do with Sam Dracoff on the stand! He'd refuse, I'd subpoena him, I'd find a way to get him back here, he'd call me at home and try to persuade me to lay off, and I'd insist on the rights of the defendant, and Sam would yell at me, *What about the rights of the dead?!* I'd threaten to unravel the government's navel in public if he didn't cooperate on the witness stand. Hell, I could build a case of a career killer who fell to his death because violence had finally made him instead of his victims helpless. They don't even have a motive. And a motive isn't evidence. Dear ladies and gentlemen of the jury, if I have injected reasonable doubt into your brain you must let this man go.

If someone else takes Farlan on and muffs it, will I carry a hump of regret on my shoulders the rest of my life?

In a corner of my brain is the intolerable image of my lord teacher Farlan in jail.

It's not my problem. It's his problem.

It's my problem. The tabloids won't be able to resist this trial, they'll dig it out of the grave, the two parts of the triangle still alive, one trying to defend the other against the charge of having done away with the third. TV would lap it up. One hell of a career builder, Farlan would have called it. *Now here's what you should do.*

Shut up, Farlan, I can handle this on my own. Oh Annie, wherever you are, my student days are over, I'll be free at last! If Dad's ghost glares, I can take it. Dad did his dirty job and now I have mine. I can defend Farlan Adams better than anyone on earth.

I looked up the phone number of the precinct. With a finger that moved as if it was disconnected from me, I pressed each numeral once.

"Seventeenth Precinct, Sergeant Witkowski."

"This is Susan Whitcomb," I said, clearing my throat. "I was speaking to my client, Professor Farlan Adams, when we were cut off."